Second Chances

Amy Iketani

Published by Amy Iketani, 2024.

This is a work of fiction. Similarities to real people, places, or events are entirely coincidental.

SECOND CHANCES

First edition. June 7, 2024.

Copyright © 2024 Amy Iketani.

ISBN: 979-8224157525

Written by Amy Iketani.

Also by Amy Iketani

Coming Home
The Last Wish
I Never Knew
Second Chances

Watch for more at instagram.com/amyiketaniwrites.

To Leo and Alisa,

There are not enough words on these pages to tell you how
much I love you!

Chapter 1

Walking around the empty apartment gave Noah an uneasy feeling. He had spent years of his life living here and now it was over. Time to move on, they said. How could he move on from all of the memories that they made here?

Everywhere Noah looked he remembered Malia. Everyday when he got home from work, Malia had dinner ready. Her hours at the outdoor supply store allowed her to be home in the evenings. Dinners were always a surprise, they could be elaborate casseroles or instant ramen. Noah smiled as he thought about it all.

He walked into the bedroom to do one final check. Noah closed his eyes and tried to remember their happy times here. He could still picture Malia, still asleep when he left for work. Noah Wagner was a Pittsburgh police officer and had pretty odd hours. Usually he was leaving so early that Malia was still snuggled in their warm bed.

The happy memories would always be clouded by the events of that night not so long ago. A night that changed their lives forever. Noah believed he could still smell her perfume. Malia always loved the floral scents of gardenia or lilac. He missed her so much.

Noah had met Malia Harris when he visited the store she worked at on his day off. He often went in when he needed new running shoes or wanted to try tennis or golf. Noah loved the outdoors and was willing to try any sport that he thought about at that moment.

When a beautiful woman approached him and asked if he needed help, he immediately forgot why he was there. Noah hesitated and could only stare at her. This made Malia laugh and Noah was instantly hooked. Her dark skin and brown eyes were flawless. Her hair was braided and that only emphasized her natural beauty. When Malia asked, again, if he needed help, Noah finally found his words.

"I, uh, am supposed to go hiking with my buddy, Steven, this weekend and I don't know what I need," Noah replied.

"Well, our hiking section is over there," Malia said while she pointed to the far corner of the store. "I can show you if you want."

Noah simply nodded and the two of them walked in that direction. From that moment four years ago, Noah knew he would not let this woman get away. He didn't. Malia moved in with him and he proposed not long ago on a romantic trip to Niagara Falls.

Malia was very understanding of Noah's job and schedule. Past relationships couldn't handle being in a relationship with a cop, but for Malia it was more comforting. She wasn't really worried about his safety. She knew Noah could handle himself and wouldn't get hurt, at least that's what she prayed for each night.

Noah ran his hand through his hair, they were supposed to be planning a wedding, not a funeral. They had plans. Noah had saved enough for a down payment on a house in the suburbs so they could finally move out of the city. Even he knew it was not the best neighborhood and didn't want to raise a family here.

Malia would always go to open houses and they even found the perfect neighborhood with a big backyard and on a quiet cul-de-sac. Noah's apartment days would finally be over, or so he thought.

That was a long time ago. It had taken a lot of therapy to get to the point he was at today. That night would always be traumatic, he just needed to learn how to move on. His fellow officers were very supportive when the sound of gun shots would make Noah freeze instead of react like a cop should. That's when they told him he needed to take some time off.

These last few months, Noah felt like he was just surviving day to day. This was no life. Every sound would send his heart racing and hands sweating. Could he still be a police officer when he was suffering from the trauma of that night?

Moving out of the apartment was a step in the right direction, he was sure of it. No one could take away his memories, he just had to make sure they were stronger than the nightmares. His therapist wanted him to do exercises that focused on his happiest memories. He tried. Somedays he was successful, but most of the time he failed.

It was Noah's parents who worried the most about him. They didn't like him living alone for the last six months, especially in the same apartment that was the catalyst for the nightmares. The place where the worst night of his life happened.

When they suggested that Noah move back home, on a temporary basis, he was hesitant. He certainly didn't want to move backwards but he knew he couldn't continue living in the apartment. He told them he would find something on the other side of town, or move in with Steven. There had to be a better option.

In the end there wasn't. Noah had given up the fight and gave in. His parents won.

"The truck is all loaded, son," Richard Wagner called from the front door.

Noah's dad had also been a police officer but was now a homicide detective. He was grateful for his father's help today, he couldn't have done it alone. His mother, Dawn, was probably waiting outside in the car. With all the heavy lifting done, she was eager to get back home and get everything organized.

"Just a few more minutes," Noah called back to his father.

Noah walked back to the living room. He could picture them snuggled up on the couch watching a sappy romance movie that Malia chose. She always wanted to watch something that would make her cry or cuddle. Noah didn't really mind. He lived the action and crime dramas in real life. Having a couple hours to wrap his arms around Malia as she cried into a tissue was priceless.

Noah knew that drawing out the inevitable wasn't doing him any good. He took his keys out of his pocket and set them on the counter in the kitchen. He took a final look back before closing the door behind him.

Noah followed the rental moving truck in his own pick up truck. The half hour ride outside the city to his childhood home was soothing. He didn't know what his future held but for now, he didn't need to decide anything. He was on a medical leave of absence and he was going home. Noah needed to recuperate from the inside out.

He imagined Malia in the seat beside him talking about their day. She would ask about his day and he would share what he could. He smiled at the possibility of her still being alive instead of the wooden box filled with her ashes that occupied the passenger seat. He knew he would never be able to move forward unless he put her to rest.

Richard drove the moving truck with his wife, Dawn, beside him. They were happy to have Noah move back home so that they could keep an eye on him. His behavior these last few months were concerning them and they believed this was for the best.

Dawn worried about the calls from his partner, Steven, when he reported that Noah had been out drinking all night. Or when he would sleep with his weapon on the bedside table, or worse yet, under his pillow. Dawn knew that trauma could make people do things that weren't normally in their character, so she was concerned about his safety.

It would be an adjustment to have their thirty year old son back home again, but it was something they were willing to do, for Noah. He needed people around him that loved him. Dawn feared that his personality was dissolving into fear and depression. She wanted to expose him to empathy and laughter.

"Are you ready for this?" Richard asked his wife.

"As I'll ever be," Dawn replied.

They both knew this wasn't going to be easy. Steven had stayed with Noah a few times, especially after nights of drinking, just to make sure he was okay. That's when he experienced Noah's nightmares. He would wake up in a panic and a cold sweat and start yelling at the top of his lungs. At first, Steven thought something happened, but soon realized that this was Noah's new normal.

Dawn was thankful for the heads up, but still wasn't sure what they were getting into. Noah still had weekly therapy sessions, so at least he was working his way out of the darkness. Even Richard, who had all the police training available to him, wasn't sure how to best help his son.

When everyone reached the house, Richard backed the moving truck down the long driveway. Noah followed them in his pick up truck and both men started unloading the remnants of Noah's life. Dawn had cleared out his old bedroom of childhood furniture and the memories of a different life.

Dawn knew that in Noah's thirty years, he had seen his share of love, violence and loss. She hoped that his old room would become his sanctuary when he needed it the most. She would try not to intrude or hover, but she couldn't promise not to worry about her only child.

Noah and his father unloaded all of the items from the truck and now he was left to unpack on his own. He rubbed his left shoulder, still sore and tender from that night. He didn't think his shoulder would ever be one hundred percent again, but it was getting better. The scar was slowly fading a little more each month.

With his bed assembled, Noah was finally able to lie down and relax. He didn't realize how tense he was until he exhaled and release the anxiety he had been feeling all day. He knew that moving on was what he needed to do, but he also couldn't help the feeling of leaving Malia behind.

Noah looked in his bag for the picture of them from Niagara Falls. He placed the framed photo on the bedside table and stared at it. It was a selfie he had taken right after proposing. Malia was smiling and holding up her left hand to the camera.

Noah had spent weeks hunting for the perfect engagement ring. Finally finding it at a small jewelry store in downtown Pittsburgh. Malia was thrilled to show it off to everyone, whether they asked to see it or not. Noah smiled at the memory. That ring was now somewhere in the bottom of his backpack.

Noah cried. He seemed to be doing a lot of that lately. He didn't tell anyone. His therapist urged him to feel his feelings, not to hold them in. When his emotions took hold of him, he felt like he was drowning, barely keeping his head above the rising water. It didn't last, though. Noah focused on the horizon and kept moving forward.

A knock on the door brought him back to the present. His mom entered with a tray.

"I thought you might like some hot tea."

"Thanks, mom," Noah said. "You didn't have to."

"I know," she replied.

She placed the tray on the dresser and handed him a cup and took one for herself. They sat together on his bed and sipped the soothing beverage. Dawn knew her son was not one for small talk. She just wanted her son to be comforted by her presence. Sometimes that was all anyone really needed.

When Noah shifted and lowered his cup, his mother took this as a sign to leave him alone. She stood up, took his tea cup and started returning them to the tray. As Dawn was turning to leave the room, Noah spoke.

"Mom," he started, "thank you for this."

Dawn smiled at her son. "You're welcome. Tea can solve almost anything."

"No, I mean all of this. For encouraging me to let go and welcoming me back home," Noah replied.

His mother set the tray back down and came over to hug her son. She kissed him on the top of his head like she had done when he was a child. "You're welcome," she said again. "Anytime."

Chapter 2

Noah tried to embrace his new life at home. He ran in the mornings, went to the gym and did chores around the house. It was freeing and stifling all at the same time, but he also knew it was the medicine he needed right now.

He yearned to get back to the streets, to his job of protecting and serving the people of this city, but now was not the time. This was his time to heal. It was an adjustment to be living at home after nearly a decade away, but he knew it was an adjustment for his parents, too.

He could feel their eyes on him. Noah knew they meant well, they just didn't know how to deal with him. It was like he was a levy ready to break and the flood would be all encompassing. He wasn't sure if they were wrong, he just knew he could only take one day at a time.

With Richard at work everyday, Dawn tried to stay out of her son's way. She tried to act like everything was normal by going out with her friends and hemming new curtains for the kitchen. She fought every urge to go and sit with him or get him to open up. That would come when Noah was ready.

Noah was no where near ready. He didn't want to talk about that night and couldn't image ever letting anyone in about how he felt. He was trying to get past it, not dwell on the worst day of his life. Every time he did, he subconsciously touched his left shoulder. The only physical evidence that anything was wrong.

His mother called out to him on the couch that she had lunch ready. She didn't believe him when he said he wasn't hungry. He hadn't eaten anything all day.

"It's my homemade chicken noodle soup," she said, "your favorite."

Noah stood up and walked into the kitchen. Dawn smiled as he sat down in front of the steaming bowl of soup. It was chilly for the end of May, probably the last chance she could get away with a hot lunch until the fall. Plus, she did know it was his favorite.

She came around behind him and placed a plate of warm biscuits next to him. That's when she noticed the hand gun tucked into the back of his jeans.

"Noah, I wish you wouldn't wear your gun in the house," she said.

"Sorry, mom, it's just habit," Noah replied without removing it.

Dawn simply sighed and ate her soup. She knew there would be small battles like this one and she chose to let it go. She knew what being married to a police officer was like, but she was concerned that Noah was taking it a step further. Today, they would just enjoy their soup.

Noah had plans to meet his old partner, Steven, for drinks later. It would be good to catch up and hear the latest gossip from the station. His parents were glad that he was at least still keeping in touch with Steven. They also knew that if there was anything that concerned him, Steven would let them know.

NOAH WALKED INTO SULLIVAN'S Bar and saw Steven sitting on a stool. Steven waved when he saw Noah approach and asked the bartender for another beer for his friend. They hugged and Noah joined him.

Noah laughed at his stories from the police station. He had been partnered with Greg and they weren't an easy fit at first, but they were getting better.

"I miss my old partner," Steven said.

"Me, too," replied Noah.

"How much longer do you think you'll be out?" Steven asked.

Noah didn't know how to answer that. Should he tell Steven that he still walks around with a gun in his belt? Or that he still wakes up thinking about what happened? Or that he flinches when he hears a loud noise?

"I don't know," Noah said. "I think I need to get away for a while."

"Where would you go?" Steven asked, concerned.

"I was thinking about Virginia."

Steven looked confused. "Why Virginia?"

"It's where Malia's family lives," Noah replied. He took a sip of his beer before continuing. "I want to give them Malia's ashes. It's only right that they decide where to bury her."

Steven watched his partner and friend wrestle with his decision. "Are you sure?"

"Yes, I've been thinking about it a lot lately. I know they weren't on good terms, but they are her parents." Noah paused then looked at his friend. "Since living at home, I know how much parents love their children and would do anything for them. I can't keep her from them, even if they did disagreed with our relationship."

Steven patted his friend on his back. "That's pretty amazing. I'm proud of you, man."

Noah smiled.

"When will you leave?" Steven asked.

"Soon," Noah replied.

Steven turned towards Noah and raised his glass. "This calls for a toast. I believe there is hope for you, yet. To safe travels!" Steven said loudly.

Noah raised his glass. They both took a drink and remained silent. Steven wondered if this was really a step forward or more running away from his problems. Noah knew this decision was a hard one to make but now that he had said it out loud, he felt better.

He didn't know what he would be walking into. Malia had always made it clear that she was not welcome back home in Virginia, not while she was still with Noah. Well, he didn't have to stay long and they certainly couldn't refuse him while returning their daughter's ashes.

When she was pronounced dead at the hospital, it was Steven who called her parents. Noah couldn't do it. He was ashamed that he couldn't protect their daughter, his fiancé. This could very well end badly but it was a risk he was willing to take, for Malia.

The next day, Noah told his parents his plan to drive to Virginia. At first they tried to convince him that he could send someone else, he didn't need to be the one to deliver Malia to her parents. What if they were still angry and tried to hurt Noah, a child for a child?

Noah tried to assure his parents that they wouldn't do anything to him, but deep down inside, he wasn't completely sure. Her death wasn't his fault, but he was a cop, he still blamed himself. He also knew that he needed a complete change of scenery and this was the perfect opportunity.

Noah had never been to Virginia. Malia never went back home, so there was no reason to go. He knew the Shenandoah Valley was beautiful, so he would stay a little while. He would need to build up the courage to meet them face to face, so a few days of exploring the outdoors would be good for him.

Who knows? He may even find a new path for his life. He wasn't finding it at home, so maybe Virginia would be a good place to start.

It was the only thing he hadn't tried already. He wouldn't let himself sink any deeper into his depression and planned to leave the day after tomorrow.

Richard was more skeptical that this was the answer his son was searching for. Dawn had her doubts, too, but was willing to let him go. Richard wouldn't stand in his way either, but he had a bad feeling about the whole trip. He was stirring up hornets that were better left to their nest.

Noah knew his parents had concerns about his trip south, concerns they didn't voice to Noah, himself. He did, too. It was the hard decisions in life that built character. Wasn't that something his father always said? He went for a walk to clear his head. He was at peace with his decision, but he still felt anxious. Noah was jumping into the unknown and that would be scary for anyone.

His walk quickly turned into a run. Noah found himself running nearly six miles before finally returning home. He needed to clear his head and the stillness of the evening was perfect for that. As he looked around, he realized that he didn't even know any of these neighbors any more. This was his parent's home, it was no longer his.

Noah needed to find his place in the world again. He thought he did once. He had a whole future planned out but that evaporated in one night. The thought made him touch his left shoulder, still tight and sore. Noah feared that his wounded shoulder would be a constant reminder of that night.

He thought carefully about what he would take. Not even sure how long he would be gone, he packed for a couple of weeks. His gun would be tucked into his belt, hoping to keep the nightmares at bay.

Finally, he packed Malia's ashes. He sat on this bed and looked at the picture of them at the happiest moment of their young lives. A whole future was ahead of those two. Noah had grieved and felt the anger, now he was trying to accept what had happened. He felt like he had made tremendous progress, until he was reminded that he was sitting in his childhood bedroom.

Noah placed the picture in his bag, he would bring it with him on this journey. He was going to need all of the strength and encouragement he could get. He even called Steven to let him know he was leaving in the morning.

Steven wished him well and reminded him that he was only a phone call away. Noah knew he could rely on his partner to help in any way he could. He had even once offered to come with him, but Noah knew this was something he had to do on his own.

That night, his father cooked burgers on the grill. The June evening was warm and getting warmer. It was a nice dinner on the back patio with the barbecue and his mother's famous macaroni salad and baked beans. A real cozy sendoff before he left for a couple of weeks. At least, that's what he told them. In reality, he didn't know when he would return.

Noah felt that he would know when the time was right to come home. He was going to play this by ear and do what felt right at the moment. He may even keep driving south until he ran out of land.

His parents watched him. They tried not to be obvious about it, but they desperately wanted to know what was going through his mind. They did not see this one coming. When Noah announced his trip to Virginia, they were both caught a little off guard.

They knew coming home was temporary, but they expected him to eventually move back into the city, to his old life. Perhaps his old life was just that, old and worn out. He was searching for his new life, his new path.

Dawn had made a cake for dessert. She was treating this like a celebration even though she wasn't sure what it was. She just knew that a cake felt like a fitting going away dessert. Part of her wondered if he intended on returning. There was a knot in her stomach that wouldn't go away because she believed this might be a one way trip.

The three of them ate their cake in silence, all deep in their own thoughts. Richard hoped his son could find closure in this trip and come back as his normal self. He also worried that it was too much to hope for.

Noah just wanted the nightmares of that awful night to end and prayed that this would be the solution. He feared that handing over Malia to her parents was like giving in to his own weaknesses. Noah would have done anything for Malia, anything to make her happy or to keep her alive. He would have sacrificed himself and his own safety to give her a chance at a future, a future she was denied.

Noah was betting it all and would never admit to himself or anyone how frightened he was about heading into the unknown. He would let his training take over and hoped it would be enough. He would do it for Malia.

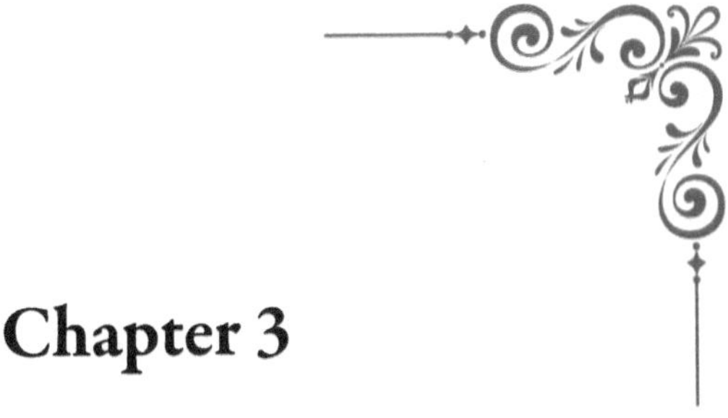

Chapter 3

The four hour drive from Pittsburgh, Pennsylvania to Virginia was refreshing. The big city slowly gave way to green hills and valleys. Noah saw corn fields, cotton fields and even tobacco farms as he drove further into Virginia. The Shenandoah Valley National Park was a place he had wanted to visit, maybe this trip he would get the chance.

Noah saw cows and horses and thought about what it would be like to see this everyday. If only Malia had wanted to visit her parents, he would have loved seeing as much of Virginia as he could. He loved the outdoors and felt like he could be happy in a place like this. Maybe.

As he approached the small town of Summer Hill, Virginia, he slowed down to get a good look. It was very small. He must have passed the downtown area because the sign announcing the next town was all he saw.

Noah turned around and drove back to the small town square. He saw a bank, a motel, a diner and a hardware store. He knew there had to be more, but for now, this is all he needed. He parked in front of the motel and asked if there was any vacancy.

"Sure, how long are you staying for?" The man behind the counter asked.

"I'm not exactly sure," Noah replied honestly. "Let me have two nights for now. I'll know more later."

The old man nodded, had him sign in and took his credit card.

"Room 106," the man said as he handed Noah a key. "Over on your right."

Noah nodded his thanks and took the key. He drove to the parking spot right in front of room 106 and carried his bag inside the room. It was as unwelcoming as he had imagined. Well, he didn't expect to be in Summer Hill very long, so it would work out just fine.

Noah was not going to try to visit Malia's family tonight, he would call later and set up a time to meet them tomorrow. He didn't want to come unannounced, this was a delicate operation.

First, he was hungry and wanted to eat. Noah had skipped lunch, too nervous to eat anything earlier, now he was starving. With limited choices on restaurants, he walked to the diner across the street.

The diner looked straight out of the fifties. As soon as Noah opened the front door a small bell jingled and every head turned to look at him. He already knew he didn't fit in. It would be obvious to the locals that he was from out of town. Noah hoped he could blend in enough to sit and eat in private, that little bell just changed all of that.

He walked slowly down the middle of the restaurant passing curious diners along the way. He opted for the counter so that he could at least sit on the end and avoid being the center of attention. Every eye stayed on Noah.

Noah's head looked up at the pretty young waitress when she yelled, "Okay, shows over! Everyone get back to eating your dinner!"

Noah smiled at her. "Thank you."

"Hi, honey," she said. "I'm Teresa, but everyone calls me Teri. What can I get you?"

"Umm, I don't know. I'm just passing through. What do you recommend?" Noah asked.

Teri smiled at Noah and brought him a menu. "Well, the meatloaf is the most popular, but the fried chicken is my favorite," she said.

Noah only glanced at the menu before ordering the meatloaf and a cup of coffee. Teri brought him his coffee and Noah took the time to look around. The customers were a mix of everyone. There were families, older couples and a few cowboys in real cowboy hats and boots.

Noah was starting to feel like he had just stepped into the backlot of a western movie. Was this really how people dressed everyday? He had never really thought about it before. Noah was a city boy that wore shorts and sneakers. Occasionally he wore a baseball cap but most days it was his police uniform.

Teri brought his meatloaf dinner complete with mashed potatoes, gravy and green beans. It was delicious. Noah noticed the cowboys were the first to leave. They glanced back at him before waving at Teri and getting in their trucks.

It was a strange feeling to be in a town where you knew no one. Noah was definitely the outsider. He was sure he was the topic of conversation at every single table. That was okay with him, as long as no one gave him any trouble.

Noah just wanted to eat his dinner and go back to the motel. Tomorrow would be another day, one that he was not looking forward to.

Teri came back to refill his coffee and asked how the food was. Noah complimented the cook and Teri laughed. He had watched her make the rounds to all the tables and flirt with all of the customers. He thought she couldn't be more than twenty or twenty-one and was good at her job of making everyone feel at home.

"Do you want pie?" Teri asked.

"Well," Noah wasn't sure. When he hesitated to answer her, Teri said she would bring him a piece of apple pie on the house.

Noah was not going to let her give him a free piece of pie and decided he would tip her extra for the thought. Perhaps this is what she says to all the customers and in turn gets great tips. Noah laughed to himself as he at his pie.

When Teri brought out his bill, Noah laid down a twenty dollar bill for the food and another twenty for a tip. Teri smiled and winked at him.

"Are you gonna stick around? Maybe come back for dinner tomorrow?" Teri asked.

"Maybe," was all Noah could say.

The little bell jingled as Noah walked out onto the sidewalk. Unsure of what to do next and unwilling to go back to the motel, he looked up and down the quiet street. He noticed some neon lights on a building further down the street, usually indicating a bar.

Sure enough, he walked into a dimly lit room with a bar on one side and pool tables on the other. He also noticed the three cowboys from the diner were playing pool in the corner. Noah walked up to the empty bar and ordered a draft beer. He chose a seat that gave him a good view of the whole room.

He wasn't expecting any trouble, but didn't want to be questioned about why he was here, either. There was one cowboy not playing and Noah watched him as he approached the bar. The man purposely chose the corner closest to Noah when ordering another round of beers.

"I don't think I know you," the cowboy said. "I'm Mason, Mason Fisher."

Mason held out his hand with a casualness that his eyes did not have. Noah knew this was a test. He would play his game and remain calm.

"I'm Noah Wagner."

"Well, Noah Wagner, how long are you staying in Summer Hill?" Mason asked.

"I'm just," Noah hesitated, "making a delivery. I'm not staying long." Their eyes locked onto each other.

Mason took the beers, tipped his hat and said, "See ya around," before heading back to his buddies.

Noah's police officer senses were telling him that Mason Fisher was a man to be avoided. A man who had a bad side and was not afraid to show it. Noah made a mental note of the name, he would have Steven run it if he needed to. Mason wasn't going to scare him off.

Noah just kept reminding himself that he would not be staying here long enough to encounter anyone's bad side. He would make his delivery and keep moving. This town might just be too small to be a long term stay, lucky for him, that was not his plan anyway.

After a couple of beers, Noah pulled out his phone and summoned the courage to call Malia's parents. Since he had never met the Harris's, he wasn't sure of their address. He thought he knew where they lived, but would definitely want to confirm it before heading out there.

Noah's palms were sweaty as the phone rang. He let it ring long enough before he determined they weren't home. Well, he took a chance. He would try again tomorrow.

When Noah set his phone back down on the bar, he noticed the group of cowboys had gone, Mason with them. He was glad and breathed a small sigh of relief before ordering another beer.

Noah wanted to call his dad next and let him know he was okay. He gave a quick update on where he was and how the day went. He said how he tried to call the Harris's but there was no answer and would try again later. They didn't need to worry about him, he survived the day.

His father said that they both wished him well and hoped he accomplished what he set out to do. He knew his father suspected that he had ulterior motives. Maybe he did, he wasn't even sure what he was even doing here sitting in the bar on a Monday night.

They talked a bit more before his father was pacified enough to let his son go. Noah wished them both a good night and hung up. Maybe it was the three beers or the three cowboys, but he was suddenly feeling a little unsteady. He knew it was time for him to leave.

It was late and Noah suddenly felt tired enough to sleep. It wasn't a particularly eventful day, but it was mentally exhausting. He needed to get to bed. He paid his bar tab and walked out into the cool mountain air. Even when he closed his eyes, he could tell he wasn't in Pittsburgh anymore.

Noah turned right and walked past the diner again. It was closed at this time of night. He decided that he would come back here to eat tomorrow. He had no where else to go anyway and wasn't about to leave without finishing his task. He would let Teri flirt again and offer free pie.

Noah crossed the street and entered room 106. He locked the door and even put a chair in front of it. He showered and looked around at the depressing room. He sat on the edge of the bed and turned on the television. He found a sappy movie that he knew Malia would demand to watch, but instead changed the channel.

He realized early on that he would encounter many things in the course of a day that would remind him of Malia. A scent, a taste, a laugh, but he had to keep moving. These were fleeting moments, not Malia. He would not let these things make him sad, he would acknowledge them and push forward. Some days were easier than others.

After six months, Noah found that the saddest moments were also fewer and farther between. He was encouraged when he could quickly glide past the triggers and simply remember her. That was always the goal. It didn't always work. Grief and trauma were a work in progress.

Noah felt that she would be proud of him. He would never forget her, but it was less painful to think of her now. He subconsciously touched his left shoulder. That ache would always be there. There wasn't anything he could do about that.

After flipping through every channel the motel provided, he found a late night news channel that gave the sports scores. He particularly wanted to hear how the Pirates did tonight. His life back home felt like lightyears away, even though he had only traveled four hours. Unfortunately, as soon as Noah's head hit the pillow, he went right to sleep.

Chapter 4

The sun coming in through the worn curtains woke Noah from a restless night. He had awoken with another nightmare but it went as quickly as it came. The rest of the night he was reminded that he was in a strange city because of the lumpy mattress and scratchy sheets.

Noah was eager to start the day if it meant the night time was over. He tried calling the Harris's again but still no answer. He decided to take a chance and drive out to their place, unannounced. It wasn't how he wanted to do it, but he felt he had no other choice. He couldn't keep hanging out in this town waiting for them to pick up the phone when they lived only five miles away.

He stopped at the gas station to fill up and grab some coffee and a donut. Fueled up, he headed to their last known address. He was surprised to feel nervous and anxious as he headed in their direction. His palms were even sweaty as he made the last turn onto a dirt road.

He pulled over to the side of the road when the large white house came into view. He nearly ducked behind the dashboard when an older woman walked out into the front yard. He surmised that this was Mrs. Harris, Malia's mother.

She went around to the side of the house and turned on the garden hose. She proceeded to water the rose bushes that lined the perimeter of the house. Noah watched as this woman went about her morning routine, unaware that her daughter had been brought back to her just feet away.

He continued to watch as she put the hose away and went to the large chicken coop in the backyard. She threw out feed and collected eggs. Noah hated being a voyeur as this woman went about her tasks, but in truth, he was losing his nerve.

What started as a mission to deliver their daughter's ashes, felt more like a disruption of their daily routine. Was he doing this to make the Harris's feel better or himself? He didn't know and it didn't matter, Noah put his truck in gear and drove away.

He told himself he would try again, call this time. It didn't feel right to just show up. Noah did not want to be responsible for ruining their day, again.

Noah followed the signs to the Shenandoah Valley National Park. He spent the afternoon walking the trails and enjoying the scenery. It was a great place to pass the time and be surrounded by nature. He found a shady place to sit and relax.

What was he doing here? Why had he really come to Virginia? He didn't have any answers. If it was solely to deliver ashes, he would have done it by now. There was something else drawing him here but he didn't know what it was, not yet.

He listened to the birds and felt the cool breeze. Noah took out the water bottle in his backpack and sipped the water eagerly. He missed having a companion on days like this. He had gotten used to having a partner in life who loved doing things together. Realizing this didn't make him sad, though, it made him feel alone.

Noah didn't like to feel alone. He had always had someone near him whether it was his fiancé or his partner on the streets, he was never alone. That's how he liked it. Today, here, he wasn't just alone, he was lonely. There was a difference.

After several hours passed, Noah decided it was time to head back to town. He didn't have any cell phone service out here, so he had to rely on his sense of direction to get him back. That was a bad idea. After getting lost a few times, he finally had to pull over and ask directions. Confident he was finally on the right road, he relaxed a bit more.

What should have been a twenty minute drive turned into an hour. Noah was starving. He parked at the motel and went inside to shower and change. He knew he was sweaty from the afternoon hike and didn't want to walk into the diner like that.

The little bell chimed to announce his arrival. All heads turned in his direction as he walked up the center of the diner to the same stool at the counter. Teri's big smile was surprisingly comforting as Noah sat down and was handed a menu.

"Well, well, you did come back after all," Teri said.

"I'll have the fried chicken tonight," Noah replied.

Teri's smile lit up her face as she said, "Coming right up!"

As she poured his cup of coffee, Noah looked around the restaurant tonight. It was a different crowd, no cowboys. He was secretly glad that they had somewhere else to be tonight. He didn't want any more questions about why he was here.

"So, sticking around are you?" Teri asked as she brought his fried chicken and french fries.

"Only another day or so," Noah replied as vaguely as possible.

"Well, it's nice to see you every day," Teri answered with a wink.

Noah smiled back and ate his dinner. He was sure she used these lines on all her customers, but it was nice to be flattered once in a while. She was not on his radar, being ten years older than her, but it was fun to have her flirt with him.

Customers came and went, emphasized by the jingle of the bell as Noah ate in relative peace. Aside from the occasional questions from Teri about whether he needed anything, he was free to let his mind wander.

He knew he still needed to call the Harris's again and his parents. It was an unusual feeling to have no one else concerned with his whereabouts. Noah finished his fried chicken and had to admit it was delicious.

"Pie?" Teri asked as she cleared away his dishes.

Noah shook his head but Teri was not convinced.

"Tonight I'll bring you pumpkin, on the house, of course."

Noah was soon looking at a large slice of pumpkin pie complete with whipped cream on top. He did like pumpkin pie and ate it all. He liked coming to this diner and smiled to himself. Teri was good at her job and when she brought the bill, he paid with a twenty and tipped with another twenty.

Outside, he walked to the bar down the street. He was creating a routine and it was comforting. He sat at the same corner of the bar as the night before and thankfully, no cowboys. He was sure that if he encountered Mason again, it would turn into a confrontation.

Noah was in no hurry to start a confrontation with anyone, let alone the resident bad boy. He ordered a beer and took out his phone. He tried dialing the Harris's again and still no answer. Perhaps they had trouble with their phone line.

The next phone call was to his parents. This time his mother answered. Noah assured her that he was safe and having a nice time. He talked about the park and left the rest out. He didn't want her to worry about him, there wasn't anything she could do for him anyway.

Noah ordered another beer and found himself wondering what he was going to do tomorrow. He didn't have a plan. He couldn't just keep sitting here and eating at the diner. He wasn't moving forward.

He decided that unless something changed, he would drive out to the Harris's place tomorrow, whether they answered their phone or not. He couldn't keep putting himself through this. Maybe this time tomorrow he would be in Atlanta or Miami. The possibilities were endless, but he had to make a decision.

Noah ordered a third beer and was reminded about the days he would need to be carried out of the bar. Those were dark days and

Steven helped him through it. He knew he was drinking too much and it was all in order to avoid reality. Well, he was living it now and reality sucked.

Three beers were his limit, maybe he should make it two. Tomorrow. After paying his tab, he went outside and walked back towards the motel. Again, he hesitated in front of the diner. He liked this place and actually looked forward to going back again.

He was just about to move on when he noticed a sign in the corner of the diner's window. It was a Help Wanted sign but not for the diner. It was for the Patterson Ranch. They were looking for temporary help at the ranch, no experience necessary. Well, that was exactly how much experience he had with working on a ranch, none.

At the bottom there was a name and number listed. The sign instructed interested people to call Katharine at this number. At first, Noah was going to just keep on walking, but decided to go back and copy down the number. This could be just what he was looking for.

The next morning, Noah actually woke up from a restful sleep. He didn't have a nightmare which was something to celebrate. He decided to try the breakfast at the diner and then give the number on the sign a call.

Noah didn't see Teri, she must not work the morning shift. Instead, it was an older woman with a questionable attitude who brought him the menu and filled his coffee cup. He ordered the eggs, bacon and toast and pulled out his phone as he waited.

Noah was surprised when it was picked up on the first ring. "Hello?"

"Hello, I was calling about the help wanted sign at the diner for the ranch," Noah said.

"Oh yes," a female voice replied. "Are you interested?"

"I think so, is it still available?"

"Yes, it is," she answered. "Can you come by today and we can discuss the details in person and give you a quick look around and you can see if you're interested."

"Sure, that sounds good," Noah replied. He copied down the address she gave.

"Just ask for me, I'm Kate."

Noah hung up after telling Kate he would meet her in an hour. This was a surprising turn of events and he started to actually look forward to driving out to the ranch and see what this was all about. He had nothing to lose, Kate made it clear that he could hear what the job entailed and still decline if he wasn't up to the job.

That arrangement suited him just fine. A temporary job with no strings or commitments. It was just what he wanted right now. Physical labor would do him good. He had never worked on a ranch or a farm before, so it was actually exciting when he thought about it.

After paying his bill, he went back across the street and packed up his belongings. He had debated about whether to check out of the motel or pay for another couple nights. He opted for checking out. If this ranch job didn't work out today, he would head out of town anyway.

Everything depended on what Kate had to say. Noah loaded his bags into the back of his pick up truck. It wasn't much, so he headed down the road in time to meet Kate at the ranch. He followed his phone's navigation as best he could.

Noah's cell phone service was spotty but it managed to lead him to the right location. He pulled up to the front gates of the Patterson Ranch and waited a moment. He was starting to feel a knot in his stomach. He realized that all of the corn fields that he had been passing for the last few miles were all owned by the Patterson Ranch.

What was he getting into? This ranch was massive. Even from the road he could see horses grazing in the field and a long dusty road leading to the main house. He reminded himself that this was what he wanted, an opportunity to find another path and try something new.

Noah took a deep breath and exhaled as he turned his truck into the long driveway that led him closer to the main house. This was it, he could feel it under his skin that his life was about to change. Good or bad, he was heading straight for it.

Chapter 5

Clayton Patterson was maneuvering his wheelchair through the kitchen doorway and was getting frustrated. His front wheels were getting caught up in a throw rug and he could not get past it.

"Ashley!"

"What is it dear?" Ashley said from behind him.

"Why is this rug here? You know I can't have any rugs downstairs, they just get caught in my wheels." Clayton was backing up the wheelchair so that his wife could remove the offending object.

"I didn't put this here, one of the kids must have moved it," Ashley replied.

Clayton was in no mood for explanations. He wanted action. He hated having to live life out of a wheelchair. Something the doctors and physical therapists kept telling him was temporary. That was two years ago.

Clayton was a proud man, a great farmer and a former champion rider. He had medals and trophies all around the house to remind anyone who forgot that about the man in the wheelchair. Sometimes it was Clayton, himself, who needed the reminding.

"I have your breakfast ready, dear," Ashley said.

Ashley was Clayton's bride of thirty years. They inherited this farm from his father after his parents passed away a couple of years ago. He was always here to help out, but now it was his full time responsibility. Its success solely rode on Clayton's shoulders.

He was realizing that the task was harder to accomplish from a sitting position. His physical therapist told him that he could get out of the chair with hard work and determination. He had that in abundance and it still wasn't enough. Then they would say, 'give it another year'.

Clayton was tired of giving away his years. He didn't know how many more he had to give. He was only able to get himself to a standing position. Walking was still a long ways away. He needed help. The ranch was suffering along with him. He couldn't get out and do the things he used to.

If it wasn't for the fall off the horse, he would be running the farm equipment like he used to. He couldn't blame the horse, it was spooked by the lightening while they were bringing in livestock during a storm. He knew better and still did it.

The fall broke vertebrae in his back and he had multiple operations to fix it. Now his body just needed to heal and learn to walk again. It would just take time. Time was something Clayton was stingy with. He would go through bouts of depression and take it out on his family. He hated when he did this, he just didn't see any way out.

Ashley took good care of her husband. She was a registered nurse but quit to stay home and take care of Clayton full time. This saved them money by not needing to hire a care nurse, but spending all day and night with each other was wearing them both down.

She knew her husband was not always like this, he was a great rider and an even better rancher, but not being able to do either was effecting their relationship. Not to mention their marriage. They haven't shared a bed in over two years, let alone be intimate with each other. All of these factors led to fights and arguments about even the simplest of a things.

Like the need to hire a ranch hand. They needed help, that was for sure. Kate's boyfriend helped out when he could, but he had a full time job as a car salesman in the next town. They couldn't rely on him for daily chores or even big jobs because he couldn't commit that long.

Ashley hoped that placing an ad for a temporary helper would get things back on track. Kate agreed. Their eldest child was twenty-five. She has been with her boyfriend for a few years now and hoped he would love the ranch as much as she did. He didn't. He complained when she asked for his help and left as soon as he could escape. He loved him, but it was a sore spot in their relationship.

Now that it was summer vacation, she had to make sure the two youngest siblings had just enough chores to keep them out of trouble. The youngest was Lorna, she was thirteen. She had a trainer coming to build up her riding skills. Lorna's dream was to be a championship rider like her father.

If Kate couldn't find her around the house, Lorna was either in the barn with the horses or in the field riding and practicing. Kate loved riding, too, but didn't have much time for it lately. With her mother busy taking care of her father, she was left with he daily decisions of running the ranch.

The next youngest was Henry. He was seventeen and would be a senior in high school next year. Henry wasn't very interested in the running of the ranch, which was a disappointment to his father. He had hoped to pass it all down to Henry someday, but that was not Henry's dream.

Henry was a musician. He played guitar, wrote lyrics and sang. Kate and her mother loved listening to him, even though they knew their father disapproved. Henry couldn't help it, he could be found everywhere and anywhere around the ranch with his guitar.

The fourth child, right behind Kate was Teresa. Teresa was twenty-one and no one knew what her dreams were, they changed too frequently. She didn't go to college, something Clayton and

Ashley didn't like and tried to push onto Henry. Teresa worked at the local diner full time. She liked her job and made good tips.

Her father would always tell her that a job is not a career. Teri didn't care, she went where the wind blew. She might be working at the diner this year, but next year she may be a bank teller. With Teri, they were just happy that she was happy.

Kate let her parents know that someone was coming in an hour to inquire about the help wanted ad. They all hoped he wanted the job. The last five people they invited out never came back. They were becoming desperate. They were even going to offer more money and the use of the small cottage out back for him to stay in.

They knew the work would be hard, but if that wasn't enough incentive to get someone to stay, then they were at the end of their rope. It was going to be a long summer and the work needed to get done.

Lorna's riding lessons must be over because Kate could hear her yelling at Henry, something about a snake. Kate just prayed that they didn't kill each other this summer. She might just have to add more chores to their day if they couldn't get along.

Henry came stomping into the kitchen yelling that Lorna wouldn't leave him alone. He would be up in his room if anyone needed him.

"As long as your chores are done," Kate called after him.

Henry's response was the slamming of his bedroom door. That was it, if this person coming today doesn't work out, she's making Henry do it. She didn't care if he was only seventeen.

Kate had to get out of the house. She walked back to the cottage to check on things. She had put fresh flowers on the table everyday and thought it looked cozy and welcoming. Next, she walked to the barn. They had a pregnant horse, Daisy, who was ready to give birth in about another month.

Kate loved brushing her and giving her treats like apples or carrots whenever she came to the barn. Daisy was her favorite, she even got to name her when they got her. This was one of Kate's favorite places in the whole ranch, the horse barn.

Her boyfriend thought she was crazy. He said the barn smelled and the horses were out of control. She always defended them but he would never understand the connection she had with these horses and the ranch. Kate wanted to be the one to inherit the ranch, not Henry.

Kate was walking back towards the house when she saw Teri getting ready to leave for work. She reminded her that there was someone coming about the job today.

"Oh, that's exciting! I hope he's cute," Teri said.

"Well, whoever he is, keep your hands off of him. He's here to work and only for a few weeks," Kate replied.

Teri just frowned as she got in her car and backed out of the driveway. She honked and waved as she made her way to town. Kate envied her free spirit. She was always happy. Even if she was a bit too flirty for her own good, but she meant well. Really, it was her father she was worried about. She suspected that he was the one scaring off the potential help, not the job description.

Kate went inside to make sure her father was busy doing something else. He was. He had taken a course on bookkeeping since he knew he'd be stuck in a wheelchair for the foreseeable future and had really gotten good at it. Now he was going over all the books for the ranch.

It was because of this that Clayton knew they were in trouble. He never confided in the children how bad it was, but Ashley knew. Supply costs were up, as well as salaries. Prices they got for their corn was down as well as demand. They needed new revenue streams and quickly.

Kate looked at the clock and realized it was almost time for the interview. She cleaned up the kitchen and put away the breakfast dishes. She put fresh flowers in the vase on the table and quickly went upstairs to change.

She could hear Henry quietly playing his guitar and singing to his latest composition. He had a great ear and voice. More people should hear Henry sing. In her room, Kate brushed her long blond hair and put it up. She changed out of her t-shirt and jeans and put on a dress.

After looking at herself in the mirror, she came back downstairs to check on her father. He was still occupied with his financial books and knew her mother would be in the garden. That was her happy place and where she knew she could escape for peace and quiet.

Kate kept an eye out the front door for a car. She wanted to greet him before her father heard the knock. It seemed like time slowed down as she stared down the empty road that led to the house until she started to see some dust being kicked up by a vehicle.

As it came closer to the house, Kate could see it was a shiny black pick up truck. It approached slowly, perhaps he was second guessing his decision to come, right up to the very last foot. She watched as the driver slowly got out and looked around.

Kate watched the man for any signs of retreat. Instead, she saw a tall man with a muscular build. He had brown hair and wore a baseball cap to shield the sun from his eyes. He wore a white t-shirt and blue jeans with a belt. His sneakers were what really gave him away. He was not a farmer of any kind.

Kate secretly hoped he would give it a shot. It was her mother's idea to add 'no experience necessary' to the ad. Kate insisted they should know their way around a farm at the very least. She watched him shut his door and then touch something behind his back. Still no hint of his leaving, though, that was a good sign.

It wasn't until Kate went outside to meet him when she was struck by the calming effect of Noah's smile. "Please," she whispered out loud, "let this one work out."

Chapter 6

Noah had slowly driven up the long, dirt driveway that led to the ranch's main house. It was a large white building with a wrap around covered porch. It even had a porch swing out front that looked so welcoming. He quickly scanned the property and could see a large barn with a smaller out building, horses, chickens and corn, lots of corn.

The Patterson Ranch had to be the largest one he had ever seen. He was more than a little intimidated by its size. He didn't even know what the scope of the job was but already felt overwhelmed. He slowly came to a stop in front of the house and sat for a brief moment considering turning around and leaving.

No, he would at least give it a try. If he couldn't do it, he would leave, but they needed the help and he would give it his best. He stepped out of the truck and looked around. It was bigger when you were seeing it all up close. He put on his baseball cap, secured his gun in his belt and shut the door.

There was no going back now, Noah was committed. He was surprised to see a woman coming out the front door. He wasn't sure if this was the Kate he was supposed to meet, so he wiped his sweaty hand on his jeans and offered it to the woman approaching.

"Hello, I'm Kate," she said. "You must be here about the job."

"Yes, I'm Noah Wagner, we spoke on the phone."

"Of course, won't you come inside," Kate replied. She led him into the kitchen where she had a pitcher of lemonade waiting with two glasses.

Kate gestured to one of the chairs and Noah sat down. "Thank you," he said as she offered him a glass of cold lemonade.

Noah tried to discretely look around the house and kitchen. Kate tried to discretely look at him. She cleared her throat and their eyes met.

"Well, I will briefly tell you about the job and then I can even show you if that is necessary," Kate started. "We need to replace our entire fence line around the fields."

Noah tried to focus on the crude map she had obviously drawn in an attempt to show the size and scope of the job. She showed the area of the corn fields, the house, the barn and other various smaller buildings but around all of that land was a fence.

"We can't risk any of the horses getting out or other animals getting in. There are areas where the fence has completely collapsed and we've done some temporary fixes, but it all needs new posts and wooden beams to make it complete again." Kate looked from her map to Noah.

Noah looked from the map to Kate. "Okay," he said.

Obviously stunned and taken aback, Kate simply stared at Noah with her mouth slightly open. "Um, great, yes, that's very good," she stammered.

"When do you want me to start? I checked out of my motel this morning, but I'm sure I can get my room back if I speak to them," Noah replied.

"No need, we will let you stay in the cottage out back as well as a fair salary for the work involved." Kate looked into Noah's kind blue eyes and knew without a doubt that he could be trusted. It was just a feeling, but she always trusted her gut feeling.

"Great," Noah said. "Lead the way."

Kate stood up and asked him to follow her. She showed him the cottage and explained that he was more than welcome to join them for dinner, but she also stocked the pantry with staples that he could use.

"Tonight is spaghetti. Come to the house around 6:30pm and you can meet the rest of the family. My boyfriend will come tomorrow to show you how to do the fence and hopefully you can catch on quickly because he can't come very often," Kate explained.

Noah didn't know why but when she said the word 'boyfriend' his thoughts veered and he missed the rest of the sentence. This woman that he just met was already permeating his thoughts. Why should he care if she had a boyfriend or not? She has to be about twenty-five, of course she did, she was beautiful, too.

She led him back into the kitchen so they could exchange phone numbers, in case he needed to get in touch with her and vice versa. Kate also suggested that he should get some boots and a proper hat.

"I don't have any," Noah replied. "I'll be fine."

Kate shook her head. "Noah, there are areas of this ranch that are only accessible by horse and you are going to need to walk in the fields, sneakers aren't going to work. You need the proper footwear and headgear."

Noah took off his baseball cap and ran a hand through his hair. He was starting to not only feel unqualified for this job, he was starting to question why he had even come in the first place. Was it too late to turn around and leave?

"Hold on, what size shoe are you?" Kate asked him.

"Eleven."

"Daddy might have a spare pair of boots and a hat. Wait here while it go get them," Kate said as she went up the stairs.

Noah took this time to look around the kitchen. He noticed trophies on a shelf, pictures of kids at various ages and then the view. Beyond all of the furniture, cabinets and shelves were windows. The expansive windows wrapped all along the back of the house which allowed an amazing view of the property.

Noah stood up, walked to the windows and took it all in. He could see the corn fields, the horses running in the field and the barn. It was all Patterson Ranch as far as the eye could see, impressive.

Kate returned to the kitchen with boots and a hat that miraculously fit Noah perfectly.

"There, a proper cowboy," Kate proclaimed while looking at Noah.

"Thank you," Noah answered.

After all the details of the job were finished being explained, Noah went out to his truck to get his bags. He went around back to the small cottage that Kate had said was his to use. Noah opened the door and immediately felt at home in the space. He sat in the chair in the small living area and propped his feet up.

The cowboy boots looked alien on his feet but they were comfortable. The cottage was sparsely furnished but it had everything he would need. It had a bed, dining table with chairs, a living room with couch, coffee table and a television. It was perfect.

He had a lot to get used to and fast. The job started tomorrow and he had to be a quick learner. Kate never asked what he did for a living. Maybe she assumed he was out of work and needed this job. Well, he did need the job. He wanted to stay busy and it would give him a chance to work through his issues.

Being outside everyday was a dream come true for Noah. How hard could the job be? He was invited to dinner in the main house in approximately one hour. He decided to use that time to shower and change. He noticed a washer and a drier in the closet and threw a load in. He could get used to this and was looking forward to this summer.

Noah knocked on the back door at 6:30pm sharp. Kate opened the door and welcomed him inside. He was surprised to see so many people around the table, Kate never did say how big her family was. Noah stood for a moment in the doorway, not sure where he should sit.

Kate made an announcement to the family that he was here to help with the fence and he was introduced to everyone around the table. Noah was surprised to actually see a familiar face.

"Well, hello stranger," Teri said.

"Teri, so nice to see you again," Noah replied.

"Noah was such a great tipper at the diner," Teri explained out loud to the family. "I knew we'd run into each other again."

Noah went up to Clayton and shook his hand. Ashley stood up and gave him a hug. Henry and Lorna looked only slightly interested. Clayton told Noah to sit as everyone passed dishes around and started eating. It was the youngest child who actually asked the most questions. Apparently her interest piqued when he said he was from Pittsburgh.

Noah was asked about his favorite teams in baseball, football and hockey. When they asked what he did for a living, he simply replied that he worked for the city of Pittsburgh. He didn't really feel the need to go into the details of being a cop. He wasn't really sure why he hid his actual job, his instincts just told him to not give away too many personal details right now.

When they asked Noah why he was in Summer Hill, Virginia, he said he was visiting someone. He didn't elaborate and they didn't press him on it. As the dinner progressed, the conversation turned to the corn crop and Clayton was more than happy to talk Noah's ear off.

Ashley and Kate started clearing away dishes and brought out strawberry shortcake for dessert. Noah couldn't remember the last time he had such a wonderful meal. His mother was a good cook, but something about being here and enjoying great company made it all taste better.

After dessert, Henry escaped into his room to play guitar. Noah could hear the music from the kitchen.

"Is that Henry playing?" Noah asked Kate.

"Yes, he's really very good at playing guitar and singing," she replied. "He writes his own stuff, too."

Lorna and Teri went into the living room to watch television. Clayton excused himself and went into the office. He slept downstairs since Ashley converted the office into his bedroom. It was just easier for him and they were so used to it now. It wasn't until strangers came to the house that they realized having a bedroom in the downstairs office wasn't normal.

"Dad is working on getting his leg muscles stronger. He can stand, but only for short periods of time. Physical therapy really wipes him out," Kate said.

"I get it," Noah replied. "I hated mine when I had to do it, too." He was feeling comfortable with Kate to share some bits and pieces of his real life. "As long as he sticks with it, it'll happen."

Kate couldn't help but be drawn in by Noah's blue eyes. His smile was warm and caring, too. Whatever job he had with the city needed to involve the public. Noah had a way of making someone feel safe. There was sadness in those eyes, too. Kate didn't know what brought Noah to this place, but he was not only searching for something, he was healing from something, too.

Noah helped clear the table and load the dishwasher.

"If you want, you can come for breakfast," Kate offered. "There's always plenty and it'll be a long day."

"I'll see," Noah replied. He didn't want to commit to too much. If he relied on this family for all of his needs, he would never be able to leave. He had to be as self sufficient as possible, for his own peace of mind.

Kate simply nodded. She liked spending time with him. She knew this was dangerous, to get too close to someone who would only be here a few weeks, but she couldn't help it. Her biggest concern was not letting her boyfriend think there was anything to worry about. Especially if he was living only a few yards away from the back door.

Noah said he was going to turn in for the night. He went around the downstairs to say good night to everyone. Only Henry was left out since he was upstairs in his room. Kate watched him as he walked down the path that led to the cottage.

"He's a cutie, right?" Teri asked from behind her.

"Um, yea, I guess," Kate replied.

Teri just laughed as she placed her glass in the sink. "Maybe I can get him to open up more. He might just need some one-on-one time, if you know what I mean," Teri said with a smirk.'

"You'd better leave him alone," Kate warned.

"Or what?"

"He's only here for a short time," Kate replied.

"That's long enough," Teri said as she went back into to living room.

Kate couldn't worry about Noah, he was old enough to take care of himself. She thought that he might be almost thirty. He probably wouldn't be interested in Teri anyway.

Before heading to bed, herself, Kate went in to check on her father. They needed to go over the financial statements again even though they both knew the numbers weren't going to change.

Chapter 7

Noah paced the small cottage trying to convince himself that change was good. This wasn't just change, this was cultural differences. How could a mere four hour drive lead him to a farm where he was now wearing cowboy boots and matching hat? He thought about calling Steven, but Noah already knew what he would say, 'Go for it!'.

Noah was too wired to sleep just yet. He felt like he had been on high alert and tense all day. Only now was he able to relax and take a moment to calm down. He always felt he could hide how he really felt by projecting a calm and cool demeanor to people even when his insides were a literal hurricane.

Right now Noah needed to go for a walk. The moon tonight was big and bright and he could easily make out where all of the buildings were on the property. He decided to stay on a trail he found along the fence line. He felt pretty confident that he wouldn't get lost if he just followed it back towards the house.

Noah watched the tall trees swaying in the breeze, even the corn field seemed to move against the weight of the moonbeams. Mostly, Noah listened. He heard some birds, but mostly the crickets and frogs. He knew there must be a lake nearby because the frogs seemed to be carrying on their own symphony.

He hoped that this slow paced life in Virginia would be exactly what his turbulent soul was searching for. He suddenly felt closer to

Malia, but in a different way. It was as if she was leading him here, to this place, her hometown.

Noah suddenly found himself at the barn. This one housed the horses. There had to be over twenty stalls. He found one that was isolated and soon understood why, she was very pregnant. Her sign read, 'Daisy'.

"Hello, Daisy. I'm Noah," he said.

Daisy approached the stranger and she was close enough for Noah to stroke her head. Even Daisy felt he was safe. Noah pet her head and neck in long smooth strokes. Daisy watched him with her big brown eyes but didn't back away.

Noah wished he had some kind of treat for her. "Next time, Daisy. I promise."

The sound of footsteps approaching made Noah step back and place his right hand on his handgun, the trusted Glock 17 that he carried and was always at his fingertips for circumstances like this. He took his hand away when he saw that it was Kate.

"You startled me," she said. "I wasn't expecting anyone else out here at this time of night."

Noah, still trying to calm his racing heart, "Well, I was not expecting anyone either. You're lucky, I've got some mean karate moves, too."

Kate and Noah both laughed as she came closer to Daisy. She had two large carrots in her hand and offered one to Noah.

"These are Daisy's favorite. Go ahead and give it to her, you'll be her friend for life," Kate said with a smile.

Noah did as he was told. He watched the horse devour the pieces of carrot, content to call this stranger a friend. Noah also watched Kate. Her face lit up when talking to and petting the horses. She went from stall to stall to make sure they were all doing okay.

"You're really good with them," Noah said.

"I love horses. Some people see them as just animals to ride or beasts to control. I see them as caring souls that want to be loved and respected just like humans do."

"Do you come out here every night?" Noah asked. It wasn't any of his business, but he liked being here in the barn, with her.

"I try to. I can't always get away, but especially now that Daisy is so close to giving birth, I make time," Kate replied. "What are you doing out here?"

"Couldn't sleep."

"I'm sorry," Kate said. "It must be hard being away from friends and family. But hopefully this job won't take more than a few weeks and you can be off, again."

Noah knew Kate meant that as encouraging, but to him it just reminded him that he was lost. He felt like he was sinking deeper into quicksand and he was grabbing at anything that could save him. Was this it?

Noah simply smiled and nodded. There was no need to go into detail with Kate, not now, not here. He wasn't ready to let anyone in just yet. He still had healing to do on his own.

"Well, I'd better get back," Kate said, interrupting his thoughts. "Daisy looks happy and healthy, I'll check on her tomorrow."

"Yes, I'd better turn in, too," Noah replied. "Goodnight, Katie."

It had slipped out before Noah could stop himself. He didn't mean to call her what he had been thinking in his head, Katie. She turned her head at the more playful and familiar version of her name. She didn't say anything, she just turned back and kept walking to her house.

Noah walked back to his cottage, eager for this day to end. He just hoped that he didn't ruin anything with Kate. All she needed to do was tell Clayton that he was being disrespectful and Noah would get kicked out even before he started the job.

Kate tried not to let anyone see how shaken she felt inside. When Noah called her Katie, she felt a little flutter of butterflies in her stomach. No one had called her that since she was twelve. Even her boyfriend never used it as a form of endearment because he thought it made her sound twelve. She hated to admit that she liked hearing it.

In her room, she called her boyfriend to confirm that he was coming tomorrow to show the new guy what needed to be done. He needed to be here before seven and to plan to stay all day.

"Yes, Kate, I know," he said, annoyed.

"I don't think he's ever done this kind of work before," she said. "Just be nice to him."

"I'm always nice," he said with a laugh.

Kate just rolled her eyes and they said good night. She was more than a little afraid of how tomorrow would go. She was pretty sure Noah could hold his own, but ten hours alone with her boyfriend could be a bit much for anyone, even her.

THE NEXT MORNING WAS chaos. Noah knocked on the back door at six in the morning but no one heard him. No wonder. Slowly, he let himself inside and he saw Kate at the stove scrambling a massive amount of eggs, Lorna was buttering what seemed like a loaf of toast and Ashley was frying a pound of bacon.

Clayton was sitting at the head of the table dropping pancake batter onto a griddle and Henry was pouring juice into eight glasses. As if Noah needed another reminder that Kate's boyfriend was coming today, there were also eight chairs around the table.

"Noah!" Kate yelled. "I'm so sorry, we didn't hear you knock. Come, sit down."

"Is there anything I can do to help?" Noah asked.

"No, not really. It's probably best if you just sit this one out," Ashley replied.

Noah went to sit next to Clayton, who had just finished stacking about two dozen pancakes. The griddle was whisked away and Teri came over with syrup, butter, ketchup and hot sauce, any type of condiment one could need for breakfast.

"Good morning, Noah," Teri said. "How did you sleep?" She asked with a wink.

Not used to such direct flirting, Noah raised his eyebrows, wiped his hands on his jeans and glanced at Clayton before answering, "I slept fine, thank you."

Clayton just smiled, knowing how Teresa could be around men. "Let's eat!" He proclaimed.

"We're still waiting for one more," Kate replied. She gave a quick glance at Noah before sitting down opposite him.

There was still a flurry of activity as more plates and platters were added to the mounting breakfast feast in front of them. Noah was both impressed and amazed at the amount of food this family had arranged.

"You do this every morning?" Noah asked.

Ashley laughed. "No not really, but today is special. We have a guest and you're going to need this to get through today. We'll even pack you both a lunch for later. You will probably be starting on the far side of the field today and eventually, work your way around to the front."

Noah didn't know how to feel about that. The far side of the ranch could mean a mile or two out in the middle of nowhere.

"Just eat, it'll be cold by the time that one gets here," Clayton replied.

Noah glanced uneasy at the empty seat next to Kate. They all piled eggs, bacon, toast and pancakes onto their plates and dug in. It was delicious. Noah enjoyed the sound of animated conversations all around the table. Only Henry remained quiet.

"So, Henry," Noah started, "I'd love to hear one or your songs someday."

Henry looked up, shifted in his chair and glanced over at his father before answering, "Sure, anytime."

Noah smiled and nodded as he took another bite of scrambled egg, unaware that this was a source of tension between father and son.

Henry wanted nothing more than this happy family gathering to be over. He had places to be and people to see. He had tried to slip out last night, but there were too many people at the house to get away unnoticed. His parents never took his music career seriously, anyway.

"I'm done, can I go feed the chickens now?" Lorna asked.

"Okay," her mother replied. "Just be careful and don't break any eggs this time."

Lorna stood up and slammed her napkin on the table. "I said I was sorry!" Lorna exclaimed.

"Watch your tone, young lady," her father scorned. "That's your mother you're talking to."

"Yes, sir, sorry," Lorna said before leaving out the backdoor.

"Maybe he's not coming," Teri said, gesturing to the empty chair.

Kate exhaled deeply. "He'll be here, he's just late."

Noah saw Teri roll her eyes at this statement. He suspected that Kate made lots of excuses for her boyfriend. Noah tried not to have any negative feelings towards this mysterious man that he hadn't even met, but it was hard to not get a less than stellar opinion of the guy.

Ashley had already packing two lunches for the men to take with them. Kate started clearing the dirty dishes and Henry took this opportunity to slip upstairs. Clayton sipped his coffee and read the paper.

Noah thought this scene could even be playing out at his own parent's kitchen right now. Such a normal morning of washing dishes and reading the paper. However, there was nothing normal about this setting. He was wearing cowboy boots and could see the cowboy hat sitting by the back door.

"He's here!" Kate yelled from the living room. Noah suspected she was anxiously awaiting his arrival by the front window. Well, it was her boyfriend for goodness sake. He would be waiting by the door for his girlfriend, too, if he could.

Noah could hear their muffled greetings to one another and then kisses. He suddenly felt uncomfortable and was eager to get started. As Noah heard footsteps approach from down the hall, he stood up to greet Kate's boyfriend.

Kate entered the kitchen first, holding hands with the man who entered behind her. She was smiling at her family and then looked directly at Noah.

"This is my boyfriend, Mason Fisher. Mason, this is Noah Wagner," Kate said.

The two men stared at each other a moment without saying anything. Shock was not a strong enough word to describe what each man was feeling. Kate just stood and looked from one man to the other. She didn't know why Mason wasn't being more of a gentleman and shaking Noah's hand.

Then, Mason's mouth formed the most devious smile she had ever seen. Noah simply sighed. What kind of joke was the universe playing on him.

"We've met." Mason said with a smirk.

Chapter 8

Noah's head was still spinning after learning that Kate's boyfriend was Mason Fisher. The one person he had the worst feeling about. How could Kate get involved with a guy like that? It was starting to make sense how he was never around and she kept making excuses for him.

Noah also had a hunch that the whole family didn't think too highly of Mason Fisher. He wasn't exactly sure what he would do if Mason gave him any trouble, he didn't want to cause any waves. He would just learn how to do the job and leave Mason alone.

He helped Mason load the supplies and equipment they needed into the back of his truck. They would sometimes catch the other one staring, but they each kept their thoughts to themselves. Neither one said a word to the other since leaving the kitchen a half hour ago. He was sure Mason was sizing him up just like Noah was doing to him.

Once they finished, they both got in the truck and Mason drove down the long driveway and out onto the main road.

"So how far is it?" Noah asked.

"Not far, the other side of the ranch," Mason replied, looking over at Noah. "It's the farthest point on the ranch, but it's accessible by dirt roads and trails."

Noah nodded and looked out the window at the passing scenery. He didn't know what else to say or ask, better to just say nothing, Noah thought.

"I thought you were only here a couple of days to make a delivery?" Mason asked accusingly.

Noah cleared his throat. "I, uh, haven't done it yet."

"So why are you here?" Mason asked with a harsh edge.

"I needed something to do in the meantime, until I can make my delivery," Noah replied. He knew it sounded fake and vague, but he was not giving this man any more details about his life or why he was really here.

Mason simply nodded his head and glanced over at Noah. Noah felt his stare and knew his questions weren't finished, but he accepted the silence the rest of the way to the job. They drove along the fence line and Noah was pretty sure this wasn't a real road. They bumped along the field for another ten minutes before finally stopping.

They had passed areas of the fence that were damaged from fallen trees and other places that had simply rotted away. Noah understood now how fixing the fence had taken on the urgency it had. He looked up and down the fence line thinking that this job would definitely take longer than Kate imagined.

Mason was the first one out of the truck and walked to the back. Noah got out and followed. Mason showed him how to replace the rotten pieces and dig another hole if necessary. They added more lumber and reinforced with wire when needed. Some parts of the fence were still in decent condition and could be passed by.

It was grueling work but Noah welcomed the physical labor. He would have to stop and wipe his brow or rub his left shoulder once in a while, but he was actually keeping up with Mason, or so he thought.

"You need to dig those holes deeper," Mason would say or, "That wire isn't tight enough, a horse could walk through that like it was a piece of string."

Noah corrected his work without complaint. He suspected Mason was trying to get a response from him each time and when Noah didn't, he tried again.

"If you aren't going to do it right, then go home!" Mason yelled.

"I am," Noah replied.

Mason stopped what he was doing and came up to Noah. Mason was standing his full six foot four frame with his dark hair in a pony tail. Noah saw his eyes, so dark and full of hate at that moment that his instinct was to reach for his handgun.

Mason spoke low and slow, emphasizing each word as he spoke, "I said you're not."

Noah straightened up to show his height of six feet. They couldn't be more different. Noah had brown hair that barely touched the collar of his shirt and his blue eyes were serene.

"Maybe you need to show me, again," Noah taunted.

A vein in Mason's temple grew more pronounced as he clenched his jaw. Noah knew he would not win a physical fight against this man with the build of a fighter, but he certainly wouldn't go down without giving it his all.

To Noah's surprise, Mason backed down and grabbed another piece of lumber. "Let's just finish this fence," he said and went back to work. Noah knew this was just a test to see how far he could push him. He thought he passed.

Mason didn't like the guy. It took every ounce of his self control to not knock him out right there in the field. He thought of Kate and the Patterson's and knew it would not look good for the boyfriend to hurt the new guy. And he was sure he could really hurt him.

Mason didn't trust Noah. He was hiding something and he would find out what it was. He knew there had to be a reason he was here on the ranch, it was not a coincidence. When he had met him at the bar, he said he was only here for a couple of days. Why is he accepting a job that would take weeks?

He also mentioned a delivery. Maybe this guy was up to no good. Was it drugs? He had heard from his buddies that there were some overdoses at the high school, could Noah be involved in that? Maybe he should come around the ranch more often to keep an eye on him.

They both stopped their work when they heard a horse approaching. Kate had on a white cowboy hat and her long blond hair flew in the wind behind her. She came to a stop and jumped off her horse.

Noah didn't recognize this horse, there were too many to learn. She brought two soft sided coolers down from her bag and handed one to each of the men saying that they had forgotten to take their lunches.

"How's it going?" Kate asked.

"We're making progress," Mason replied and leaned in to kiss Kate.

It was obvious to Noah that Kate didn't appreciate the public display in front of him and she kissed him awkwardly. Mason simply smiled.

Noah nodded in agreement and added, "I think I got the hang of it."

Mason shot him a side glance and smirked. "Yea, he might be just fine on his own. But I don't mind checking on him from time to time."

Noah didn't like the ominous insinuation and Kate didn't even pick up on it.

"Great! Glad to see you both getting along," she replied.

Noah and Mason went to sit on the back of the truck to open their lunches. Kate hung around a few more minutes and then rode back to the house. The men ate in silence and Noah was thankful for the peace and quiet. Noah believed he could feel the animosity coming off of the other man in waves, but he wasn't going to give in to it.

No, if Mason wanted a fight, he would have to be the one to start it. Noah was glad he never told anyone in the family he was a cop and he hoped that detail didn't come out. Noah was sure that if Mason knew that about him, it would make the situation much worse. He didn't want to find out how much worse it could get.

The two men worked their way up the fence line the rest of the afternoon. It was hard work but Noah took the time to enjoy the surroundings and scenery. It was beautiful here in the valley and mountains with beautiful vistas in every direction you looked.

It was late, the sun was setting and Mason said they should call it a day. They loaded up their supplies into the back of the truck and headed back towards the house. Noah and Mason were hot, sweaty and tired. Too tired to talk or ask anymore personal questions.

At the house, Kate saw them drive up the lane. As the men cleaned out the truck, she brought their dinners to the table. Her parents had already eaten. Lorna and Henry had finished as well and were upstairs. Teri was working tonight at the diner, so it only left Kate. She had waited to eat with the guys.

Kate didn't want to let on how anxious she had been while waiting for them to return. She was afraid of what Mason would say to Noah and hoped that Noah wasn't going to quit. Mason had that effect on the workers. He liked to taunt them until they had had enough.

Mason entered the kitchen first and grabbed Kate to kiss her on the lips. Noah simply walked past them and sat down at the table. He took the same seat he had at breakfast and Kate sat opposite him. Mason was next to Kate and glared at Noah during dinner.

The three of them ate in silence, only their eyes gave away what they were thinking. Kate's eyes displayed sympathy to Noah and his reflected it back to her. Mason didn't like the looks that were being exchanged when they thought he didn't notice.

He noticed. He would make Noah regret it, too. Kate was his girlfriend. That might not mean anything to Noah, but it did to Mason. Kate was his.

Kate felt the tension, how could you not? Outwardly they were calm and cordial, but she knew Mason. Inside, he was plotting something. His kisses were a way of marking his territory. There was really nothing Kate could do about it, Mason was going to do what he liked. She knew that better than anyone.

Noah ate his dinner and tried to ignore the looks that Mason was giving him. He savored every bite of the roasted chicken, mashed potatoes and corn. Kate even had homemade biscuits. Noah made a point to compliment every item on his plate. He also made a promise to never eat meals in the family home again.

Noah would do his own grocery shopping and cooking in the cottage. He didn't want to give Mason any more reasons to question his intentions or prove his dominance. Noah wanted to do the job and move on without any trouble.

Mason had no other choice but to leave. He gave a warning look to Noah and then to Kate as he walked out the front door and into his truck. He had to be to work at the car dealership tomorrow and he still had to drive home and shower.

It was late, but Noah wasn't ready to turn in just yet. He said good night to Kate and went to the cottage. His body begged for sleep but his brain was too active to rest. He decided to take a walk to the barn.

Daisy was happy to see Noah, especially when he produced a carrot from his pocket. He made sure to have an ample supply in the cottage. Noah gave Daisy lots of attention until he had to admit he was exhausted.

As he left the barn, he thought he saw a dark figure on the front porch of the house. He tried to get his eyes to focus in the moonlight and determined that it was someone but they weren't trying to break in, they were sneaking out.

The small build of a teenaged boy slowly and quietly walked from the house to a car in the driveway and went to the trunk. The silhouette of a guitar case was visible in the dim light. Noah watched as the car drove down the lane.

Noah finally turned to leave when the tail lights faded in the distance. He would not get involved. If Noah could have his secrets, so could Henry.

He had half expected Kate to meet him in the barn tonight. Perhaps she had already checked on Daisy earlier. Noah had better stop expecting Kate to meet him anywhere. That was exactly what Mason was silently warning him about tonight.

If Noah knew what was good for him, he would heed Mason's warnings.

Chapter 9

Over the next couple of days, Noah got used to his new routine. He woke up and ate breakfast in the cottage before loading his truck with the supplies he needed for that day. He wasn't specifically trying to avoid Kate but it was helpful that it worked out that way.

His plan wasn't one hundred percent effective because Kate still rode out to meet him with a homemade lunch. They talked a little, but conversations were awkward. Noah just didn't understand how she could be with a guy like Mason.

"You've really made a lot of progress the last few days!" Kate exclaimed.

"Thanks," Noah replied. "I've tried my best."

Kate had brought a lunch to eat with him. This was the first time she had done this, usually she just delivered his lunch and rode back home. Noah didn't know if there was something she wanted to say to him or if she just wanted the company. They ate in silence.

"Is everything okay?" Noah finally asked.

Kate seemed to be deep in thought and the question made her look at him. "Yes, why?"

"You just seem... sad," Noah replied.

"I'm fine," she answered. "Just a lot on my mind. Between the ranch, the crops, Daisy and Mason, well, it's just a lot."

"And you have to deal with everything yourself?"

"Not exactly, but sometimes it feels that way," Kate admitted.

Kate didn't bother Noah with the details. That the bank was threatening foreclosure, her father's physical therapy was costing them a fortune, the price of corn had dropped, Mason was pressuring her to move in with him and that the vet was worried about Daisy.

"Mom and Dad try to help, but they have their own things to worry about," Kate replied.

It was clear that Kate wasn't going to give him any more details and Noah wasn't going to pry. It wasn't any of his business, he just wanted to help. Noah knew how hard it was to ask for help. It was easier to drown in silence.

Noah credited the hard work and other distractions for his lack of nightmares, at least in the last week. Maybe he was finally healing from the trauma, time would only tell. Noah subconsciously touched his left shoulder. Kate saw this.

"Are you hurt?" She asked.

"Oh, no, it's just an old injury," Noah explained. "I'll be fine."

Kate expressed concern, but didn't press him. She made a mental note to offer an ice pack later tonight. She knew very well how to keep a secret if you really wanted to. They all had their secrets.

"Well, I'd better let you get back to work. I've kept you from it long enough," Kate said.

Noah thanked her for lunch and watched her ride away. He enjoyed the time they spent together, but he was also enjoying the time alone. As a cop, he always had a partner next to him. Here, he had the great outdoors.

He wasn't lonely, but he was alone. That was okay with him. He certainly didn't want the company of Mason Fisher. He would take the horses and chickens to Mason any day. He was making progress, he had to admit that to himself.

The work was getting easier and his physique was changing. This was more upper body work than he was used to and it showed. Kate noticed, too. When she had met him for lunch, Noah had already been stripped down to his sleeveless undershirt, too hot in the mid-June sun to wear anything more.

Kate hadn't seen him in anything sleeveless before and she was drawn to his shoulders and biceps. She had only known Mason to have larger muscles than Noah, but he was a close second. She knew she shouldn't be thinking about Noah that way, he was only here for a little while longer, anyway.

Kate entered the kitchen and was surprised to see her father standing! It was obvious that Clayton was in pain, but he was actually standing while hanging on to the kitchen counter.

"Daddy!" Kate exclaimed.

Clayton tried to brush her off with a wave, but he smiled at his daughter. Ashley was close by with the wheelchair for when he was ready to sit back down.

"My physical therapist yelled at me for not standing up more often," Clayton explained.

"You should be trying to take steps, too," Ashley added.

Again, Clayton waved off the comment. He would do what he was good and ready to do, nothing more and nothing less. As much as Clayton would love to run up and down the road, he just didn't feel he was able to take a single step.

"It doesn't matter anyway, I don't think we can afford to keep paying him," Clayton said as he sat back down in the wheelchair.

Kate and her mother exchanged concerned looks as they watched him wheel himself into the living room.

"Mom, what are we going to do?" Kate asked.

"We have to pray that things turn around for us," her mother replied. "We can't keep skating by as we are. We won't survive."

Kate knew her mother was right. They had to come up with another revenue source and fast. Paying for labor that certain people should be doing for free is not helping. She thought about Mason and how he gave the bare minimum to her and her family. That had to change, too.

NOAH RETURNED IN HIS truck just as the sun was falling behind the mountains. He had worked another solid day and was tired. He walked around back to the cottage and stepped into a hot shower. He was still thinking about how Kate had come to eat lunch with him today.

It was nice, but he hoped it wouldn't be a habit, for both of their sakes. He let the water run over his body, letting his tension wash down the drain. If only it were that easy. He looked at his hands, now calloused from working on the fences. He had tanned only on his arms. He was beginning to feel different, alive.

Noah liked having something to do and look forward to every day. He was outside under the big open sky and was pretty much his own boss. He had a time frame but not a time clock. Noah felt he could get used to this.

Kate had watched Noah return that evening and also saw that he avoided the house and went straight to the cottage, again. She had tried to engage with him at lunch and invite him to eat at the house, at least in the evenings, but she lost her courage. Noah seemed to be happy alone.

Kate was lonely. Mason wanted her to come and live with him. He had a nice house in the next town and he was sure she could find a job either at the dealership he worked at or anywhere else. Kate had been putting him off for years, she loved the ranch. More than that, she felt a part of it.

Mason would never feel that way about it, she was sure. No matter how many days he volunteered to help out, it was foreign to him. He was a city boy pretending to be a cowboy. Kate wasn't interested in the city. She even enjoyed the dirty side of the ranch and farm life. This was were she belonged.

This was often the cause of most of their fights. When they first started dating, she had tried living in the city with him. It was loud, confusing and she hated it. When her father had his accident, it was the perfect excuse for her to move back home. It was still a good enough reason to stay now, but she knew Mason would get tired of waiting, eventually.

Teri got home from work just as Kate was putting the leftovers from dinner away. Teri wasn't hungry, but noticed a plate off to the side filled with food.

"Who's that for?" Teri asked.

"Noah," Kate replied. "He came home and I'm not sure he ate dinner."

Teri's face lit up. "I'll take it to him!" Teri grabbed the plate and ran out the back door before Kate could protest.

Teri knocked on the cottage door and waited. It took a few minutes for Noah to answer, not sure who would be coming out here at night. He only had a towel wrapped around his waist.

His lack of clothes took Teri by surprise but she didn't miss a beat. She walked right past him and into the small kitchen. She glanced around as she placed the dish on the kitchen table.

"I brought you dinner," Teri said.

Noah deeply regretted his decision to not get dressed first. He closed the door and slowly turned around to face Teri.

"Thank you," Noah said. "I'm sorry, I just got out of the shower and wasn't expecting anyone."

Teri could tell he was genuinely embarrassed. As Noah walked into the kitchen, she let her eyes wander over his body, taking in his biceps, abs and a large pink scar on his left shoulder. As she circled around behind him, she noticed the matching pink scar behind his shoulder, too. Teri also checked out his butt.

"Well, I prefer this outfit anyway," Teri said with a smirk. Teri softly touched his back with her hand as she walked back towards the front door. "Maybe another time, though," Teri said as she left the cottage.

Noah waited for Teri to leave before going to get dressed. He had to admit, the food smelled delicious. He was going to just make some instant noodles, so this would be a far better alternative. Noah devoured the fish, rice and beans.

After dinner, he didn't want to just sit in the cottage. He hadn't gone out to the barn in a couple of days, so he grabbed a carrot and walked out into the cool night air. He enjoyed this time of night the most. The sun had set and there was a slight breeze as he crossed the field to the barn.

As he got closer to the barn, he noticed a faint light, like the light from a lantern coming from inside. Noah grew concerned thinking something might be wrong with Daisy and hurried up his pace. He was both relieved and apprehensive when he saw it was only Kate petting Daisy's neck.

"I'm sorry, I didn't know anyone else would be here," Noah said as he walked slowly towards the horse, and Kate.

"Oh, hello," Kate said, equally startled at the surprise company. "I didn't get to check on her earlier, so I thought I'd better before going to bed."

Noah pulled out the carrot from his pocket and fed it to Daisy. The look of appreciation on Kate's face let him know that she was touched by his gesture. Kate and Noah were only inches apart as they both pet Daisy. Kate, however, was only watching Noah.

He caught her staring and smiled. "So how much longer do we have to wait to see the new baby pony?" Noah asked.

Kate laughed. Noah thought it sounded musical. "Baby ponies are called foals," Kate corrected. "And the vet thinks another couple of weeks."

Noah watched her, Kate's whole face lit up when she talked about the ranch. It didn't matter if it was the corn, the chickens or the horses, it was obvious that she was in love with it all.

Kate turned to Noah and suddenly realized she forgot to give him an ice pack. "The ice pack! I was going to bring it to you with the dinner but Teri beat me to it."

"It's okay, my shoulder feels better," Noah replied. Their eyes stayed locked on each other. He was getting more attached than he wanted and there was still something he wanted to know. "Katie, why are you with that guy?"

Kate's heart jumped at his use of her childhood name but the question actually made her upset. "That's really none of your business," she replied.

"I'm sorry," Noah said. "You're right. I have no right to question who you love."

Kate's breathing grew quick and shallow as she looked at Noah, still with wet hair from his shower. She looked at his lips and could imagine kissing him. What was she doing?

"I have to go. Good night, Noah," Kate said as she ran out towards the house.

"Good night, Katie," Noah said out load in the empty barn.

Chapter 10

Noah was eager to get started on the fence today. After what he said to Kate last night in the barn, he wanted to forget it ever happened. As he walked around the house towards his truck, he was frozen in place when he saw Mason loading up his own pick up truck.

"Good morning, partner," Mason said.

Noah did not like Mason calling him that and it sent shivers up his spine. He tried not to respond to his bait and continued walking.

"Good morning," Noah finally replied.

"I told Kate I had time to help out today, actually only the morning, so don't be too sad," Mason said with a smile.

Noah knew he could get through the first half of the day, he just needed to keep conversations with him to a minimum. He also didn't know why Kate didn't tell him, a warning would have been very helpful.

After the truck was loaded with supplies, they took off. Noah was thankful for the quiet on the way to the job site. Mason didn't seem to be a talkative mood, which suited him just fine. They bumped along the dirt road and stopped at the place Noah left off yesterday.

Noah could tell that Mason was distracted today. He kept checking his phone whether he got a notification or not. He was clearly waiting for something or somebody. He assumed it was work related, but he also could believe it was something darker. Noah couldn't pin it down with a guy like Mason Fisher.

Noah was a good judge of character and knew the guy was trouble, but what kind of trouble was yet to be decided. He didn't want to find out, either. The less he saw of Mason, the better.

"Where are you from, Noah?" Mason asked as they were midway through the morning.

"North, a few hours away," Noah replied. He knew he was being vague but he wasn't going to give Mason any information.

Mason laughed but kept on working. "What are you doing here? It's been over a week, isn't your delivery late by now?"

He had put a particular emphasis on the word 'delivery' and Noah knew that explanation wasn't going to work much longer. In fact, the delivery still didn't happen because he never did call the Harris's back. A fact he wasn't proud of.

He wanted to tell him to back off and mind his own business, that he was being a bully. He also wanted to catch him doing something illegal so that he could arrest him. Instead, Noah simply said, "No."

The Mason from a week ago would not have given up so easily. That Mason would have kept asking questions until he got a straight answer. That or punch him in the face. This Mason was too distracted to care. That was fine with Noah.

At lunch time, Kate came up on horseback. As she jumped down and approached the two men, Mason went up to her and kissed her on the lips. She tried to wiggle away, but he grabbed her around the waist and held her still.

When Mason finally released her he said, "Not for me today, babydoll. I can't stay."

Kate and Noah both watched as Mason got in his truck, backed up and drove off. Noah realized his mistake when he was suddenly stranded at least a mile from the house. He threw his hat on the ground and ran a hand through his hair.

"It's okay, Noah," Kate said, knowing what he was mad about. "Let's call it an early day and ride back with me."

Noah looked at the one horse and realized what she meant. They would have to ride together on the back of one horse. He didn't mind walking, but what was he trying to prove.

"Okay," Noah relented. "But let's eat first."

Kate smiled as she laid out a blanket and they sat down together. She didn't actually intend to stay and eat, not bringing a lunch for herself, but since Mason had left, she ate his. At first they ate in silence, letting the birds be the only sound they heard. But Noah needed to apologize.

"Katie, I'm sorry for what I said the other night," Noah started. "I was out of line and I shouldn't have said it."

"It's okay. I know not everyone sees the good side of Mason," Kate replied.

"There's a good side?" Noah didn't mean to say that out loud and apologized, again.

Kate didn't respond. She finished her bite and looked at him. "He just doesn't like the ranch. He wants me to give it all up and move in with him. He lives in the city, I tried it once and hated it."

Noah was surprised with how open she was being with him. He was given a small glimpse into her life with Mason and it wasn't what he wanted for her. She deserved a man's attention, love and loyalty. This moment of raw vulnerability made Noah want to share something of himself with Katie.

"I was engaged once, last year," Noah said.

Kate waited for more, but he didn't elaborate. There was a sadness in his voice. "Did she call it quits?"

"No, she died."

Without thinking, Kate grabbed Noah's hand and squeezed it. He looked up at her and saw his own sadness reflected there. He was caught off guard by her touch and they just stared into each other's eyes for a long moment.

"I'm so sorry," Kate said, and Noah believed her. He knew that her heart empathized with his. He felt it in her touch and saw it in her eyes.

"It's partly the reason why I came to Virginia, I needed to get away for a while," Noah said. He even surprised himself with how candid he was being with his private life. He was breaking his own rule about not divulging too much personal information. But this was Katie.

They finished their lunch and packed up all of the things that Kate had brought with her. She jumped up on the horse first and Noah climbed on behind her. It was intoxicating being this close to her. Her hair brushed against his face as the horse walked slowly towards home.

Noah could smell the faint scent of lavender in her hair. It reminded him of Malia, but only slightly. Malia wasn't here anymore, but Katie was. She was so close he was touching her. His hands were on Katie's hips as the movement of the horse moved them in a rhythmic motion.

Noah closed his eyes, imagining that Katie was his girl and he was hers. He was falling for this woman. As much as he tried to fight it, it was happening.

"I want to show you something," Kate whispered just loud enough for him to hear. It snapped him back to reality and the horse veered to the left.

Noah watched as the landscape changed. It was greener and more lush here and he could hear the sound of water. Lots of water.

Kate stopped the horse and they both jumped off. Kate took Noah's hand and led him to the base of an amazing waterfall. The water came from a cliff that was about twenty feet high and fell to a pool of water that was so clear and welcoming.

"What do you think?" Kate asked, smiling.

"It's beautiful," Noah answered, but he was looking at her.

Kate blushed and led him to the edge of the pond. "Do you want to go in?" She asked.

"Now?"

"Yes, silly," Kate replied.

Noah watched as she took off her t-shirt and shorts to reveal a bikini underneath. She carefully stepped into the pond and walked over to the waterfall. She looked up and let the water fall down her body. Noah couldn't help but admire her. She wasn't shy or embarrassed and asked him to come in, too.

Noah didn't have a bathing suit on under his pants, just briefs. He wasn't shy either. He was thirty years old and they were both adults. He could keep his hands to himself, maybe.

He took his shirt off and slid his jeans down. He had to be careful to hide his gun in his pants pocket so she wouldn't see it. He wasn't sure why he kept it hidden, Noah was pretty sure Kate had grown up around guns her whole life, probably was pretty good at handling one, but he had never told anyone about it and thought that was for the best.

Noah stood on the edge of the pond with only his briefs on. Kate watched him as he eased into the water and made his way to join her under the waterfall. Their eyes never left each other's the entire time. Kate admired his body as he made his way closer.

Under the waterfall, Noah exhaled. He didn't realize he had been holding his breath until this moment. They sat under the rushing water without saying anything. They were both occupied with their own thoughts. Then Noah turned to Katie.

"Thank you for bringing me here," he said.

"It's my favorite place on the whole ranch," she said.

"I understand why," Noah said and took her hand.

Kate turned towards Noah. They were standing just inches apart when Kate leaned forward and kissed him on the mouth. The kiss didn't last long but the feeling of her lips did. Noah didn't know what to do, he knew he shouldn't be kissing Mason's girlfriend but here she was kissing him.

"I'm sorry," Kate said.

Noah didn't know what to say. He wasn't sorry at all.

The physical attraction was too much and Kate had already overstepped the boundary. "We'd better go," she said.

They made their way back to the edge of the pond and got dressed. Neither one of them were eager to leave but it was inevitable, they had to get back.

"Thank you for this, Katie" Noah said, again.

Kate simply nodded her head and climbed back on the horse and so did Noah. They rode in silence, nothing more could be said. The kiss said it all. Kate could feel his warm body against her back, it was all she could think about.

Noah's hands started off on her hips but slowly moved up and rested on her waist. He didn't dare move them any further. Kate was not his girlfriend, he had no right to want her. He wished they were miles away from the house, but they could see it in the distance.

Kate led the horse into the barn and Noah helped her take off the saddle. They checked on Daisy and hesitated. Kate didn't want to leave and lingered as long as she could, but she had to get back to the house. She had been gone for hours and that wasn't like her.

Noah said he was going to stay behind and he watched her leave the barn. He was playing with fire and knew that it wouldn't end well for him. What did he care? He would be gone in another week or two anyway. Still, he knew better.

Just as Noah was about to head towards the cottage, he spotted someone sneaking out of the house, again. Henry was getting into a car with his guitar in the backseat. Noah watched as he put the car in reverse and backed up slowly. Just when Henry thought he had made a clean getaway, he locked eyes with Noah.

Henry didn't know Noah that well and he wasn't sure if he would tell on him. Henry didn't wait to find out, he continued out the drive way and turned onto the main road. Whatever Henry was up to, it was none of Noah's business. He wouldn't say anything to his family, but he might have a talk with him.

Noah went back to the cottage and took a hot shower. It reminded him of the waterfall. It reminded him of Katie.

Chapter 11

Noah enjoyed the solitude of his work. It was better for him to avoid the house anyway. Out on the land there was no temptation or regret, just him and nature. He was starting to feel guilty, though. He had another nightmare, the first in a long while, but it took him back to that night. It took him back to Malia.

Part of him never wanted to leave this ranch. Another part couldn't wait to leave. What was he going to do? He never did have a plan other than bring Malia's ashes to her parents. Beyond that he just wanted time alone.

He didn't really know how long this fence would take. Some days were easier than others but it was nearly two weeks already and it was only half way finished. Noah was pretty sure that when Kate told him about the scope of the job she didn't really know how long it would take, either.

Well, he was determined to finish it. Noah was not a quitter. He may be broken and alone, but he wasn't a quitter. During his off time, he loved just exploring the land. He never needed to even leave the ranch. There were so many hidden gems to explore just in this radius.

Noah wasn't so sure he could go back to wearing a uniform and being confined to a police car every day, he had a lot to think about. Virginia had changed him and it was most definitely for the better. He kept in contact with his parents. They were concerned with how long he was staying away, but couldn't deny the change in his voice and attitude that they noticed.

He looked forward to Kate coming on horseback to deliver his freshly made lunch each day, but today was different. Teri rode up to him and jumped off her horse.

"Hey there, cowboy," Teri said. "Hungry?"

Noah stopped what he was doing, took off his hat and wiped his brow. "Yes, thank you."

She didn't make a big deal about the lunch as Kate did, there was no blanket to sit on or plates to lay their food out on. Teri just handed Noah his cooler and they sat right on the grass in the shade.

"So you have the day off today?" Noah asked.

"Yes, the diner is pretty flexible with my schedule," Teri replied. "They know that if they need me at the ranch, I can't come in."

Noah didn't ask why the ranch needed her, he just ate his lunch. Perhaps if he didn't ask personal questions, she wouldn't either. No luck.

"So what really brought you to Summer Hill?" Teri asked.

The directness of the question made Noah choke on his water. "I had to deliver something here." It was Noah's story and he was sticking to it.

"So did you?"

"Not yet."

"Why?"

Noah didn't know how to answer that one. He had been asking it himself for days, even weeks. He's tried calling, but never followed through beyond that.

"I don't know," Noah said and paused. "It will be very difficult."

"So you're hiding," Teri replied.

Noah smiled at her. "Not exactly," Noah said, trying to think of the proper word. "Procrastinating."

"So you don't like to do things that are difficult," Teri responded, accusingly.

Noah shook his head and was reminded of his years as a cop. "No, it's not that. It's just...this is different, this is personal."

Teri ate her food and watched Noah struggle with his answer. She knew he was choosing his words very carefully. He was hiding something. Teri wondered if Mason wasn't right after all. Kate always said they could trust him, that he was a good guy. Mason insisted he wasn't.

She would try to give Noah the benefit of the doubt. Maybe he was just someone passing time until he built up his nerve to do something he didn't want to do, or he had ulterior motives. Time would tell, she just hoped they wouldn't be hurt in the process.

Teri looked at Noah and decided to take a chance. "I want to show you something," she said.

"The waterfall?" Noah asked.

Teri smiled. "No, that's my sister's favorite place, I want to show you mine."

Noah wasn't sure what to expect, but it was safer to hang out with Teri than it was with Kate. He was also open to see places of the ranch he might not have seen yet.

"Sure, what is it?" Noah asked.

Teri jumped up and held out her hand. She seemed excited for him to join her. "It's the lake and it's not far from here. We can walk."

Noah took her hand as she helped him up. They walked together through a small group of trees and into another clearing. Teri was right, it wasn't far. In front of them was a large lake, complete with a boat, a dock and an out building presumably with supplies for each.

The lake was beautiful. The trees provided shade to half of the lake and it felt ten degrees cooler there. It was a large enough lake that it was difficult to see the other side and the Pattersons owned it all.

"This is my favorite place," Teri announced. "We come here a lot for swimming, fishing and hanging out."

"I can see why!" Noah replied. "It's wonderful."

Noah was too busy admiring the view to notice that Teri had stripped down to a bikini. "Last one in is a rotten egg!"

Teri's playful spirit made Noah smile. He had no intention of reliving the intimacy of the waterfall, so Noah simply stood on the bank and watched. Teri knew he probably wouldn't join her, but it was fun to watch his reaction.

"Come on, cowboy," Teri said from the water.

"No, I'm good right here," Noah replied with a smile.

He watched as Teri would climb on the dock and jump. She was like a little kid on a summer holiday. Noah had to admit that Teri was pretty, but he was not interested, not in this sister.

Noah laid down in the cool grass under the shade of the trees. He closed his eyes and let his mind wander. He couldn't stop thinking about the waterfall and Kate's kiss. He was starting to have real feelings for her and that worried him. As much as he tried to avoid her, his thoughts always betrayed him.

Noah's thoughts were interrupted by drops of water on his face. He opened his eyes to see Teri hovering over him as her wet, blond hair dripped into his face. Noah tried using his arm to shield his face as he sat up and laughed.

"I've been trying to get your attention, cowboy!" Teri said. "We can leave now, I need to get back to the house."

Noah waited for Teri to get dressed and they walked the short distance back to her horse. He helped her up and thanked her for the pleasant afternoon.

"Anytime, cowboy," Teri said as she turned the horse in the direction of home.

Noah knew he should get right back to work, but instead he sat off the back of his pick up truck. He had a lot going on in his head right now. Noah didn't know how much longer he could keep being vague about why he was here. He didn't want them to get the wrong impression of him and be suspicious.

He needed to be honest about who he was and what he has been through. There was only one person he could envision telling his truth to, he just needed to find the right time. He didn't know if he could say it all at once, either. It would be a lot for anyone to handle, even him.

Noah decided to work a little bit more on the fence and head back early today. He just wasn't into it anymore that evening. He worked a couple more hours and then hopped in this truck to head back to the house. The flexibility the Patterson Ranch offered him was going to be hard to leave someday.

He waved at Kate from the kitchen window as he walked to the cottage out back. If she wondered why he was home early, she didn't say. He just walked past the main house and into the small cottage to be enveloped by its cozy familiarity. He was suddenly relieved to be indoors and in the comfort of his own untamed emotions.

Noah kicked off his boots and sank into the chair near the door. He ran his hands through his hair and looked around him. He had gotten used to this little cottage. The picture on his bedside table caught his eye. It was the engagement photo of him and Malia at Niagara Falls. Happier times.

AS SOON AS TERI HAD walked in the front door after delivering Noah's lunch, Kate let her know she was upset. Teri knew she shouldn't have taken him to the lake, but she couldn't help it. Immediately Kate wondered what took her so long, why was she dripping wet and what did she say to Noah?

Teri tried to calm her sister down, but she had to say that she was starting to agree with Mason. She wasn't sure Noah was as sweet and innocent as he led them to believe. Mason had said this to everyone in the family but Kate always defended Noah, unwilling to believe Noah was anything but a nice guy that needed time away.

"Maybe you just don't want to see it," Teri said accusingly.

"Nonsense, I can tell he is not here to hurt anyone," Kate replied.

Teri just looked at her older sister. "We will see," she said ominously.

Yes, they would, Kate said to herself. They will see that Noah isn't hiding anything, nothing more than any of us are hiding pieces that we are ashamed or embarrassed about. It's normal and natural to not give strangers every last detail about their past. But were they still strangers? Perhaps they were.

Kate wasn't sure what all happened between Teri and Noah today and she knew her sister wasn't going to tell her. Maybe Noah would. Kate had seen him come home earlier than usual and wondered if it had anything to do with Teri.

Kate hadn't finished preparing dinner, so she decided to make Noah a sandwich and take it to him, perhaps he would fill in some details. He didn't join them for family dinners and she understood why. Nothing like being interrogated by six people all at once, seven if you include Mason.

She tried her best to keep Mason away from Noah. She saw how Noah reacted to him and it was for the best to keep them separated. It was the best for all of them. But, when Mason offered to help on the ranch, she just couldn't say no, she actually liked that he offered when he had the time.

It seemed like Mason didn't have a lot of time for her lately, though. He didn't usually stay away so much and hoped that everything was okay with him. She knew Mason Fisher could take care of himself, but it also concerned her when he was this quiet. They would have to have a talk soon.

Kate walked out the back door and down the lane to the cottage. Holding the tray of food, she managed to knock on the door without dropping anything. She didn't know why she suddenly felt so nervous waiting for Noah to answer the door.

Noah heard the tentative knock on the front door. Not wanting another episode of getting caught in only a towel, he made a point of getting dressed as soon as he finished his showers now. Noah opened the door expecting to see Teri. It was Kate.

"Katie," Noah said with surprise in his voice. "Come in."

"Thank you," she replied.

Noah held open the door wide enough to accommodate her and the tray she carried. He watched as Kate walked into the kitchen and placed it carefully on the small table along the wall. She turned to him and gestured to the modest feast under the towel.

"I thought you might like some dinner but it wasn't actually ready, yet, so this is just a sandwich and some side dishes," Kate said. "There are a couple cold beers, too."

Noah could tell she was nervous, fidgeting with the towel in her hands that was, a minute ago, covering the tray of food. Noah slowly approached her. Kate couldn't look him in the eyes, she just looked from the table to the towel she now twisted in her hands.

They were inches apart now, they could even feel each other's quick and shallow breaths. When Kate finally brought her eyes up to meet his her breathing became unsteady. Sensing this, Noah reached out his hand and took one of hers.

"Thank you," he said. "That was very nice of you."

Kate didn't trust herself to speak. She just nodded her head and smiled. Noah smiled, too. He knew he could trust her but could he tell her the truth about him, here...now? They both spoke at once.

"Well, I'd better...." Kate started.

"Katie, there's something...." Noah started.

They both stood in awkward silence until Kate moved past him. Her shoulder brushed Noah's, his left shoulder. Subconsciously he rubbed his shoulder and turned just in time to see Kate exit the cottage.

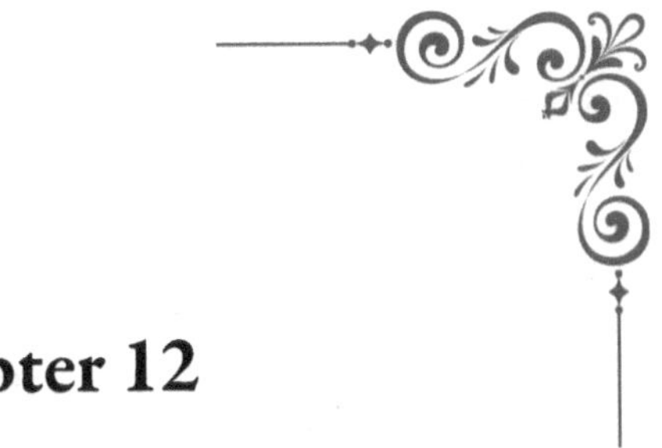

Chapter 12

"It doesn't matter how many times you look at the statements, Kate, they always say the same thing! We don't have the money." Clayton Patterson was upset. The ranch's finances were dire. He had been pouring over the numbers for weeks, months even, and they always said the same thing.

"Maybe we need to sell," Clayton said quietly.

"It can't be that bad," Ashley replied.

The couple looked at each other, Ashley had always let her husband handle the finances and she knew deep down that if that was the conclusion he made, then it must be bad. This ranch had been in Clayton's family for generations and they had hoped it always would be. Henry was next in line, however unlikely that might seem.

"Dad, there has to be another way," Kate said, trying to project a confidence she didn't feel.

Clayton simply shook his head and wheeled himself into the other room. He was tired of discussing it or even thinking about it anymore. Kate and her mother looked at each other, a loss for words. Kate felt the tears pooling in the corners of her eyes and turned towards the sink. She made an effort to wash a coffee mug while staring out the window.

Today was a day off for the ranch, apart from the normal chores. Kate still had a lot to do. The fiery discussion this morning with her father was enough to make her want to drive away. But she didn't. Instead, she went to the barn.

The vet said that Daisy could give birth very soon. That was exciting for Kate. They hadn't had a foal born on the ranch in several years and this would be cause for celebration. She produced a carrot and an apple to Daisy when she came to her stall.

"Well, now you're just spoiling her," a voice said from behind her.

Kate turned to see Noah, a carrot in his hand, too. She laughed, it was easy to laugh around Noah. It felt natural to be relaxed and calm around him.

"Nothing is too good for my Daisy," Kate replied.

This time it was Noah who laughed and joined her in front of the pregnant horse. "I'm sorry, I don't mean to keep putting you in an awkward position," Noah said.

Kate looked confused. "What do you mean?"

"It just seems like we are always alone together," Noah started. This was harder to articulate than he expected. "It's hard to be alone with you. Plus, there's Mason to consider."

Kate looked at Daisy and shook her head. "I like being with you," Kate started. "It's...calming." She risked a quick glance at him to see his reaction.

Noah smiled. "You don't look calm, Katie" he said.

Kate waited until Daisy finished her treats and exhaled deeply. She put both hands in her pockets and stood facing Noah.

"The ranch is in trouble," Kate said matter-of-factly. "Financial trouble." She didn't know why she told him, maybe the weight was just too much for her to bare alone any longer.

Whatever Noah was expecting her to say, this was not it. He was a little taken aback, not just with the information, but that she was being so open with him. It made him want to do the same. But not now, this was her time.

"Why?" Noah asked, genuinely interested. "I thought the corn crops were doing well."

"They are, or were," Kate replied. "It's just that the price we're getting for them is down and it's hurting us."

"Sounds like you need another means of creating revenue," Noah said. He started rubbing his chin and walking in circles. He desperately wanted to help this family and Katie. "Have you considered tourism?"

"What do you mean?" Kate asked, interested.

Noah came over to Kate and took her hand. It was not meant as a romantic gesture, he wanted to lead her to the entrance of the barn.

"Look at all of this land, you could use it to your advantage, your financial advantage," Noah answered.

Kate looked around but was still confused. "How?"

Noah smiled. "I think people would pay to ride your horses, to rent out your lake or even the cottage."

Kate shook her head. She didn't think people would want to come here and pay to ride their horses. She thought Noah was just making jokes. "No, they wouldn't."

"Yes, I believe they would," Noah insisted. "If you market it to the cities as a weekend getaway or even a destination for groups to use the lake, it could be a hit with the city folks wanting a taste of the country life."

Kate was trying to see his vision, but wasn't completely onboard.

"Just suggest it to your family," Noah encouraged. "I'm telling you as someone who drove four hours to come to Summer Hill, I could see my friends and family doing the same thing on the weekend."

"Maybe."

Noah turned to her, "Weddings!"

"What?"

"Have you ever considered offering the ranch as a venue for weddings? The ranch has so many possibilities such as the barn, the lake...even the waterfall," Noah said with a smile.

This made Kate's face lift into a near smile. She hadn't thought about being a wedding venue, why hadn't they? It did seem more logical than a weekend rental but she would bring all of Noah's suggestions to her father.

"Come to family dinner tonight," Kate said. "You should be the one to tell my father your suggestions."

Noah shook his head, "No, it should come from you. I don't want him to think that I have any ulterior motives," Noah replied. "I just want to see you happy again, Katie."

"Thank you, I do feel happier than I did an hour ago," Kate admitted.

"Good."

Just then a soccer ball came out of nowhere and almost hit Kate in the face. They both turned to the direction of the kick and saw Lorna with her hands to her face.

"Sorry!" Lorna yelled.

The big sister reassured her that she was fine and Noah and Kate joined her in a game of soccer, girls against boys, of course. It was such a lighthearted afternoon of laughter and soccer. The girls were winning and when Noah spotted Henry on the front porch, he called out to him.

"Henry, I need your help! These girls are kicking my butt," Noah said.

Henry smiled and nodded but made no attempt to get up. "Nah, I'm good," Henry replied and continued playing his guitar on the porch swing.

Henry was not the soccer type. He had a gig to get to later tonight and with everyone home, he wasn't sure how he could sneak out without anyone seeing him. Noah had seen him the last time and was afraid he would say something to Kate or his parents. To his credit, he hadn't.

To Henry, music was his life. He didn't dare tell anyone in his family that the bar in town let him play at night for tips. He was nervous that someone he knew would say something, like Mason. Mason knew what he did, even tipped him pretty well the nights he performed, but never told his family.

Henry liked Mason, but knew he wasn't good for his sister. Mason had secrets and he was pretty sure they weren't good ones. Henry had watched Mason flirt with all of the waitresses at the bar. He would pinch their butts and stuff dollars down their shirts. It was disgusting but he could never tell Kate any of that.

Henry wasn't worried about what his sister would say, he was more afraid of what Mason would say. Mason would know it was him that told and he was sure that Mason would hurt him. He was as sure of this fact as the sky was blue. No one messed with Mason Fisher unless you were prepared for the consequences.

Henry hummed his latest composition as he strummed the guitar. He watched the soccer game out on the field and wondered about Noah. Everyone wondered about Noah. He was an enigma and seemed to be trying to move in on his eldest sister. He just hoped Noah knew what he was doing. He was teasing the viper and that could only end one way.

"Who wants some cookies and lemonade?" Ashley came out onto the porch and yelled in the direction of the kids.

All heads turned to the porch and they made their way to the shade. Henry took this as his cue to go back inside the house. Groups weren't his thing, either. Noah sat on the swing and Kate joined him. Lorna sat on one of the many wicker chairs. They all commented on how great the lemonade tasted on this hot day.

"Yes, I needed a break," Lorna agreed.

Kate and Noah both smiled and took a cookie. Kate knew her mother made the best chocolate chip cookies in the state and Noah agreed. It wasn't just the cookies and the lemonade. This part of the country was a little slice of heaven that Noah didn't even know existed.

He couldn't believe that Malia grew up in this town and then chose to live in the big city. Compared to this, Pittsburgh could have been Los Angeles or NYC for all she knew. Of course, leaving home was her decisions, not being able to return was all because of her parents prejudices.

He knew that things would have been easier for her if Noah wasn't white, but he was and she loved him. Because of that, her parents refused to be a part of her life. It was hard for him to swallow sometimes. Malia could have any race of friends she wanted, but not a boyfriend or fiancé.

He was sure they blamed him for her death, whether it was directly or indirectly. The violence of the big city, living with Noah or not coming back home even when they begged her. Pick any or all reasons and Noah was sure it crossed their minds.

This was why he never went to the Harris's. He was afraid that even stepping onto their property was like pouring salt into a gaping and festering wound. But he had to do it, he had to make it right with Malia. She belonged back with her family.

"Are you okay?" Kate asked. "You seem a million miles away."

Noah blinked his eyes and brought himself back to the present. "Sorry, I was thinking about something I need to do."

At this, Noah stood up and left the porch without any further explanations. He walked around back to the little cottage and laid down on the bed. He let the tears come. Noah thought he had cried the last for Malia months ago, but it was funny how grief worked. Grief had no rules.

Noah showered and climbed into bed. It wasn't his usual bed time, but he was suddenly very tired. He looked over at the picture of the happily engaged couple and let the sadness envelope him. He would be fine tomorrow, he knew.

Tonight he let himself be sad. He was sad for the woman who's life ended too soon. He was sad for the ranch who might have to be sold. But mostly, he was sad for a woman he was falling for and couldn't have.

Chapter 13

After breakfast, and with the family still gathered around the table, Kate decided to relay all of the suggestions Noah had mentioned in regard to alleviating their financial headache. She had watched Noah leave in his truck already, so she knew she was on her own in this.

Kate cleared her throat and wiped her palms on her shorts. "So, I've been thinking about the ranch and how we might be able to save it," Kate started. All eyes were on her, waiting. "I think we should open ourselves up to tourism."

Everyone looked at each other and then back to Kate. She continued, "There are a few ways we can go about this and depending on the season, we could even do several simultaneously." Kate sat up straighter and talked with more confidence than she felt at the moment.

"We could do weddings, at least be the venue. We could clean up the barn and have ceremonies in there, or out on the field. Even the lake or waterfall could be a great place once we get a decent access road ready." Kate had their full attention.

"We could also rent out the cottage, like on a nightly rental site. It could even be combined with a wedding if they wanted it." Kate paused and took a sip of her coffee. "Another option is to rent out the lake for parties or reunions, that kind of thing. They could have access to the boat and boathouse. It's private enough that loud music wouldn't be an issue."

Encouraged by their interested looks, Kate went on. "Winter could be ice skating. We do that anyway, why not charge the public. We could do sleigh rides and corn mazes, maybe even plant pumpkins for next fall and have a whole fall festival."

Kate watched her father. He was starting to actually smile. The first smile she had seen on him in weeks. "What do you think, dad?"

"I think these ideas actually have potential," Clayton agreed. "Some are more readily doable, for sure. It could really make an immediate impact, Kate. Thank you."

Kate felt her whole body relax. She wanted to give Noah the full credit, but now was not the time. Baby steps, she thought. Let's get some of these ideas up and running and when they are successful, she can mention Noah. Not now, not yet.

"I'll call some people and see if we can't make something happen," Clayton said before leaving the kitchen.

Her mother smiled at her. "Kate, that was unexpected but wonderful news this morning."

Kate couldn't wait to tell Noah the good news, his ideas were a hit with her family. She was proud of herself for trusting Noah enough to let him in on her troubles and that she actually followed through with telling her parents about the new ideas. This could be a turning point for the Patterson Ranch.

She busied herself with chores until she could meet Noah for lunch. Kate caught up on the laundry that she had been avoiding for days. She was even able to pick enough vegetables in the garden to serve with the meatloaf tonight. Kate made Lorna and Henry clean their rooms and asked Teri to collect the eggs.

Today her spirits were up, it was a good day. She packed lunches for her and Noah and after looking at the sun high in the sky, decided to put on her bikini. She wanted to take him back to the waterfall.

Kate rode the horse to where Noah was working on the fence today. She noticed how handsome he was with his cutoff sleeves and jeans. She would never have guessed that he wasn't from this town, wasn't raised in cowboy hats and boots. All the Patterson kids got new ones practically every Christmas.

Noah stopped working and smiled as Kate approached him on the horse. He helped her down and they were again just inches apart. Noah stepped back and Kate turned to produce two coolers filled with their lunches.

"Do you want to eat here or at the waterfall?" Kate asked.

Noah smiled. "The waterfall," he replied.

Kate's face beamed at his answer. She felt like a teenager around Noah. Kate got back on the horse and Noah settled in behind her. He placed his hands on her waist and breathed in the lavender scent of her hair. Noah would not hesitate getting in the water today.

They ate first. Kate had laid out a blanket for them to sit on and they watched each other as they chewed each bite. The anticipation of touching and kissing her again felt endless. When they finished, Kate stood up and undressed to reveal her bikini. Without any encouragement, Noah undressed down to his briefs.

He followed her into the water and met her at the waterfall. They were playful today, laughing and splashing until Kate ended up in his arms. As the water poured down from above them, they stayed like that, looking into each other's eyes.

It was Noah this time who kissed Kate. He wasn't sorry about it, he wanted to do it. He had been wanting to do for a long time. Kate, however, was in too much of a playful mood to linger. She was out of his embrace just as quickly as she had gotten into it.

Noah looked around but Kate was already swimming away. She continued to laugh and splash all the while swimming towards the bank of the water. Noah followed her, eager to kiss her one more time. She crawled to the blanket and used it as a towel.

Noah sat beside her and shook his head making his hair spray water on her like a wet dog. They both laughed and she offered him half of the blanket. He wrapped it around his shoulders just like her. The stayed huddled under the blanket as the sun warmed up their skin.

"You're in a good mood," Noah said.

"Yes, I am!" Kate confirmed.

"Tell me why."

"It's all because of you," Kate said. The surprised look on Noah's face made her realize how that sounded to him. "I mean, your ideas," she corrected. "I told my family about the suggestions you made and my father loved them, all of them."

"I'm glad I could help, truly, Katie."

"I know. Thank you for that," she replied.

There was so much that they wanted to tell each other. Still so many secrets to share. Noah wanted to but he was also afraid of her reaction. He decided to keep his secrets for as long as he could. He appreciated the fact that Kate never pushed him to explain.

He knew she saw his scar and knew she had questions. These were answers he wasn't ready to talk about, yet. Maybe later. Noah was getting good at putting things off. His 'to do' list was getting longer with each passing day.

"Well, I'd better get back," Kate said without moving.

"Me, too," Noah replied.

Neither one wanted this moment to end. He knew these stolen moments were going to catch up with them. Mason didn't come around very often which was good for Noah, but he still couldn't understand why she didn't just break up with the guy. They didn't even spend much time together.

Noah was the first to stand up and get dressed. Reluctantly, Kate followed his lead and loaded up her things. They rode on horseback and Noah held her waist one last time. At his truck and they said their goodbyes. Noah worked the rest of the afternoon thinking about what changes were coming to the ranch. He had started a wheel of change around him that was gaining momentum.

He loved the ranch as it was, quiet and private, but it would never grow this way. They needed income and the only way he could see it happening was to open it up to the public. He knew several people who would want to be first on their list of paying visitors. It would have made a great wedding venue. Noah shook the images from his past away, he would focus on his future.

At the house, Kate's father was more animated than she had seem him in weeks. The new ideas had sparked new excitement in him then ever before. It was July and the Fourth of July Carnival was only a couple of days away. Clayton wanted to run some ideas past his friends and get their opinions, too.

Kate had been so preoccupied she had completely forgotten about the carnival. She and Mason went together every year. She made a mental note to call him about it later. It was odd that she hadn't heard from him or seen him in a few days. Kate hoped he wasn't up to his old tricks, again. It was getting old.

The carnival was a big deal in the county. Everyone came for the food, rides, petting zoo and fireworks. She realized that this was probably Noah's first carnival in Virginia and knew he would love it. Kate couldn't wait to bring him and show him around. Then she thought of Mason.

How was she going to suggest to Mason that they bring Noah along? Well, she would. He had to admit that Noah was doing a great job on the fence and it was only right that he attend the carnival with the Patterson family. It would be like the whole family was inviting him along, not just Kate.

She decided to give Mason a call.

"Hello, babe," Mason said.

"Hi, how are you? Is this a good time?" Kate asked.

"Yes, why?"

"Well, I really haven't heard from you in a long time, I figured you were extra busy with...things," Kate replied.

Mason laughed a deep laugh. "I've always got time for you, Kate."

"Are you planning to go to the Fourth of July Carnival? It's coming up," she reminded him.

"Oh, I know," Mason answered. "I've been meaning to talk to you about that. I think I have to work, a new client and all."

Kate was not only disappointed, she was angry. "Really, Mason!"

"Listen, I know you're upset. I'll come over tomorrow and we can discuss it. We can spend some time together to make up for it," Mason replied.

Kate didn't want to discuss anything, not now. She said good bye and hung up the phone. She was sitting on her bed and after the conversation with Mason, she laid down and cried. How had their relationship gone so off course? Weren't they happy together anymore?

There was nothing she could do now. Kate must have dozed off because the high pitch beep of the weather alarm woke her up. It was evening and the alarm said that a major storm was rolling in later tonight. She would have to close up the barn and make preparations.

They had a generator for power failures that happened during storms. It only worked at the house, not the cottage. She would just have to make sure Noah had candles, other than that, he would be fine. Her biggest concern was Daisy.

Mason was now the furthest thing from her mind. Noah had asked why she was with him and to be honest, she didn't have a good enough reason to put up with his games. She supposed they were just comfortable with each other at this point. After years of being together, you either got married or gave up. She wasn't sure which would come first for them.

Kate went downstairs to start making dinner. She wanted to get as much done before the storm as possible. If the weather alarm was alerting them, it would be a big one. At least she had some time to prepare.

As Kate was pulling items out of the freezer to cook, she was relieved when she saw Noah return in the truck. She knew it was nearly time for him to return, but if she didn't see him soon, she would have called him. Apparently, the dark sky did that for her.

Dark clouds were rolling in fast, in more ways than one.

Chapter 14

Noah had awoken from a deep sleep. He didn't know if it was because of the nightmare he just had or the clap of thunder he just heard. Either way, he was now wide awake. Lightening made the cottage look like midday and Noah tried the light switch. It worked, for now.

He got dressed and then looked out the window. Rain was coming down at an angle and the trees were swaying so far that he thought they would snap. Noah had lived through strong storms before, but not in Summer Hill. Kate had warned him that it could get pretty bad.

Bad was an understatement. He thought the cottage was pretty solid and that he wasn't in immediate danger but he did worry about the main house and the barn. Daisy was ready to give birth and this could be the catalyst for that event.

Just as Noah decided to head for the barn with blankets in hand, he lost power. He opened the door and saw darkness all around. He figured the power was out in the whole area. He pulled up the hood of his raincoat and made a run for the barn.

Noah's boots were sloshing through puddles. He tried to avoid them, but in this rain, it turned everything to mud so deep he could lose a boot. Noah headed straight for the barn. He could see a faint light coming from inside the closed doors and hoped nothing bad happened.

When Noah came bursting through the closed doors of the barn, Kate jumped. Neither one was expecting company out here but both were grateful to see the other one.

"I can't get ahold of the vet!" Kate said in a panicked voice. She had been walking in circles and trying desperately to get ahold of their vet.

"Why? What's wrong?" Noah asked.

"It's Daisy, I think she ready to have the baby, but the vet isn't answering!"

Noah walked over to Kate and held her arms to her sides. "Breathe, Katie. Take deep breaths and calm down. Panicking isn't helping Daisy, either." Kate did as she instructed. "Now try one more time to call the vet."

The vet picked up on the third ring. Kate was visibly relieved as was Noah. She explained that Daisy was ready to give birth, she could see the feet. However, her relief turned to panic, again, when the vet said she could not come.

"I'm sorry," said the vet. "I'm at the Leary farm right now, their cow is sick and there's no way I can make it across the county in time. Daisy will be fine. Just let her do her thing. Feet, legs, nose, head and back legs, in that order, if not, call me again."

The phone disconnected and Kate looked like she was about to faint. Noah was prepared for emergencies, not exactly this situation, but he knew how to calm people down and talk them off of ledges. That training would come in handy now.

"Everything will be okay," Noah said as calmly as possible. "You heard the vet, Daisy knows what to do. We can help her."

Kate was still taking deep breaths and simply nodded her head. The storm was making it impossible for her to relax but she tried focusing on Daisy. They entered her stall and sat down, both stroking her and giving her encouragement.

"Good girl, Daisy," Kate said. "You can do it."

Noah watched Kate. She was so good with the horses, so good with the ranch. He thought she would make a good veterinarian herself. The thunder and lightening made them both jumpy. Kate was so glad Noah was there, with her.

They watched as Daisy pushed and then relaxed. The foal slowly emerged just as the vet described. The front feet came out followed by very long legs. The nose was next and then the whole head. The rest of the foal came out fast, the body and back legs, it was miraculous.

Daisy licked her new foal until it took its first breath and within a couple hours was standing and ready to nurse. Kate and Noah witnessed it all. It was with extreme relief that they didn't need to call the vet again. Daisy did it all by herself.

They sat in the barn until they knew the new foal was okay. They were sitting shoulder to shoulder facing Daisy's stall. Kate couldn't help but notice the way Noah flinched whenever a loud clap of thunder rang through the darkness.

It was easy to talk in the dark, it afforded an ambiguity unavailable in the light. Even though they knew they were talking to each other, the darkness shielded conversations and allowed only the inner most thoughts to come out.

"Noah, are you okay?"

"Yes, why?"

"I can feel your whole body tense up at the thunder," Kate said. When no answer came, she continued. "I never asked about the scar on your shoulder..."

Noah knew this conversation would happen eventually. He took a deep breath and responded. "I was shot," he said.

Those words hung in the air for a minute before he summoned the courage to continue. Luckily he couldn't see the look of pure shock on Kate's face or he would never have been able to say what he wanted to say.

"That's how my fiancé died. We were both shot. I survived, she didn't. It left me a little...shell shocked."

Kate was stunned. She could feel him exhale and relax beside her. She was glad that he couldn't see the silent tears running down her cheeks. She cried for his dead fiancé, she cried for him. In the darkness, grateful for his honesty, Kate reached for his hand and squeezed it.

Noah was lost in his thoughts of that night. There was more, of course, but not now, not tonight. Tonight they mourned a death and celebrated a life. Daisy and her foal were bonding and thriving, so were Kate and Noah.

She had so many more questions to ask him, but she restrained herself. So many thoughts ran through her mind and even doubts that Mason had planted had resurfaced. Why would someone get shot unless they were doing something they shouldn't have been? Was Noah a bad man like Mason had suggested?

The storm seemed to be subsiding, the worst of it was passing. All that was left was a steady rain, even the lights came back on. This was their cue to leave. The intimate moment had passed but left in its wake was something more, something deeper.

They were still holding hands when they stood up. Noah saw the wetness on her cheeks and wiped it away with his hand. His hand lingered on her cheek and she leaned into it. They gave each other a small smile.

Noah lowered his hand and Kate gave him a hug. It was warm and loving. Her hug said so much more than her words ever could. It conveyed sympathy and sorrow, and love. Her hug was full of love.

It was well after midnight and she needed to get back to the house. They said good night to each other and ran through the rain in separate directions. In the cottage, Noah was emotional. He didn't feel like crying, he did that already. He felt...happy.

Kate ran onto the front porch and shook herself off. She was so focused on not falling in the mud that she didn't notice the truck, Mason's truck. She walked slowly into the house as if he would jump out from around a corner.

She saw him sitting at the kitchen table drinking a beer when she walked in. He was waiting for her, but why?

"I was worried when I heard the news report and I came right over," Mason said.

"What news report?" She asked.

"Flash flooding, trees down and no power in half the county," Mason replied. He actually sounded annoyed that she didn't know. "Where have you been?"

"In the barn with...Daisy," she replied, catching herself. "She had her foal tonight. I guess the storm was too much for her."

Mason looked at her skeptically, but stood up to give her a hug. "I missed you, Kate."

"Me, too," she said. "You haven't been coming around much lately."

Mason released her and stepped back. "I've been busy, like I said on the phone," he answered. Again, he sounded annoyed at her comment. "You know I work so hard for you, for us, right? So that we can have a better future for us."

"Better than what? You know I love this farm and don't want to move," Kate replied. She didn't want to fight about this in the middle of the kitchen. "I'm going upstairs."

Mason followed her up. He had a bag on his shoulder and set it on the bed.

"What's that?" She asked.

"I'm staying over," Mason said, matter-of-factly. "I thought you were just complaining about how we don't spend enough time together and now that I said I'm spending the night, you don't want me to."

"I didn't say that," Kate replied. "I was simply asking a question." Kate shook her head in frustration and went in the bathroom to take a hot shower. How could this magical night turn so sour?

Mason had changed and was waiting for her in bed. Kate entered her room without looking at him and sat on the edge to brush her hair.

"So, how's the fence coming along? Shouldn't it be done by now so he can get on his way?" Mason said.

"It may take another week or so. He's doing a good, thorough job."

Mason sat up. "Teri said he has a scar the shape of a bullet wound in his shoulder. I told you he was trouble. Probably a drug deal gone bad." Mason spoke with such animosity, Kate had to stop what she was doing and turn to him.

"It was not from a drug deal, his fiancé was killed." As soon as the words came out Kate instantly regretted them. She had betrayed Noah's trust by telling Mason of all people.

Intrigued, Mason came around the bed to face Kate. "So you do know that he was shot. What else do you know about this mystery man?"

"Nothing. Let's just go to sleep," Kate said. Inside she prayed he would let it go.

Mason did let it go, for now. He would get to the bottom of it all, later. He had his ways and it might not be the conventional way of getting information, but he would get it. Nobody made a fool of Mason Fisher. He never liked that Noah and didn't like how close he was getting to his girlfriend.

Someone needed to teach Noah a lesson and Mason was happy to volunteer for that job. He would get with his buddies tomorrow and try to find out more about this Noah Wagner from Pittsburgh. He never really thought he needed to, until tonight.

Kate laid in bed beside Mason and pretended she was asleep. Mason tried to kiss and touch her but she knew he was too drunk to try very hard. She laid quiet and still until she heard the gentle snoring beside her. That was the only time she let herself relax.

She knew how to handle Mason, it was Noah she was afraid for. She was furious with herself for letting Noah's personal information slip out. He had trusted her and she let him down. Maybe Mason would let it go. He was too busy to get involved in Noah's life anyway.

The fence would be done in a week or so and Noah could go on his way, away from here. The thought of the Patterson Ranch without Noah here made her stomach twist up in knots. It was like a piece of her would be ripped out forever. Kate didn't want that to happen. Maybe it was finally time to break up with Mason.

The thought of telling Mason Fisher they were over added another knot to her stomach. Did she have the courage to do it? And what if she did and Noah left anyway? Her head was spinning and it was causing a terrible headache. She needed sleep.

Everything would look better in the morning, it had to.

Chapter 15

Today was the Fourth of July, the biggest celebration of the summer. Mason's ominous warning had been ringing in Kate's ears since the night he stayed over. She didn't tell Noah about the conversation, she was too embarrassed and scared to bring it up.

The Pattersons had a tradition of having their own cookout before going to the carnival. They all had their part in preparing the feast. Clayton made the burgers, Ashley made the macaroni salad, Teri made the cupcakes, Henry made the fruit salad and Lorna opened the cans of baked beans. It was simple but it was tradition.

Noah was outside with Lorna playing soccer again. Later when Kate looked out the window they were throwing a football. Mason never did any of those things with her siblings. It was when she saw Noah and Henry talking as they walked towards the barn that she felt that he could really fit in here at the ranch, with her.

Kate often felt that Henry was largely ignored by her parents. They expected so much from him that he wasn't willing to give an inch. She knew they wanted him to run the ranch, but he was the most uninterested out of all the kids. Even Teri would be a better fit than Henry and she was only here half the time. It put a lot of pressure on Henry.

Henry had other goals, ones that their parents didn't approve of. He loved music. He wasn't a rancher, he was a singer. She hoped he would be able to show them how much he loved it and how good he was at it someday. Henry had a good heart, he just needed more people to see it and appreciate it.

Everyone could smell the delicious aroma of the burgers cooking on the grill. Clayton's physical therapy was really coming along and he was putting in the work. He couldn't take more than a couple steps, but it was progress. That's all they could hope for right now.

It took several people to get him and his wheelchair down the back steps in order to access the grill, but once he was there, everyone knew Clayton was in charge.

"Burgers are ready!" Clayton announced.

With that, everyone ran to the food and got busy assembling plates. It was organized chaos as everyone filled their plates and sat down and the tables that were arranged outside. Everything tasted delicious. Clayton said the burgers were a secret family recipe and they all laughed. It was a running joke every year because they all knew what it was.

Noah laughed, enjoying the camaraderie of this family dynamic. He was an only child and envied those who grew up in a large family. To him, a family of six was enormous. The Pattersons were more than happy to include him. Noah was a welcome addition to the family and Ashley secretly hoped it would lead to something more.

She wouldn't dare say anything directly to her daughter, but she could pray for it each night and no one could stop her. She never liked Mason, he was a typical used car salesman. No one should trust anything out of his mouth, especially her daughter.

He would say he didn't want anything to do with the ranch, which she believed, but that wasn't going to stop him from continuing a dead relationship with Kate just to marry into it. She wanted her to see that, but she had to see it on her own.

Teri passed around her cupcakes and everyone ate them greedily. She never really bothered to make them red, white and blue. Today they were chocolate with chocolate icing and they were excellent. Noah complimented everyone on their contribution to the feast.

As plates and dishes were cleared away to the kitchen, they had a little bit more time before they left for the carnival. Noah took Lorna to see the new foal. Clayton had a smaller pen inside the larger field for just this reason. Mother and baby could live uninterrupted until they were ready to join the rest of the horses.

"We still have to name her," Kate said, coming up from behind them.

"What's it going to be?" Lorna asked.

"I don't know, yet. I have to think about it," Kate replied.

"Can I name her?" Lorna asked.

"Maybe."

Lorna ran back to the house which left Noah and Kate alone.

"Thanks, again, for that night. I couldn't have done it without you," Kate said.

"Yes, you could have, Katie." Noah said with a smile.

They watched as the little foal ran and danced around her mother. They were very lucky there weren't any complications. Kate looked at Noah. Maybe they were just plain lucky. Their intense gaze was only interrupted by the sound of her father's voice.

"Let's go!" Clayton yelled as Ashley pushed the wheelchair to the car.

Everyone wanted to drive separately. Henry would go, but he didn't want to stay. Clayton would go, but he got tired easily and Ashley would just end up bringing him home early, too. Teri and Lorna rode with their parents but would probably want to stay longer, so Noah said he'd take his truck so they could all stay a little longer.

Kate rode with Noah. Mason had called earlier to confirm he wasn't going to make it, to have fun without him. She would. All three vehicles pulled into the parking lot and everyone went their separate ways.

Noah had never seen anything like this before. They had fairs and festivals back home, but nothing like this. There were pens with pigs, cages with rabbits and pony rides. There were eating competitions, cooking competitions and Noah even saw a karaoke singing competition listed for later that evening.

Kate loved the atmosphere of the carnival. Everyone felt like a kid here, even a thirty year old man could have some fun here. She weaved her arm through Noah's and steered him towards the games. There was basketball throwing, baseball throwing and even a target shooting game.

"I'll give this one a try," Noah said, feeling the toy gun in his hand.

Kate was very impressed when he shot down all the plastic ducks without missing any.

"How did you do that?" She asked.

"Just lucky, I guess," Noah replied.

"Pick your prize, sir," the game attendant said to Noah.

"What do you want?" He asked Kate.

Surprised at the gesture, she quickly scanned her options and said, "The dolphin!"

The game attendant handed Kate the dolphin and she hugged it. Noah was glad to win it for her but wondered why she chose the dolphin.

"I thought you would have picked the horse," Noah said.

"I see horses all day long. How often do it get to see and hold a dolphin?" Kate beamed.

Noah couldn't argue with that logic. He just smiled as they passed by all the other games. He did try the dart game, but didn't win. Instead, they spent money on food. Kate wanted cotton candy and Noah wanted popcorn.

They ran into Clayton and Ashley as they were sitting down and eating a funnel cake. "Have either of you seen Henry?" Clayton asked.

They hadn't, but assured them he was probably around here somewhere getting something to eat. There were people everywhere and the carnival stretched out for as far as the eye could see. Noah and Kate walked up to one of stages to see a hot dog eating contest. It was fascinating to watch, but not for very long.

Another stage had dancers. A third stage, near the back had the karaoke competition. Normally they would have kept on walking, but a familiar figure on stage made them stop and listen.

Henry was singing along to the words on the screen and he sounded great. Kate stood there in amazement and listened to her little brother sound just like the original artist, but better. She had heard him humming and singing softly for years, but never like this, never in front of people.

Henry didn't see them or he probably would have bolted off the stage. He didn't look nervous, he looked like a natural. Kate was mesmerized by her brother's voice. Noah agreed that he needed to pursue his music, he shouldn't try to hide a talent like his. He was sure his parents would agree if they could hear him.

"Let's ride the ferris wheel," Noah suggested after Henry's performance ended.

Kate nodded and they bought two tickets. From up high, they could see the whole carnival grounds. When it came back down low, they could focus on the details. It was while they were up high that Kate thought she spotted Mason. Surely, she was mistaken. He said he couldn't come with her.

As the wheel came back down, she was sure it was him. Mason was here and he was with another girl. She saw them walking arm in arm, cuddling, laughing and then kiss. Mason had the nerve to kiss another girl at the carnival. A carnival he knew she would be at!

"I need to get out of here!" Kate demanded.

"Katie, we aren't at the bottom, yet," Noah replied, concerned. "What's wrong?"

"Mason...with a girl...here!"

As soon as the ride stopped to let them off, Noah was out and walking in Mason's direction. Kate was running right behind him to stop him.

"No, Noah!" Kate pleaded.

He wasn't listening. She had to stop him. Mason was dangerous and shouldn't be confronted here. A crowd would not deter Mason Fisher from saying or doing anything.

"Stop!" Kate yelled.

Noah finally stopped and turned around. "Give me one good reason why I shouldn't go over there and punch him in his smug face!"

"He knows!" Kate's face changed, she had gone from angry to terrified in a split second. "I told him...I'm so sorry...about your bullet wound." Tears starting coming down her face. "He's bad news, Noah!"

Noah let the realization of what Kate said sink in. "I can handle Mason." Noah was going to go, he wasn't afraid, he even had his hand on his Glock tucked into the back of his jeans. The look on Kate's face stopped him, it was terror.

Instead, Noah took a deep breath and tried to calm down. He embraced Kate who was now shaking and terrified. Noah finally took the warning seriously and they walked away. Noah was sure that whatever he would have done would also have gotten him arrested. He could see the headline now: Pittsburgh cop arrested at carnival...for murder.

They found an empty table and Noah went to get Kate a sweet tea. They both needed a moment to calm down and catch their breath. It also gave him time to focus on what Kate had said. She told Mason he was shot.

"Why did you tell Mason I was shot?" Noah asked.

"It just came out, I'm sorry. He assumed you were involved in illegal activity and I wanted to prove it wasn't true and I said that you and your fiancé were shot," Kate said.

Noah would never understand how Mason's mind worked. If he was spreading lies and rumors about him, Noah wanted to know. Kate was still crying, this night started off nice and ended in a disaster. He tried to reassure Kate that he wasn't mad at her.

It was definitely not something he wanted to hear, but he couldn't be mad. He had confided something personal to her and she let it out to the one person he wished she hadn't. He was just glad he didn't say anything else.

"Let's go home," Noah suggested.

Kate nodded her head and stood up. They found Teri on the way out and said they were leaving. Either come now or find another ride. She said she would stay. Everyone else wanted to stay, too. They didn't even stay long enough to see the fireworks.

Noah glanced beside him on the ride home. Kate was quiet.

"Katie, why are you with him?" Noah asked for the second time.

Her eyes were sad. "I don't know anymore."

"Maybe this is a sign, that you need to move on," Noah said.

"He said he wouldn't do it again and I was stupid enough to believe him," she replied.

Hearing this made Noah grip the steering wheel so hard his knuckles were white. He clenched his jaw and wished he would have punched him. It wasn't his place, he knew it. Until Kate made the final decision to leave him, it was up to her.

Noah released his grip on the wheel and reached over with his right hand to take hers. She offered a small smile in return.

"It's okay, everything will be okay," Noah said. It had to be.

Chapter 16

Kate was restless. She knew in her head that it was over between her and Mason, she just needed to tell him that. Kate was grateful that he never came over, she didn't think she could pretend everything was okay between them. She had to find the right moment to break up with him.

Today was not it. Today she woke up with the birds chirping and the sun shining. She was determined to have a good day. It was a warm July day and she thought about going to the lake after breakfast.

Kate felt too embarrassed after the other night to face Noah. She had been sending his lunches with Teri or even Henry and Lorna. She knew she couldn't avoid him forever. The worst part was that she actually yearned to see him. She knew his days here would come to an end when the fence was completed and that would be soon.

Kate knew the arrangement she made with her father when hiring a helping hand, it was only to be for a few weeks and it was already stretching out into nearly twice that. They simply couldn't afford it. She felt sad, almost empty, when she thought about her daily life around here without Noah.

She knew she would be okay. She didn't need a man to prove her worth, it was just that she could really see a future with Noah. He saw her as an equal, not a less-than. That was the big difference between Noah and Mason. They had very different ways of treating women.

After breakfast, everyone in the family went their own directions so Kate went to the lake. She was pretty sure she wouldn't run into Noah there, he would now be working on the fence closest to the corn field by now. She could relax.

She packed a bag and took a horse. The ride was peaceful and it gave her more time to think. She decided that she would do anything she could to keep this ranch. It was her one true love. She felt that as long as she took care of it, it would take care of her.

Kate tied up the horse when she arrived at the lake. She found a lounge chair on the dock and settled in for the morning. She didn't want to take the boat out or swim, today she wanted to just feel the warm sun on her body.

MASON THOUGHT HE HAD gotten away with it. He always felt that way. What he didn't know was that Kate saw him with that girl at the carnival. He didn't even remember her name. She was the waitress from the rest stop he passed through coming back from the other side of town.

Mason didn't even like carnivals, it wasn't his thing. He liked seeing more action. He liked boxing, wrestling and trucks... and women. Maybe even in that order. He never intended to mess things up with Kate, he just couldn't help it sometimes.

Kate used to be fun to hang out with until she started paying more attention to the ranch than to him. He knew it had to do with Clayton's accident, they all felt bad about it, but Kate really took over from that moment on.

Mason didn't want to be a farmer or a rancher, he grew up on one and didn't want to do it anymore. He did like the size and scale of the Patterson Ranch, though. It could come in handy when Kate inherited it.

Noah was getting in the way and Mason didn't like it. He was sure that Noah was involved in something, he just had to find out what it was. He told himself that he would figure it out for Kate's sake, but really it was jealousy and revenge.

Mason would find out, even if he had to go to the man himself. He decided to make a special trip back out to the ranch soon to pay everyone a visit. Just to be nice, of course. He never expected Noah to stick around as long as he had, he was now becoming a liability.

The first night he saw Noah enter the diner and then again at the bar, he pegged the man as a weakling. Whatever he did as a real job was definitely not physical labor, that's why he wasn't concerned at the beginning. But the longer he stayed out at the ranch, the more Mason grew suspicious of his true intentions.

NOAH WAS TORN BETWEEN wanting to get the hell out of here and wanting to spend the rest of his days here. It was a fine line and it changed daily. All he knew right now was that the fence should finally be done in a few days. He could actually see the house in the distance as he worked. It brought Noah a feeling of accomplishment to know he never quit doing something at which he was totally unexperienced.

He had decisions to make before then, big decisions that would effect his future. Noah really hoped that Kate would finally call it off with Mason because he wanted to stay. He really wanted to stay on the ranch with her.

Perhaps he could even join the local police and help at the ranch when they needed him. Or he could live on the ranch, he could see it, him and Kate. Noah had to snap himself out of the dream. There was no him and Kate, not yet. He even had to face the fact that it may never happen.

At the end of the day, Noah returned to the house. He parked his truck right next to Mason's. Noah immediately tensed up when he thought about seeing him again. He nearly punched, or shot, the man the other night at the carnival.

What could he be doing here? If he was apologizing, Noah hoped Kate would not accept it. Would Kate even tell Mason she saw him with another girl? Noah didn't even know if she would. He just kept his head down and walked around to the cottage.

Stay out of it. It's none of your business. He kept repeating these in his head to prevent him from bursting into the main house and confronting the man himself. Keep walking. Don't look back. Noah didn't even realize he was holding his breath until he closed the door behind him.

The evening felt cool. There was a slight breeze that took the worst of the day's heat away. Noah came back outside after he showered and changed. He walked over to the fence and watched the horses run as they enjoyed the cool evening, too.

Shouting coming from the house made Noah take notice. He looked in that direction but couldn't see who it was. All he could make out was a male and female voice. It could be Clayton and Ashley having a fight about something. Or it could be Kate and Mason.

Stay out of it. It's none of your business. Noah gripped the fence harder and stayed where he was, for now. Everyone had their fights, it was not unusual. He suspected that the night of the carnival was the topic of the yelling, but he couldn't know for sure.

He did notice Henry come out from the back door and stop. Apparently he, too, needed to leave the house and the fighting behind. Henry saw Noah and walked towards him.

"What's going on in there?" Noah asked, trying to sound casual.

"The usual, Kate and Mason," Henry replied.

Noah nodded his head as if he understood. "Hey, I heard you sing at the carnival. You're really good."

Henry looked embarrassed. "Thanks."

"Seriously, you should pursue it. There are plenty of music programs and art schools who would love to help you," Noah said.

"I don't know if college is for me," Henry replied.

"What are your plans, then?"

"I want to record a demo."

"Doesn't that cost a lot of money, to rent studio space and all?" Noah asked.

Henry looked down at the ground and started moving his shoe back and forth. "Well, I've kind of been making money and saving it." Henry looked up at Noah. "Don't tell my family."

Noah didn't appreciate the last sentence. It was putting him in a very awkward position, but he reluctantly agreed. Maybe he could encourage Henry to tell them himself.

"How are you making money?" Noah asked.

"The bar in town lets me play some nights for tips. I make pretty good money and I've been saving it all. There's a studio in the next town that I can rent to record a few of my songs, too. I've already asked." Henry answered.

Noah had to admit he was impressed. "Why are you afraid to tell your family? It sounds like you have a solid plan, and talent to back it up."

"My dad mostly," Henry confessed. "He wants me to take over the ranch." Henry looked back at Noah. "I don't want to. Don't get me wrong, I love it here, but I think I want to give music my full attention and I can't do that here."

"Sounds like you want to live in a big city."

"I don't know, I've never lived in a big city," Henry said. "Maybe I just want a bigger one than this."

"Well, I'm from Pittsburgh. It's only four hours away and I know it would have lots of opportunities for someone like you," Noah replied. He wasn't sure he should have said that, he didn't want Henry telling his family that Noah offered to take him to Pittsburgh. "You have to finish high school first, though. And go to college."

Henry smiled. "Yea, I know. There's no way my dad would let me do anything before I graduated. But I don't know about college..."

Henry didn't finish his sentence, but Noah got the point. He wanted out. Maybe Kate was the only one who truly wanted to stay.

While Noah was talking to Henry, he hadn't noticed that the fighting had stopped. He wasn't sure if that was good or bad. There was now a commotion on the front porch and Noah wondered if Mason was leaving.

Noah and Henry watched as Mason walked into the barn and proceeded to bring out one bail of hay and place it in the back of the field. Then he went into the barn to bring out another bail of hay and place it next to the first one.

Mason then went to his truck and came back with a bag that he recognized as a rifle bag. What was he up to? Then Mason secured a large target on each of the bales of hay and walked back to where he left the rifle.

Noah watched with an uneasy feeling in his stomach as he saw Mason take ammunition from the bag and load the rifle. He could see members of the house come out onto the porch to watch the demonstration as well. No one knew what he was up to, all they could do was watch.

Noah watched with curiosity but also a sinking feeling in his gut. This was not just a demonstration. There were two targets. This was turning out to be a competition, with weapons.

Henry stayed next to Noah, he also felt the tension in the air and didn't want to go anywhere near Mason. Nothing good could come from mixing those two elements, Mason and guns.

Noah wanted to just go back into the cottage. He took his hands off the fence and tried to slowly back away. He gave a slight nod to Henry as if telling him to do the same. Henry started walking towards the house and Noah started walking towards the cottage.

Noah nearly got away. Keep walking, he told himself. Stay out of it. Noah tried but he wouldn't get the chance.

"Hey! Noah, come over here!" Mason shouted from across the field. "You and I are gonna have a friendly competition. Target shooting."

Noah stopped in his tracks and turned to face Mason. "No, thank you." He turned back around and had his hand on the door handle. So close. Then Noah heard the telltale sound of the rifle being loaded and ready to use.

"It was not a suggestion!" Mason called out.

Chapter 17

All eyes were on Noah as he slowly walked to where he was being summoned. Mason stood with a smirk on his face holding a loaded rifle. Noah had to admit to himself that he was genuinely frightened. There was no telling what was going on in that man's mind.

As he slowly walked past the house, he glanced up at the porch. Kate's eyes were red from tears she had probably been shedding for the last hour. He supposed the fight did not end well for her. This was the result.

Noah figured his name had come up during the argument. Mason was jealous, that was clear. It was probably something he had been battling for a while and it had finally come to a head here and now. Mason had to show everyone who was really in charge around here.

Noah was in no hurry to reach the spot where Mason stood, waiting. He could tell Mason was growing impatient but Noah took his time.

"Come on! I haven't got all night!" Mason taunted.

It was true. Noah definitely didn't want to do this in the dark. The light was already fading and he didn't want this to be any more reckless and dangerous that it already was. Mason was enjoying this but how far would he take it. Noah wasn't sure.

Noah approached Mason as he would any armed person. He put his hands up as if to say he wasn't a threat. Mason laughed.

"I'm not aiming it at you. See, it's pointed safely up," Mason said.

Noah knew it was loaded, safe was not a word he would use to describe anything about this situation. But here they were. At least they weren't alone, there were witnesses. Mason couldn't be planning anything too criminal with witnesses.

"Okay, here's how we're gonna do this," Mason started. "We each have our own target. We will take turns shooting at the target. Best out of five wins."

He made it sound so simple. Wins what? Noah didn't know. Wins the girl? It was archaic and asinine, but in Mason's brain, perfectly normal. Who wouldn't shoot rifles at targets to win over a girl?

"I'll start," Mason said.

Mason lifted the rifle to his shoulder. Up close, Noah saw that it was a Kimber Hunter in 308. Noah was better at hand guns but he could hold his own with any weapon. What happened if Noah lost? What happened if he won? Winning was probably more dangerous for Noah.

Mason looked through the scope and squeezed the trigger and the sound reverberated through the valley. He lowered the rifle and smiled. Mason's shot was good but not perfect. He was happy with it, though. Mason looked at Noah. There was evil in his eyes but Mason's smile remained the same.

"Your turn," he said.

Noah took the Kimber Hunter in his hands. He felt the weight of it and looked around at the terrified spectators who had gathered on the porch. He gave a quick nod to the family and then slowly turned back to the target. Noah's heart was beating fast and he had to take a deep breath to calm himself.

Noah didn't look at Mason, he didn't need to. He knew that Mason watched every move he made. Noah raised the rifle to his shoulder and looked through the sight towards the target. He could feel the pressure on him. He was relying on all of his skills and training and would do his best to hit the bullseye.

He did. Noah felt relief has he lowered the rifle and handed the Kimber back to Mason. Mason's face changed, he was no longer smiling, he was angry. Noah risked another glance towards the house. Kate had stopped crying, she was glued to the spectacle in front of her as well as the others.

Noah had won that round and Mason wasn't happy about it. He was more rough with the rifle which also meant more unstable. He didn't take as much time to line up the sight for accuracy before he pulled the trigger, he was being reckless.

Noah didn't need the sight to tell him that Mason had missed, again. Noah was feeling nervous and his palms were getting sweaty. Mason held the Kimber Hunter out to him. Noah wiped his palms on his jeans before reluctantly taking it.

Noah took his time looking through the sight and finding a good stance before shooting. Another perfect bullseye. Noah smiled when he thought about his partner, Steven. He would be proud of his performance here today.

When Noah handed the Kimber back to Mason, he misread Noah's smile to be gloating. Noah was so relieved to have hit the center of the target he didn't realize his bale of hay had fallen backwards. Mason was fuming. This whole competition was backfiring on him and he didn't like it. Why was Noah turning out to be a better shot than him?

"Go fix the target!" Mason demanded.

Noah stiffened. He had been in front of loaded weapons before but he was usually dressed in uniform, with a bullet-proof vest. This was different, he suddenly felt naked. Noah looked from Mason to Kate.

"Now!" Mason yelled again.

"Secure your weapon!" Noah yelled back.

Mason pointed the rifle to the sky and waited.

"I'm not walking down there while you're holding a loaded weapon. I'm not stupid!" Noah said, angrily.

Mason laughed. "I'm not gonna shoot you, if that's what your afraid of."

It was, but Noah didn't say it. He didn't want to do what Mason was asking, but Noah felt like he had no choice. He slowly walked down towards the target, glancing behind him every few steps. Every fiber of his being knew he shouldn't turn his back on Mason, he himself was a like a loaded gun.

Noah was nearing the bale of hay when he heard the familiar click of the Kimber Hunter being loaded. Noah stopped in his tracks and slowly turned around. It only took a second to see the rifle pointed directly at Noah.

Instinct and training took over. Noah was on autopilot. He quickly ducked behind the upright bale of hay as cover and pulled out his Glock 17, his own handgun that was safely tucked into his belt at this back. The motion was fluid and swift.

He knew the hay was no defense, but it was all he had. Noah ducked low and held his arms out straight, weapon in his hand.

"Lower your weapon!" Noah demanded.

Mason didn't move a muscle. It was a standoff. Mason with his Kimber and Noah aiming his Glock. Noah knew he could take him out at this distance and Mason probably did, too.

"I said, lower your weapon!" Noah repeated. "I'm a police officer and I said to lower your weapon, now!"

Kate had her eyes closed until she heard Noah's voice. When she opened them to see the two men with guns pointed at each other, she screamed. Kate's shrill scream could be heard for miles, Noah was sure.

It was as if her scream broke Mason's focus because he lowered the weapon to the ground and put his hands up. Mason would not be shooting anyone today.

"I didn't mean no harm, officer," Mason teased with a smirk. "We were just having fun, right?"

Noah remained behind the hay with his gun firmly pointed at Mason. Firm, until the flashback of that night came to him. Memories and panic quickly overtook him. Noah stood up straight and let his arm fall to his side with the gun pointing down. His other hand reached for his chest. In his mind he was no longer on the ranch, he was in his bedroom in Pittsburgh.

Noah started breathing in short and shallow breaths and clenched his shirt over his heart. Was Noah having a heart attach? Noah buckled over and let his Glock fall to the ground. Both hands were on his knees as he bent over, struggled to catch his breath.

Noah was having a full blown panic attack. He remembered everything about that night, it was coming back to him as if he was reliving it. Masked men, intruders. Guns pointed at them. It was dark. Then pain and blood, lots of blood.

Noah looked up at Mason and ran towards him, rage taking over. He ran fast and hard and he took Mason by surprise. Noah yelled as he got closer to him and ran his shoulder into Mason's torso. The momentum caused Mason to fall backwards. They wrestled on the ground until Mason got his footing. In his mind, Noah was fighting back, fighting the intruders who came into his home.

Mason's boot connected with Noah's ribs. Noah winced and got on his knees. He avoided another kick by grabbing hold of Mason's cowboy boot. Mason took a hard fall to the ground and it knocked the wind out of him but they continued to struggle together.

Noah took the opportunity to get on top of Mason and started punching him in the face. Noah wouldn't stop. He was punching the demons who followed him everyday, the ones who killed Malia. The ones who left a permanent reminder in his shoulder every time he looked at himself in the mirror.

Mason managed to knock Noah off of him and pinned him to the ground. This was Mason's turn to return the punches until Noah's face was a bloody mess.

Kate was still screaming and everyone was trying to break them up but they didn't know how. It seemed like a fight to the death was happening right in front of them. When Kate couldn't take it any longer, she grabbed the rifle and shot up into the air.

The sound made Mason stop his attack. He rolled off of Noah and they both laid on the ground. Ashley was already by Noah's side with her medical bag and he moaned when she tried to touch his face.

Mason simply stood up, put his rifle back in the bag and walked back to his truck. He spit out some blood onto the gravel and took a handkerchief from his pocket and dabbed at this bloody nose. Mason didn't look as bad as Noah did, though.

Noah tried to stand up and talk but the women made him stop. "Take me...to...cottage," was all he could say. The two women told him to stop talking as they did what he asked.

With Kate on one side and Ashley on the other, the women helped him walk to the cottage. Kate hoped that the look of unmasked anger she gave Mason would make him get the hell out of here. Mason knew he messed up but would never admit it. He had pushed her further into Noah's arms.

Inside the cottage, the women laid Noah gently on the bed. Kate ran to get towels from the bathroom and a bowl of water from the kitchen. Ashley tried her best to clean the wounds and bandage them up.

Henry let himself inside. He walked quietly and stood next to his mother. He laid Noah's Glock 17 down on the bedside table. Noah nodded weakly.

"So, you're a cop?" Henry asked.

Kate and her mother both told Henry to wait outside. Noah didn't need to talk or explain anything right now. They just needed him to get better. Henry had so many questions, but did as he was told.

They all had questions. Questions were all they had. After Ashley gave Noah some pain medicine and turned off the light, she motioned for Kate to meet her outside.

"I think we should call a doctor," Ashley whispered. "He could have broken ribs."

"Well, there's nothing a doctor can do about that anyway, right?" Kate asked.

Ashley slowly nodded, but she knew Noah had many more injuries, not all were easily fixable. "What do you think happened? One minute he was pulling out his gun, the next he had a panic attack and lunged at Mason."

"I don't know, mom," Kate replied. "We just have to wait until he gets better. Maybe he can explain."

"Well, I should probably stay with him tonight," Ashley offered.

"No, you go check on dad and the kids," Kate replied. "I'll stay with him."

Her mother had to admit it made more sense for Kate to stay. She was also worried about what else Mason would do. Ashley figured Mason would be long gone by now, but that didn't mean he wouldn't return tomorrow.

When Kate and Noah were finally alone, she pulled up a chair close to the bed and carefully held his hand. Noah opened his eyes briefly and smiled. How did it come to this? Kate knew it was all her fault. She had tried to end things with Mason today and he wouldn't let her.

He said that he would win her back, show her how much she meant to him. She had no way of anticipating that this would be

Mason's way of demonstrating it. This wasn't love. Kate almost believed that Mason would have killed Noah tonight. He was capable of anything.

Kate touched Noah's hair softly and kept smoothing it back as if comforting a sick child. She wondered what demons he was fighting inside of his head. She wished he would have felt able to confide in her earlier. It was darker than she had ever imagined.

"Sleep, Noah," Kate whispered. "I'll make it up to you, I promise."

Chapter 18

Neither one of them got any meaningful sleep. Kate knew Noah was in pain and had tried giving him some more medicine throughout the night. Every time Noah tossed and turned, Kate woke up. She needed to make sure he stayed in bed.

In the morning, things became more clearer to her. Noah could have died yesterday at the hands of Mason. Also, Noah was a cop and he had been hiding that fact for weeks. These details could be discussed later. Right now he needed to eat something.

Kate tried to sit him up as best she could and made soup for him to sip. Noah was grateful to have her here. He also knew it was his fault he was beaten as bad as he was. If he would have just deescalated the situation rather than rushing at the guy, they all could have walked away peacefully. Maybe.

The flashback to that night was too strong to just push out of his mind. The trauma was still too raw. He had been able to live through the nightmares that were slowly fading away, but yesterday was different, something had taken hold of him.

Seeing the gun pointed at him was all too real. He looked to his left to imagine Malia laying there covered in blood but all he saw was Kate. Beautiful and kind Kate who was now feeding him and helping him heal. He remembered her bone chilling scream and hoped to never frighten her again.

Noah vowed to never let Mason push him that far again, either. Noah drifted from wakefulness to dreaming most of the day. Kate was in and out that day as well as her mother. Ashley changed bandages and applied ointment where she could. The rest was up to Noah.

Kate went to the main house and prepared dinner. The ranch could wait. There was only a little bit of the fence left and Henry was working on it now. Maybe there was hope for him after all. Kate noticed that Henry had become very quiet since the...fight, quieter than usual.

She suspected that he and Noah had a real bond and the fact that Noah almost died had an effect on her brother. She would have a talk with him after dinner. Her father was also shaken since the incident, he had a new level of hated for Mason.

Clayton never liked Mason and was now ready to ban him from the property. Kate begged him not to, not yet. She would talk to him, again. Hopefully this time it would end better. Her father warned her that if she didn't get him under control, he would call the police.

Kate knew she couldn't promise anything, but she would give it a try. But right now her priority was getting Noah back on his feet. She quickly put the chicken in the oven and the potatoes to boil then ran back to the cottage.

Noah was sitting on the edge of his bed and gently touching his wounds.

"Don't do that," Kate said as she came in the door.

Noah looked up at her and smiled. She joined him on the bed and brought the damp cloth to his face. It was still swollen and bruised but the scabs looked better. They determined he didn't have any broken ribs. Noah knew what those felt like and this wasn't it.

He was just sore from Mason sitting on him and the punches. Other than that he was fine. Noah wanted to go outside and sit. He didn't like being cooped up in the cottage and wanted fresh air. Kate helped him walk to the chairs that were right outside the door.

She gave him some iced tea and they sat watching the horses run in the field. They didn't need to say anything, even though Noah knew she had a million questions.

"First, let me say thank you for taking care of me and then, sorry for starting the fight," Noah said.

"You have nothing to be sorry for! You didn't start anything," Kate replied. She was still upset with Mason about the whole thing, in her eyes, Noah did nothing wrong.

"Well, my part of it anyway. I shouldn't have provoked him. I knew better."

"About that..." Kate leaned towards Noah. "Why didn't you tell us, or me, that you were a cop?"

Noah shifted in his chair and looked away. He hoped he could find the right words in the mountains beyond the ranch. Instead, he looked down at the ground and tried to start at the beginning. Noah took a deep breath, winced at the pain it caused, then looked at Kate.

"I am a Pittsburgh police officer on leave," Noah started. "I took a leave of absence after my fiancé was killed."

Kate's eyes remained on Noah's face as he looked away. She hung on every word knowing how hard this was for him. He had been hiding it for so long, reluctant to let anyone into his world of pain.

"We were the victims of a home invasion." Noah quickly glanced at Kate to see her reaction. She remained focused on him. "It happened in the middle of the night. There were two armed men dressed in all black with face masks. They were quiet, too quiet for us to hear or I could have gotten to my gun in time."

Noah paused. It was obviously hard for him to tell the story, having to relive every detail, but he continued, for Kate.

"I think they thought our apartment was empty. We had been away for a few nights prior to the invasion, so maybe they were watching the building? I don't know."

Noah shook his head as if doing this would bring about a logical explanation for any or all of it.

"They demanded money, which after being awoken from a dead sleep, I said I didn't have any. They didn't like that answer. They could have taken anything in the apartment and I wouldn't have cared, but they took...Malia. I just remember watching the gun as it shot me and then shot her, laying beside me."

Noah looked to his left, as if seeing her again. "My left shoulder hurt, so I knew I was shot, but Malia was covered in blood, so much blood. I called to her and tried to get her to wake up, but she was already gone."

"The men left as quickly as they came. I grabbed my Glock and tried to chase after them, but it was too dark and I knew I needed to call 911. They never solved the case." Noah looked over at Kate, a tear ran down her cheek.

Noah tried to give her a reassuring smile. "I've been going to therapy and even stayed on the force for as long as I could. But when I froze in a situation one day, I knew I needed to take time off. I also decided that it was time to bring Malia's ashes to her parents, in Summer Hill."

"The delivery," Kate said.

Noah half smiled. "Yes, the delivery. I still haven't done it. They never approved of our relationship and refused to acknowledge it. Malia said it felt like they kicked her out and disowned her. It was hard for her."

"That must have been so heartbreaking, knowing you would get married and her parents wouldn't come," Kate responded. She suddenly felt sorry for Malia and Noah. They must have really loved each other to go up against those obstacles.

"So what will you do now? I'm sure you want to get out of here as soon as possible," Kate said.

Noah didn't respond. He just looked at her and took her hand. It was a hard question to answer. He had been trying to answer it for weeks. "I don't know anymore."

"Well, you can stay here as long as you need," Kate replied.

Noah squeezed her hand. He would love to stay like this forever and not deal with the outside world at all anymore. He wasn't sure he wanted the same things any longer.

Kate's head was spinning from the story Noah had just shared with her. She hated to leave him but had to go check on dinner. Before she went inside, she asked if he wanted help back inside the cottage. He said he wanted to stay outside a little longer.

Noah noticed someone coming in from working in the field, it was Henry. Noah called him over to sit with him.

"Where have you been?" Noah asked.

"Working on the fence," Henry replied. "It's nearly finished."

Noah looked at young Henry with a new appreciation. "Wow, great job!"

Henry smiled and blushed. "How are you feeling?" He asked.

"Oh, I'll be fine. Just a few bruises. I'll be as good as new in no time," Noah said.

Henry looked at Noah. Noah knew he had questions that he wanted to ask but was probably too polite to ask them.

"I'm a police officer from Pittsburgh," Noah started. "I'm sure your sister will fill you in on all the details that I just told her, but I wasn't really hiding anything, I just wanted everyone to get to know me for me, not that I'm a cop. Does that make any sense?"

Henry nodded his head. "I was just surprised was all. I think it's kind of cool."

Noah laughed. "Well, good."

"It's just, I liked talking to you and when Mason did what he did," Henry paused. "It scared me. You're not the kind of guy my sisters bring home and it was nice having you around."

Noah knew there was a compliment in there somewhere. "Thanks, Henry. You know you can call me anytime, to talk."

"Why, are you leaving?"

"Well, eventually," Noah answered. "I have a life to get back to." Noah wasn't so sure about that, but it was partially true. He didn't really know what he was going back to. He wasn't working and was living with his parents.

Henry went to the house leaving Noah alone with his own thoughts. Noah was tired and must have fallen asleep because it wasn't until Kate came out with a plate of food that he realized the sun was setting. Kate helped him back inside the cottage.

"It smells good," Noah said.

Kate fed Noah the roasted chicken, so soft that it fell right off the bone. She also had mashed potatoes and gravy along with green beans and cornbread. Noah ate it all. He thanked her for the meal and for the help.

Kate said it was the least she could do, she felt responsible. It seemed like everyone was blaming themselves for Mason's hot temper and jealousy. He needed to be held accountable. Mason hadn't been back and that was definitely a good thing.

For dessert, Kate had brought a small carton of vanilla ice cream. She went to the kitchen to get a spoon and sat next to Noah. Their eyes never wavered from each other's. Kate continued to feed Noah the softened ice cream, even though he could do it himself.

Noah let Kate feed him. It was intimate and sensuous and they were both enjoying it. In between feeding Noah, she would take a spoonful for herself. Her hand rested on his thigh and Noah did the same. They were only inches apart and when a drip came down the side of Noah's mouth, she kissed him.

Kate was careful of his bruises but she continued to kiss him. Noah kissed her back and he brought his hands to her face. They stopped long enough to look at each other and smile. Noah kissed her again and they moved closer together. Their legs were touching and the ice cream was forgotten.

It was Noah who pulled himself away. He was feeling lightheaded and it was not only because of the injuries. Kate took that moment to stand up and put the ice cream away. Noah walked to the bed and got under the covers.

Kate came back and got in bed with him. She cuddled up next to him as Noah leaned over to her.

"I love you," Noah whispered.

Kate smiled and looked over at him. "I love you, too."

Chapter 19

Noah woke up to the sun shining in the front window of the cottage. His sore movements reminded him of what happened with Mason, but the warmth beside him told him that Kate had spent the night. He leaned over, kissed her forehead and turned to get up.

"You're awake," Kate said, yawning.

"Thank you for staying last night, you didn't have to," Noah replied.

"I wanted to," she said, rubbing at her eyes.

They both got up and looked around the small cottage. Noah had been stuck here long enough. If he was going to recuperate, he should be in the fresh air and sunshine.

"Do you want to get out of here?" Kate asked.

"Sure, where do you want to go?"

"The lake," she replied. "Let me go to the house and get things ready. I'll get you when it's time to leave."

Noah nodded and Kate left. She walked in the backdoor and froze in place. Mason was standing in their kitchen engaged in a heated conversation with Clayton. They both looked upset, she must have walked into the middle of an argument.

Mason's attention turned to Kate as soon as she walked in. "Where is he?"

"Why? Haven't you done enough damage?" Kate asked.

"Someone slashed my tires last night and I'm betting it was the policeman," Mason replied.

Kate told him to settle down and leave. He had no right coming into their home and accusing anyone of damaging his truck, especially after what he did yesterday. Kate was angry.

"Maybe it was one of your little girlfriends," Kate taunted.

Mason wasn't fazed. She could make all the accusations she wanted, she had no proof he went out with other women. He tried to brush past her and walk out to the cottage.

"It wasn't Noah!" Kate yelled, glaring at Mason.

"How do you know it wasn't? He could have easily drove out to my place and slashed my tires and made it back here." Mason said.

"First of all, he doesn't know where you live and second of all," Kate glanced at her father before saying, "I was with him all night."

Mason grew more furious. He called her names, right in front of her father. Clayton told him to leave or he'd call the police. Mason wasn't afraid of Clayton's threats, he knew he wouldn't spend any time behind bars. But he didn't want to stick around anymore, either.

"We're done, Mason," Kate said, fighting back the tears that were near the surface.

"No, this isn't over!" Mason replied before slamming the front door behind him. They heard his truck tear up the gravel on his way out.

Kate let the tears fall. She went over to her father and apologized. Clayton just hugged his eldest daughter and wished he could make it all go away. He knew it was up to her to end it once and for all.

Still upset from the altercation, Kate almost forgot why she came in. "Oh, Daddy, I want to go to the lake. Can we take the boat out?"

"Sure," he said.

"Do you want to come with us?" Kate asked, knowing that he always refused.

"No, you guys go. Why don't you ask everyone else, though?"

Kate said she would and to her surprise all three of her siblings agreed to come. Henry went to saddle up the horses and Teri made sandwiches. When all of their bags were filled with supplies they were ready and Kate went to help Noah walk to the barn.

He was glad all of the kids were going. It would be a great chance to thank everyone for his time here. He had already decided he needed to move on. He had caused enough trouble here and needed to stop hiding from his problems.

Noah wasn't going to tell anyone his decision, not yet, especially not Kate. He wanted a nice day on the lake to be his last memory of his time here, not the fight. In the barn, they all chose their horse and Kate helped Noah on his.

The ride was slow and calming. Another perfect July day without a cloud in the sky. Noah enjoyed the ride to the lake. He could hear the birds singing and even the laughter coming from the other kids as they retold a funny story. It was family. He missed his.

At the lake, they tied up the horses and got in the boat. Henry found fishing poles and gear in the boat house and brought them along. They went to the center of the lake and cut off the engine. The girls sunned themselves while the guys dropped fishing lines in the water.

They all let the silence envelope them. It was a welcome change from the house. No one needed to speak, there was a prayerfulness to their silence. Every once in a while a fish would make ripples and then go away.

Noah allowed himself to breath deep and release the tension. He had been holding in the fear, depression, anger, hurt, sadness and love for too long. All of these things could be let go so that he could focus on the important things in life. What was important to him now?

He didn't have that figured out yet. He knew Kate was important to him, but was she a part of his life, or just passing through? Only time would tell for sure. For now, he knew he still had a delivery to do and that needed to take priority.

Kate brought out lunches and drinks and they enjoyed the camaraderie on the water. Noah had to admit that the boat was a great idea and was just the medicine he needed. It had been a rough summer to get through but worth it. He was glad he took the chance and replied to the help wanted sign in the diner window.

Noah was in a good mood and raised his glass. He tapped his fork on it to get everyone to listen. "May I have your attention please," Noah started, "I would like to propose a toast to the best ranch in the state of Virginia! To the Patterson Ranch!"

A series of laughter and giggles could be heard as everyone raised their drinks and toasted together. The mood was light and happy. The ladies decided it was time for a swim and jumped off the back of the boat. The splash was felt by Henry and Noah and complained that they had just scared away their fish.

They hadn't caught anything anyway and pulled in their lines so no one got tangled. Henry didn't want to join them, so he stayed on board with Noah. Noah closed his eyes and let the warm sun sink into his skin.

The girls in the water continued to laugh and splash water, Noah just smiled. A huge wave of water made Noah open his eyes when he saw that Henry had jumped in the lake, too.

"Traitor!" Noah joked.

"Sorry, Noah," Henry said. "It was just too tempting."

It was tempting. If he even felt the slightest bit stronger Noah would have jumped in, too.

For now, he was just a bystander. Kate came back on board and cuddled up next to Noah.

"I'll keep you company," Kate said.

"Thank you, Katie," Noah replied.

Kate turned her head towards him. "You know, I never did ask you why you started calling me Katie when everyone else calls me Kate."

"Maybe that's why, I wanted to be remembered," Noah replied. "Plus, I liked Katie better."

Satisfied with his response, she closed her eyes and soaked in the sunshine, too. The water was cool and it actually made Kate shiver when she had gotten out. Noah felt this and grabbed the towel that was within arms reach and gave it to her. She thanked him and stayed next to him as he put his arm around her.

Kate had never felt so safe in her life, especially now that she knew he was a police officer. It made sense to her now, why she always felt calm and trusting in his presence. She wished they could stay like this forever but she knew they had to get back.

The kids all climbed back into the boat and dried off. They packed up and headed towards the dock. It seemed like it took no time at all before they were back on their horses heading towards the house. There was no animated chatter on the way home, the carefree afternoon had quickly come to an end.

Ashley knew everyone would be hungry when they got back from the lake and had made dinner. It was just some frozen pizzas, but the kitchen smelled amazing. One by one, everyone came in and sat down at the table, even Noah.

Ashley came over to Noah to inspect his cuts and bruises. When she was satisfied that everything looked good, she moved out of the way so he could eat. She and her husband had already eaten, so they went out to the living room to watch the news leaving the younger crowd alone to finish the pizzas.

They all ate greedily and didn't stop until all of the pizza was gone. It was Lorna who noticed the apple pie on the counter and everyone took a slice. Noah hadn't eaten in the main house in a while. It just didn't feel right, he felt like he was intruding. But tonight, it did feel right. He had gotten closer to the family over the last five weeks, maybe too close.

Noah thanked everyone for a wonderful day, he was grateful for the support he had gotten as well as the time to heal. They all came to give him a hug and Noah was getting emotional. He said good night, went out to the cottage and then realized he didn't want to turn in, yet.

Instead, Noah walked out to the barn to see the new foal. He heard footsteps behind him and he turned, expecting to see Kate.

"I hope you don't mind my coming out here with you," Teri said.

"No, of course not," Noah replied.

She walked closer to him, hesitantly. Not like the bold and flirtatious younger sister she was when he first met her. This Teri was the real Teri.

"I wanted to apologize for how I acted when you first came here. I didn't know about..." Teri searched for the right words. "What you had been through. I feel terrible."

"Don't, you didn't know. No one did." Noah replied.

"You must have felt so frightened and alone and I just made it worse by hanging all over you," Teri said.

Noah laughed and then smiled at her. "Really, it's okay. I didn't tell anyone because I didn't want...this, sympathy or special treatment. I wanted everyone to get to know me before I burdened everyone with all of my baggage."

Teri nodded, satisfied in his explanation.

"Besides, if I didn't meet you at that diner, I might not have ever seen the help wanted sign in the window. Your personality is happy and flattering and there's nothing wrong with that," Noah said.

"Friends?" Teri asked.

"Of course, friends!" Noah replied.

They hugged each other in the barn and Teri left feeling better. She had worried things would be awkward now that she knew the whole story, but it felt good. She liked Noah, Mason had read him all wrong from the beginning.

Now Noah was ready for bed. He was exhausted. He walked across the field and towards the cottage. He paused as he came to the house and reflected on how much love that house contained. He was lucky to have found this family, but it was time for him to leave.

Inside the cottage, Noah thought one more day would be enough. It was another procrastination and he smiled at the thought. Why stop now? If he put it off any longer, he may as well start sending out applications around town.

He thought about what it would be like to be a police officer here in Summer Hill. He knew what his first priority would be, to put Mason Fisher behind bars. Noah was sure that Mason did a dozen things on a daily basis that could get him arrested but didn't and it would have been so satisfying to be the one to do it.

That was a dream for another day. Right now Noah just wanted to take a shower and go to sleep. These simple tasks he could complete without any help. What Noah needed help with was saying goodbye to this place and these people.

Chapter 20

Noah woke up feeling almost completely healed and much stronger. He actually offered to finish the fence, which would be his last job on the farm. He didn't tell the Pattersons that, of course, he didn't want to make a big deal about his last day. Henry said he would even help him today.

Since it wasn't far, they walked to the last portion of the fence that needed repaired. It would also give Noah time to touch base with Henry and also say good bye in his own way. They arrived at the spot and got to work.

The conversation was easy between Henry and Noah. Henry really looked up to him. He never felt that way with Mason. He told Noah that he was almost ready to book studio time to record his demo. He wanted Noah to come. Noah tried to skirt the question by saying he really didn't know.

Henry knew that he was really only here to fix the fence, so it wasn't practical for Noah to make plans beyond today. The fence would be done and Noah was free to leave. Noah tried to be encouraging by saying he would try to come, but Henry knew better.

Once his job on the ranch was complete, Henry may never see Noah again. That actually made him sad. Noah reminded him that he had his phone number and was welcome to call or text anytime. Noah would be honored if he did, he was feeling like a big brother to Henry.

Noah didn't know what his future held right now. He was living in his childhood bedroom at this parents house for goodness sake, how could he even think about moving forward when he was only going backwards. He had to prove to himself that he was capable of making hard decisions and sticking to them.

Noah and Henry talked about everything from school to girls. Some topics Henry just didn't feel comfortable talking to his father about, but Noah encouraged him to do so.

"He was a teenager once, too," Noah said. It was such an old person thing to say, but it was true. Chances were his father had done or tried the same things Henry was doing. Everyone was a teenager once.

The rest of the time they worked in comfortable silence. The pounding and tightening was relaxing in itself. Henry was getting better at doing this job, Noah recognized that, even if Henry didn't.

There was hope for Henry, yet, to become a real part of this ranch. Everyone thought he would carry on the ranching tradition, not ever considering what Henry wanted. But, maybe, subconsciously, Henry did want it. It was in his blood. Everyone deserved a second chance.

Noah knew the power of dna, his father was a police officer and so was Noah. It would be the same with farming. There may be a future farmer in Henry still. The sun was getting low on the horizon. They followed the fence line home. It was finished.

Noah put his hand on Henry's shoulder, "It was a pleasure working with you Henry."

"I enjoyed it, too," Henry replied.

As they got closer to the house, Henry went inside and Noah went to the cottage. It was a great day and Henry was almost sad it was over now. In the kitchen, Kate had dinner ready. Henry saw her try to look out the window for Noah, but Noah went straight to the cottage and went inside.

Everyone else had eaten already, so Henry ate alone. That was okay with him. He heard activity all throughout the house and it was comforting to Henry. He thought about the things Noah had said today, that he needed to appreciate the family he had because you never knew when it would be your last time together.

Henry made a promise to himself that he would be more open and honest about his life with his family, starting with admitting to sneaking out at night. He would probably be punished and grounded, but Noah was right. These were the only people he could truly trust and rely on, why wouldn't he also want their support and trust back?

When he finished his dinner, Henry gave his sister a hug. "Thank you, Kate. It was delicious."

Kate was shocked but returned the hug. Henry was a great teenager, but Noah was also a great influence. She really hoped he would stay around, but she was not an idiot, she knew it wasn't really a possibility for him.

After Kate cleaned up the kitchen, she made a plate of food for Noah. She didn't know if he needed it, but it couldn't hurt. She went out the back door and down the trail to the cottage. Kate hesitated a brief moment before knocking. What if he wanted to be alone?

She took a deep breath and knocked. Kate second guessed her decision when it took a couple minutes for him to answer the door. She almost returned back to the house after she knocked a second time.

Noah was just getting out of the shower when he thought he heard a knock on the door. Not again, he thought. Then another knock. He was afraid it could be important, so he wrapped a towel around his waist and answered the door.

Kate was immediately embarrassed by his lack of clothing and nearly turned around to retreat, again. Noah stopped her and invited her inside.

"I'm sorry, I wasn't expecting company," Noah joked.

"No, I'm sorry. I shouldn't have come," Kate replied.

They both stood facing each other, staring into each other's eyes. When Noah looked down at the plate, she was reminded of why she came.

"Oh, right, here is some dinner," Kate said.

"Thanks," Noah answered, not really interested in the dinner.

Without moving, he set the plate on the table beside him. Then in one quick motion, Noah was kissing her. It was a bold decision, but what did Noah have to lose. His hands came up to the sides of her face and hers came to his waist.

Kate's touch felt warm on his bare skin and her kiss ignited something inside of him he had long since forgotten, desire. Kate's kisses moved from Noah's mouth to his cheeks and neck. He let out a soft moan as her hands moved around his torso.

Noah brought her mouth back to his and kissed with a passion he had felt from the moment he arrived. He was attracted to Kate from that very first day he met her but kept telling himself she was off limits, not now, not tonight.

Now it was Noah's turn to kiss her neck. He wanted to kiss more and started unbuttoning her blouse. Kate helped, she wanted it, too. Noah took his time to slide her blouse off her shoulders and down to the floor. When they were both undressed, he led her to the bed.

Noah kissed and caressed her body unlike anyone else she had been with, especially Mason. With Mason, she felt like she was only there to pleasure him. Noah wanted to pleasure her, too. For Noah, it had been so long since he had been with a woman, it was electrifying and intoxicating for both of them.

They made love that night and it felt like they couldn't get enough of each other. They had each waited weeks to touch each other this way and it was worth each agonizing day. The anticipation made it even more exciting. Noah didn't want to think about leaving Kate.

Later, Noah got out of bed and walked over to the table. "I don't even know what you brought me," he said while looking under the foil at the dinner long since forgotten.

"It's lasagna from tonight's dinner," Kate replied. "Are you hungry?"

"Famished," Noah said with a wink.

Kate laughed as Noah came back into bed. They were like teenagers sneaking around so that no one would discover them. It made Noah feel young again and he was in love. How would he be able to leave this woman who brought love back into his life?

Kate had never felt like this with anyone before. She felt wanted and loved, it was a new and wonderful feeling. She wanted to ask him to stay, beg him to stay, but she couldn't. She had no right to ask that of him, especially since Mason was still in the picture.

She felt like Mason would always be in the picture, whether they were a couple or not. Mason didn't like losing, he like revenge. Kate still flinched when she thought of that night. It didn't help that the scars on Noah's face would always remind her.

Maybe it was better if Noah left Summer Hill and never looked back. This town and this family had already caused him so much pain and trouble. She could never live with herself if anything else happened to Noah. Next time would be worse, much worse. As much as Kate wanted to beg him to stay right here with her, she knew he needed to forget her.

Kate could see Noah's Glock 17 on the bedside table, now she knew why he carried it everywhere. He was a cop. He was used to dangerous situations and could handle himself. He had just never encountered someone like Mason Fisher before, and hopefully never would again.

This time when Noah got out of bed, he heated up the food and came back with two forks. They savored the lasagna and even fed each other mouthfuls. It was romantic but it also made Noah sad. He knew he was leaving, Kate only suspected. There was a difference.

Kate still had hope he would change his mind. He wasn't. He had caused her enough trouble and needed to keep moving. This was their last meal together. Kate saw the sadness in his eyes but wasn't sure where it was coming from... memories, the fight or her. Maybe all three.

Noah had seen things she never would. She was sure that was a good thing, protecting her from the dark side of life, but it also made her sad to not have experienced life with him. His fiancé did and now she was dead, was that the fate of women in Noah's life.

Life with Noah could be dangerous, he had said so. But life here was, too. It wasn't practical to run from danger every time you sensed it, you had to learn to deal with it. Maybe Kate should start carrying a gun. She would mention it to her father.

They finished the lasagna and kissed. It would be dawn soon, another day. There were so many unspoken words between them. Noah would never ask her to come with him and she couldn't ask him to stay with her. There was really nothing left to say between them.

Kate got dressed and kissed Noah one last time. When she walked out the cottage door she cried the whole way back to the house. She walked upstairs and laid in her own bed, alone. No one would know what they had done, except her and Noah.

Noah got dressed, too. He also packed his things and took them to his truck. He went back into the cottage to leave Kate a note and tucked it under his pillow. She would find it, he knew. After another quick glance around, he shut the door and drove down the gravel driveway, away from Patterson Ranch.

He thought Kate was better off with him out of the picture. She could get on with her life on the ranch without him as a distraction. It was better this way, at least that's what he said through his own tears as he pulled into the gas station a few miles away.

He had decisions to make. Does he head north back to Pennsylvania or out to the Harris's like he originally intended? He knew what he should do, but was he strong enough for that.

He had been put through some personal tests this summer and he thought he had passed them. There were moments of weakness, but isn't that true of us all? It's how we moved forward that counted. Our past does not dictate our future.

Noah had made his decision. There was really only one thing he could do. He put his pick up truck in drive and headed down the road. As the sun was just coming up, he marveled at the oranges and reds in the sunrise. A new day full of choices and second chances, he would make the right one today.

Noah would do what he needed to do a long time ago. He would not procrastinate any longer. He would be better.

Today was a new day.

Chapter 21

Kate woke up with an uneasy feeling. She immediately got out of bed and went to her window. Her fears were confirmed. Noah's truck was gone. She knew he wasn't working, the fence was done. He was gone.

Kate knew this was true, even though she ran to the back cottage to check with her own eyes. Empty. All of Noah's things were gone. The place was neat and tidy, as if he was never here. She sat on the edge of the bed where, not eight hours ago they were making love.

She curled up on the bed and cried. How could he leave her? Didn't they say they loved each other? Kate thought they could have built a life together here, even ran the ranch together. Wasn't that the plan? Maybe it was all just in Kate's head.

She grabbed the pillow to hug it but something fell to the floor. She didn't know what would be tucked up under the pillow and got down on the floor to retrieve it.

A note, to Kate. But that wasn't all. There was a framed picture on the floor under the bed. Noah must have knocked it down and missed it while packing. She picked up the note and frame and looked from one to the other.

The photo was of two people in love and smiling. The woman was holding up her left hand to show off her engagement ring. She looked at Noah's face, he looked so happy there. It was a happier time, for sure. But the woman, Malia, there was something familiar about her.

Kate stared at the woman's dark face and friendly eyes. She knew this woman, but how?

Instead, she looked at the note. She opened it up and read,

"My Dearest Katie,

I'm sorry but I don't belong here.

Please be happy.

I will always love you.

Love, Noah"

How could she be happy? The man she loved, truly loved had left her. Kate didn't think she could ever love anyone like that again. She laid back down on the bed and thought about what to do next. She had been all consumed in Noah this summer, what was there if there was no more Noah?

Kate told herself not to fall apart. She would simply do what she had been doing for years before Noah entered their lives. She would run the ranch. In fact, Kate would throw herself into all of the new projects that Noah suggested for them. She owed it to her father, and to Noah.

She thought the easiest to start with would be to rent out this cottage. It was practically ready now. She just needed to do some cleaning up and it would be good as new. Kate was still sad as she took the note and picture into the main house, but she tried to have a positive outlook.

Teri saw her enter from the back door and asked about Noah.

"He's gone," Kate said flatly.

"Gone? What do you mean gone?" Teri asked.

"I mean, he left. The job is done and he had to move on," Kate answered with as much enthusiasm as she could muster. She set the note and picture on the table and went to pour herself a large cup of coffee.

Teri went over to see what they were and stared at the framed photo.

"Why do you have a picture of Malia?" Teri asked. "And how does Noah know her?" Teri spun around, confused.

"What do you mean? That was his fiancé," Kate replied.

"But this is Malia, our old babysitter. She was, of course, a lot younger then," Teri said. "In fact, I don't think Lorna was born yet and Henry couldn't have been more than one or two."

Kate came back to examine the woman's face again. Of course! That was why she looked so familiar, she just aged fifteen years since then. They knew Malia Harris as a teenaged babysitter who came to their house often.

They also remembered how strict her parents were. Her father brought her and picked her up promptly every time she babysat them. And when they asked if she could stay longer or do something with the family, his answer was always no.

"So Noah never told you he was engaged to our babysitter?" Teri asked.

"Well, he said the name, but it didn't jog any memory. Plus, I never saw a picture of her until now," Kate answered.

They both sat staring at the photograph. It really was a small world. Kate felt stupid for not connecting the dots sooner. Malia from Summer Hill, there could only be one, but it was so long ago. How was she supposed to know it was the same woman?

To change the subject, Kate told her sister about her plans to rent out the cottage. She wanted her help to clean it up and list it on a rental site. Teri was excited to help with this new project and offered to take all of the pictures, too.

"Perfect," Kate said. "Let's get started."

NOAH ARRIVED AT THE Harris's house early and decided to wait until he saw activity. He hoped he would see someone come out and tend the garden or sit outside, anything. He was still nervous about approaching the house, he felt better about approaching a person. He would wait.

Noah had left in such a hurry, he hadn't eaten. He was starting to feel hungry and hoped he could get this over quickly. He let his mind wander about what it would have been like to grow up here in this house, in this town.

Malia never complained about the surroundings, just her parents. From what he had seen so far, he liked Summer Hill. He thought he could stay here, but he had to concede that there were too many complications.

It was best for Noah to go back home. His life was on hold in Pittsburgh and he didn't want to leave it that way. He had already called Steven and told his old partner his plans. Steven was happy for him, glad he got to get away for a while.

Noah also mentioned wanting to get out of his parent's house. Steven offered him a bedroom and that he could stay until he got back on his feet. Noah said he would definitely take him up on that offer as soon as he got back.

Noah talked to his supervisors and put everything into motion about getting back on the streets. He would have an evaluation and take it from there. Everything was sounding positive and he actually let himself feel optimistic about his future.

What was once so dark and gloomy was now coming into clearer focus. He knew it would require baby steps at first and one day at a time, but he also knew he could get back to where he was before the home invasion. It would also take a long time to get over Katie.

He already felt like turning his truck around and proclaiming that it was all a big mistake, he would stay and they would live happily every after. But, no, he couldn't do that to her. He couldn't make promises he couldn't keep.

He needed to hold himself to a higher standard than he had in the past. He had come to Virginia as just a means of passing time, he didn't consider that he would make real bonds and have real relationships with these people. He thought he could just come in one day and leave the next.

Noah was fooling himself to think he didn't need someone in his life, but not just anyone. He wanted Katie but knew he couldn't have her. Life wasn't always about what he wanted, he had to learn that. He was a cop, he needed to be more selfless, he needed to let Katie go.

That was why he was sitting down the road from a house full of people who didn't like him. People who probably blamed him for their daughter's death. His hands were getting sweaty on the steering wheel and he rubbed them on his jeans. He tried taking deep breaths to calm himself down but it wasn't working.

Just the anticipation of someone walking out and seeing him, recognizing him was making his heart beat as if he was running one hundred miles and hour. His eyes were fixed on the front door. He willed someone to come out, anyone. He just wanted this to be over with.

When Noah's phone rang, he jumped so high he nearly hit his head on the roof of his truck. It was his mother. Noah had mentioned the other day that he would be coming home today. She was just checking to make sure it was true. It was.

Noah's mother said she would make his favorite dish for dinner, lasagna. Noah took the phone away from his ear. The memories of last night came crashing into him all at once. He took a deep breath and brought the phone back to his ear.

Noah's voice quivered a bit when he replied that he would see them soon and hung up. Noah was drowning in a flood of emotions at the moment all because of the house in front of him, the Patterson Ranch from his past and the new life he would start back home.

Just then a woman came out the front door and walked down the steps. She walked over to her garden and picked a few things and placed them in a basket. She looked around for a bit and then reentered the house.

Overwhelmed, Noah put his pick up truck in drive and left. He couldn't do it, again. He was furious with himself for giving up and leaving. Apparently, that was the only thing Noah was good at anymore, running away from problems.

Noah slammed the steering wheel and ran his hand through his brown hair. Why couldn't he do it? It really didn't matter what they thought about him. They probably hated him more for not returning Malia's ashes than the fact that she disregarded their wishes and was going to marry him. Noah nervously rubbed at the stubble on his chin.

Noah was making a bad situation worse, and he knew it. Even as he hit the highway heading north, he felt ashamed that he wasn't going back. It was selfish, he knew, but he would deal with it just like he had dealt with everything else, later.

Noah tried to calm himself down as the miles and hours passed in a blur of trees and corn fields. He tried to even convince himself he was doing everyone a favor by staying out of their lives. As much as he tried to deny it, he was trouble.

Distance would be his friend. He would put Virginia behind him, literally, he thought as he crossed into Pennsylvania. As the landscape changed, so did his attitude. He thought about his parents and how worried they must be about him.

Noah had put them through a lot and he knew it was hard for them. He would try to make it up to them. He would start by letting them know how much he appreciated them by helping him move, even though it was less than ideal to be back in his old bedroom, they did it for him.

He wouldn't take things or people for granted anymore. Noah understood, better than most, how easily they could be taken away from you. He would live in the moment, accept the blessings that God has given him and appreciate every last one.

Noah was actually getting excited to see his parents. He had changed his attitude and his mindset to be more focused on the people around him. That would be his new normal. He was giving himself a second chance.

When he finally turned the corner to his street and pulled into his driveway, he felt at peace for the first time in a long time. That was until he looked at the box sitting on the passenger's seat.

The ashes remained undelivered. All the positivity he had been building up during the four hour car ride home came crashing down in an instant. He had failed, again. Noah had to face the harsh reality that he was a coward.

Noah looked up to see his parents greeting him at the front door, their expressions quickly changing from smiles to concern as they watched their son crying in the front seat of his truck.

Chapter 22

Noah did his best to throw himself back into his job. It took being back for a few months to finally feel normal again, almost like he had never left. Of course there were still remnants of the past still reminding him of what he never did. Malia's ashes were still sitting in the living room.

He had actually made several life changes that he thought he had to in order to keep healing and moving forward. He took Steven's offer of moving in and it's been working out pretty good. His parents were probably relieved as well.

At first, Noah's parents really worried about him. Dawn and Richard had watched their son suffer long enough and thought the trip south would have been good for him. Noah tried to convince them that it had been a great experience, but the way he moped around told them a very different story.

Richard insisted that getting back to work would help. Noah did everything required to get his badge and gun back and resume his old duties. There was an improvement in Noah that was very encouraging to his parents, but Dawn still worried about her son.

She saw the subtle changes that told her he was reverting back to his depression. Once Noah moved out, she relied on Steven to keep them updated on anything that might concern them. His nightmares may have subsided, but there was still a sadness about him that wouldn't go away.

Steven also worried about his partner. They were back together and Steven had to know that he could trust Noah when he needed him. He insisted that he could do his job. It had been over four months and there had been no incidents of concern. Noah thought they were all overreacting and that they needed to trust him.

Steven felt like he could relax a bit more, Noah was nearly back to his old self. They could hang out on their days off and have a drink at the bar in the evening. They had a lot of catching up to do and Steven listened to the stories Noah told of his time in Virginia.

Some details Noah left out, of course, he didn't want anyone to think he was in danger while he was there. He was, of course, but it all worked out in the end. Noah ran away, that's why. It was still eating at him, too.

Noah was angry at himself for how he left things in Summer Hill, both with Kate and with the Harris's. It was permeating his thoughts during the daytime and nighttime. He didn't know how to stop it, well maybe he did.

He couldn't go back. That was not an option. He never reached out to Kate since he left that note the day he walked out. She had probably even moved on since then. He secretly hoped she found a new boyfriend and was happy with him, she deserved happiness.

Noah didn't dare try to contact her. It would be too hard to hear her voice but he thought about her more and more each day. It was the guilt that was eating at him. He was guilty of not completing his delivery, too. In fact, that was the whole reason for heading to Virginia in the first place and he failed.

It was Malia's ashes that he felt the most weight of responsibility. Noah knew in his heart that she would want her final act to bring healing between her and her parents, and Noah failed her. He had let her down when she needed him the most.

That night, Noah and Steven were being called to an armed robbery at a convenience store. These calls came in all the time, so it wasn't anything out of the ordinary. They drove over with lights and sirens and quickly learned that they were the first ones on the scene.

Even before getting out of the car they could see through the window that the gunman had his arm around the frightened cashier and was pointing his handgun and the customers. It was a hostage situation on top of an armed robbery in progress.

Steven called for backup as Noah got out of the car. They approached the store with guns drawn and as soon as the gunman saw them, he aimed his weapon at Noah. Steven came up behind Noah and they tried talking to the boy. He really was just a scared boy.

The boy probably thought this would be an easy job, he could handle it alone. Perhaps he had friends with him, but when the situation turned sour, they fled the scene. All Noah and Steven knew was that there was a person with a gun who looked like he wasn't afraid to use it.

The two officers relied on their training to diffuse the situation, biding their time until backup could come help and maybe distract the gunman. But when the boy reacted like a cornered lion, they knew they didn't have that kind of time.

The first shot hit Noah. He heard more shots fired but Noah didn't know where they went or who they might have hit. All he knew was that he was having another flashback and was struggling to fight through it. Unfortunately, he was also losing consciousness.

The last thing Noah heard before completely blacking out was Steven yelling into his radio, "Officer down! Officer down!"

NOAH WOKE UP IN THE hospital the following day. It took a minute to realize where he was and why his mother was sitting next to his bed. He was in Pittsburgh and his shoulder hurt, those were the first details that he could put together on his own. The rest would have to be told to him.

Dawn rang the nurse as soon as she saw her son's eyes open. She had been holding his hand and hadn't left his side all night. Her tears betrayed the smile she wore for his benefit. Noah knew that whatever happened, he had scared them.

"Mom," Noah whispered.

"You don't have to speak," Dawn replied. "The nurse will be here soon."

"What...happened?" He asked.

"You and Steven had a call for a robbery and you were shot," Dawn's voice broke on that last word. It was déjà vu from nearly a year ago and she felt lucky, again.

"Steven?" Noah asked quietly.

"He's fine. He shot the gunman. Everyone is okay now," Dawn answered. She touched his face to reassure herself that he was okay, at least on the outside. Dawn feared what he was going through on the inside. How many times could a person get shot before it really messed them up?

Just then the nurse came in and took Noah's vitals. She had a warm smile and assured Noah and his mom that everything looked great. He could probably go home in another day or two.

The nurse explained that he had lost a lot of blood. It took the ambulance longer than usual to reach the scene and it was touch and go for a while. They wanted to keep Noah a couple more days just to monitor him. It was all perfectly normal.

Noah didn't remember anything from last night. He knew it would probably come to him later, but for now he would let the doctors and nurses take care of him. He just couldn't believe that he was shot again, and in the same shoulder!

Dawn was visibly relieved when Noah had woken up. She quickly called her husband and he came later that evening. Richard didn't let Noah see how badly he was shaken by the news that his son was shot, again. He had gone his whole law enforcement career without a single bullet wound and now Noah had two.

None of it made sense to Noah. He thought he was doing good, getting back to normal. How could he have been sent all the way back to start like none of the progress from the past year had even happened? All the months of therapy, the time off and the summer in Virginia, was it all for nothing?

Noah was starting to get frustrated being hooked up to all the machines and stuck in a hospital bed. Panic was taking ahold of him and he couldn't shake it. Was the universe trying to tell him that he needed to stop being a cop? What else was he supposed to think?

It was in the evening, after his family went home and the hospital was quiet that his dark thoughts crept back in. He honestly didn't know if he could go back on the streets. What other option was there, being a cop with a desk job?

Noah knew he couldn't handle working inside all day, he needed to be outside, under the sky and stars. His thoughts morphed and drifted. He thought about Daisy, the cottage and Katie. It was getting harder to deny the happiness, the pure joy, he felt in Summer Hill.

He tried to get some sleep, he was sure he needed it, but the beeping of the machines made it difficult. He pulled out his phone and started looking through his pictures. He had so many to scroll through, from the horses, the waterfall, the lake, the boat and the carnival.

It all brought a smile to his face. A smile that hadn't been there in months. He was sure everyone saw it, he wasn't fooling anyone. Noah had tried to slide right back into his old life, but just a few months ago he was trying to escape this life. He couldn't have it both ways.

He clicked on his contacts and scrolled until he found the one he wanted. Even looking at the name, he got a knot in his stomach. If he reached out now, there was no going back. He would have opened up a wound so large that no amount of stitching could make it heal properly.

Noah didn't know if he was emotionally strong enough to follow through. If he returned to Virginia, it meant he had to confront everything and everyone that he avoided last time, that included the Harris's.

He would not run away a third time and be able to live with himself. Noah wasn't sure he was even stable enough to be making such a life changing decision right now. Did he hit his head? He forgot to even ask if he suffered a concussion. Surely they would have informed him if he injured his head.

Well, injury or not, he felt he was making the right decision for him. His parents may not agree, even Steven might try to discourage him from going back, but he felt like he could never fit in again here, not anymore.

Noah took a deep breath and found the number in his phone. He thought a phone conversation might be too hard, too emotional. He decided to send a text. At least that way, if he never got a text back, he knew he was not welcome.

His hands were actually shaking as he typed and stopped. He was more nervous than he thought. Noah put his phone down and told himself to calm down, it was just a text between friends. Again, he typed out a simple text and hit send.

It was read and replied to within seconds. His heart beat faster as he read the response.

"Hi, Noah, how are you?"

"Hi, Henry, I'm hanging in there," Noah replied. "How are things at home?"

"So many things have happened since you left," Henry answered. "When are you coming back? I finally made that demo!"

"I'm so proud of you, Henry! I knew you would if you put your mind to it."

"So are you coming?"

Noah didn't know how to answer that. He wasn't completely sure, but he knew his heart was calling him there. "Maybe," was all Noah could say.

Noah put down his phone and he smiled. Reaching out to Henry was a start. Baby steps, everything starts with baby steps.

Chapter 23

While recuperating at home, Noah took the opportunity to discuss his decisions to return to Virginia with his parents. He wasn't sure how they would take it. He was prepared for both eventualities, loving the idea or hating it.

Noah was going regardless. He felt that he couldn't move forward without retracing his steps and clearing up the mess he made in the past. He knew that wouldn't make sense to everyone, but it was now crystal clear to him and that's all that mattered.

It was during dinner one night when Noah brought up the idea of going back to Virginia to his parents. They had to admit they weren't surprised. Dawn had seen this coming ever since he woke up in the hospital. She was worried what being shot, again, would do to his psyche.

For Richard, the decision was a little hard to swallow only because it made him sad to see Noah end his law enforcement career. He had hoped to see Noah follow in his footsteps, but if it would keep him safe, he was all for him stepping down.

Their son's safety was always a priority. If that meant living in Summer Hill, then they would support him. Of course, they also had their doubts that he would even stay in Virginia. They knew Noah's history for running when things got too difficult, and it sounded like this could be one of those situations.

Noah tried to assuage their fears as best he could, but to be honest, he had some too. There was no guarantee that Kate even wanted him back. Henry had said that a lot had changed. Did Kate change? Noah left over four months ago, anything could have happened in that time.

He wouldn't go back without some research, though. He had a friend look up Mason Fisher. He didn't care anymore if it was right or wrong, he had to know what the guy was up to. Turns out Mason had a record. Not much, mostly drunk and disorderly that got dismissed, but there was something that caught Noah's eye.

Noah saw a report of a domestic disturbance at the Patterson Ranch the night after he left. It mentioned Mason Fisher but there was no arrest. Kate must have not pressed any charges, or was persuaded not to. He didn't have all the details and he really wanted to know.

If Kate and Mason were still together, then he couldn't go back to the ranch. He couldn't risk Kate getting hurt by that brute. He could go back to see the Harris's but not the Pattersons. That was always an option, not to go to the ranch at all.

He wouldn't try to call Henry again to ask, he couldn't put him in that position. Maybe he could just meet with Henry and catch up, he really seemed genuinely excited at the prospect of Noah coming back. He had to admit that he missed Henry, too.

When Noah talked to his parents about Virginia, they had asked him what all happened that summer. Noah tried giving details but would always stop when it was something he didn't want them to know, something that would make them worry.

He would show them pictures so they could understand how beautiful it was there. They had a feeling he wasn't being completely honest with his stories, but Noah was allowed his secrets.

In preparation for going away for an unknown amount of time, Noah moved his things back into his parent's house. Steven enjoyed having him there, but it was the practical thing to do, especially now that Steven met someone.

This was going to be a new beginning for both of them, another chance at happiness. Steven wished him well and told him to watch his back, or shoulder as the case may be. They had joked about it, but deep down, they both knew Noah was lucky to be alive.

WHEN HENRY GOT THE text from Noah late one night last week, he immediately told his family. He didn't know what happened between him and Kate, so for Henry, it was like an old friend coming to visit.

Everyone had hoped he would come back eventually, things had really taken a positive turn at the ranch and they wanted to thank Noah personally. Kate had confessed to her family that all of her ideas were really Noah's. Clayton and Ashley were surprised when Kate said he had left, especially without saying goodbye to anyone.

Kate didn't let herself be hopeful. She knew that if she expected to see him walk in that door and he didn't, she would be devastated. Noah had only said maybe when asked if he would come back. Maybe was not a yes.

Kate decided that she wouldn't think about it. She had tried so hard to not think about him the last four and a half months. Some days were better than others, the worst days were the ones when she couldn't get out of bed.

Instead, she focused on moving forward as well as helping the ranch move forward. They had all of their plans laid out and now they just needed to implement them. Everyone had a job and they all worked together, even Henry.

Henry still had time for his music career, even reserving studio time to record a demo. He had sent it out to places with positive reviews, it was just a matter of time now. Henry also enjoyed being part of the ranch. He was more hands-on than ever before and his father was proud of him. He even admitted that college was an option.

Clayton enjoyed finally doing things around the ranch with his only son, maybe there was hope for him to take over after all. They had so many projects to look forward to together. Clayton knew he had to give some of the credit to the changes in his son to Noah.

It was nearly winter and the corn maze was a huge success. People came from all over the county to participate and they told Clayton how much fun they had. He already had plans for making it even bigger and better next year. This was only the beginning and again, Noah was responsible.

Things were really turning around for the Patterson Ranch and it couldn't have come at a better time. Clayton knew that their financial stability would take some time, but revenue, no matter how small, was a blessing.

Kate still loved going to the waterfall. It was too cold to go in, but just having the memories were enough. It was an even more special place for her since sharing it with Noah. They came here so many times over the summer, it would never feel the same again.

She walked to the edge of the water and let the spray hit her. It was cold and made her shiver, but it was also like medicine to her soul. The waterfall would always be their place and it made her miss Noah terribly. Kate couldn't understand how he could leave her and it hurt that she may never know.

Kate stayed and watched the waterfall all afternoon. Here, she could escape reality. She could imagine it was still summer and she was taking off her clothes and jumping in the water in only her bikini. She laughed when she thought about how she had persuaded Noah to strip down to his briefs! She didn't think he would, but he surprised her.

Noah spent the whole summer surprising her. She imagined him now back as a police officer protecting the streets of Pittsburgh. She hoped life was treating him well and that he could find happiness and peace. Like Noah said in his note, be happy. She wanted that for him, too.

If being happy meant they couldn't be together, then that was okay, too. She had caused him enough trouble and didn't want him to suffer any more. The whole target competition with Mason was a horrible nightmare. Then she couldn't believe he accused Noah of slashing his tires.

It was Kate who had done that. She knew it was childish and if he had caught her... well, he didn't. Kate had snuck out in the middle of the night. She didn't think he would accuse Noah, Mason had already beaten him to a pulp, she never expected Noah's name to come up at all.

Mason had hurt her too many times to count and she just wanted a little revenge. Wasn't she entitled to that? Even if he never found out it was her, she felt vindicated, a little.

It was getting cold. The weather forecast was snow tonight, it was December after all. It probably wouldn't last, but it was magical to watch. Kate decided to head back to the house. She thought hot chocolate sounded good right about now.

Kate made it back to the house just in time to see her mother taking the casserole out of the oven. The house smelled delicious. With everyone gathered around the table, they each discussed their day. It was warm and cozy and Kate felt herself melting into the comfort of her family.

Lorna loved when her family was home for dinner. Teri didn't work as much at the diner, she had things to do around the ranch and she preferred it that way. Lorna was getting better at riding and will compete next spring in her first competition. Her goal was to get as many medals, if not more, than her father.

Lorna didn't know about all the drama that took place last summer. Her family tried to shield her as best they could. They couldn't keep her away from all of it, of course. She knew there was animosity between Mason and Noah, but she was unaware of the feelings between her sister and Noah.

She saw that Kate was sad when Noah left, but when Mason came over and made more accusations and implications, she saw and heard it all. When he grabbed Kate by the arms and started shaking her, that's when the police showed up.

Lorna didn't know who called them, but she was so scared of Mason that night, she was relieved when the police came in the door. It was just like the night of the target shooting. Lorna didn't like that day at all. She didn't necessarily like Mason, but she never feared him until that day.

She hoped they never saw him again, but also knew that was impossible. He always seemed to just show up and she hated when he did. Lorna tried to stay out of it, though. She trusted her big sister knew what she was doing.

Well, Lorna might think her sister knew what she was doing, but Kate didn't. She did try to keep herself busy which also kept her mind occupied. Kate was tired of being sad and angry. She had gotten on with her life and looked forward to the future, whatever that may be. She had another chance at being happy and she was going to take it.

Kate's life had remained relatively calm since that night Mason came over to start trouble. It was the night after Noah left and emotions were already running high. Mason's outburst made everything one hundred times worse. She couldn't believe he had the nerve to even come back after everything he put her family through.

Mason accused her of having a relationship with Noah. She denied it, of course, even though they had spent the night together, she would not admit that to him, ever. She told him that Noah had left, for good. Mason still wouldn't let it go.

It wasn't until the police showed up that she saw how enraged he had become. Mason's hypocritical behavior made her laugh and he really couldn't handle that. Kate was embarrassed for her family to witness Mason at his worst, but it was also necessary for them to finally see his true colors.

It was Clayton that told him to never come back, her father had had enough of that man. If he could have fought Mason, he would have, he was that angry. Clayton didn't usually get involved in his kids' love lives, but after this, he will have to. He would not let a dangerous man like Mason in their house again.

Kate had gone to her room and was ready for this day to be over. It was a good day, but she was exhausted. She put on her fuzzy pajamas and climbed into bed. Maybe she would see snow tomorrow. With her head on the pillow, she reached over to grab her stuffed dolphin and fell into a deep sleep.

Chapter 24

Noah packed with a determination he never had before. The last time he drove to Virginia, he was only thinking of it as a short stay and a round trip. Now, he wasn't so sure. He sat on the edge of his bed and considered what to bring. Would he be back?

The duration of his stay in Summer Hill would ultimately be determined by just one person, Katie. Noah wasn't even sure he would have the courage to call her let alone face her, but Summer Hill was a small town. He thought the chances were good of running into at least one member of the Patterson family.

His parents tried to be encouraging, but inside they were nervous for him. They had a feeling it ended on a bad note last time and that he would be walking into an even stickier situation. On top of that he was injured.

Noah's shoulder was still sore and bandaged. He had a clean bill of health as far as infection and damage to muscles or nerves were concerned, so that was good to hear. He would need more physical therapy but he could do that anywhere.

No one was going to talk him out of going, Noah believed this was the answer to his inner turmoil and future happiness. He had been throwing clothes into suitcases and then started packing books, laptop and shoes. He hesitated when he saw the cowboy boots in the back of his closet, but he packed them, too.

Noah hoped that this trip didn't turn into a disaster. He knew that was a real possibility and that he could be heading back home the following day. But Noah didn't want to give into that fear, he was going to head south with the hope that he would be welcomed.

He couldn't forget the ashes. This really was the main reason for going, the reason for going again. Noah would never forgive himself for not being strong enough to meet Malia's parents last summer and he was determined to not be that cowardly again.

After Noah did a final walk around his childhood bedroom and was satisfied that he had taken everything he might need, he said his goodbyes to his parents. It was emotional for all three of them.

Dawn hated to see her son so unhappy. She knew this was something that only he could figure out. Noah had to heal himself. Richard gave his son a hug, careful not to put pressure on Noah's left shoulder. His father made sure that Noah knew he always had a home with them, no matter what.

Noah focused on what his father said as he backed his pick up truck out of their driveway. He was lucky to have such loving and supportive parents, not everyone did. This made him look at the decorative box of ashes sitting in his passenger seat. He would finally make this right.

He took his time driving to Summer Hill, enjoying the scenery and leaving the big city behind. There wasn't as much green in December, not like it was in June. The trees had shed their leaves which provided a more stark view of the landscape as he drove.

Noah tried listening to music, but didn't like having to search for new stations in every town, so he just turned it off. He let his mind wander as the hum of the engine combined with the sound of the cardinals singing outside. Even rolling the window down an inch to smell the country air.

Noah had made it to Summer Hill and was surprised to find that he actually had butterflies in his stomach as he drove down the main street and saw the familiar buildings. It was a haunting feeling of déjà vu but he tried to stay positive. He was not going into this blindly like he did last summer. He was now well aware of the dangers awaiting him.

He pulled into the same motel he stayed at in June. He paid for a couple of nights without really having a plan. Noah brought in his bag from the truck and stood outside in the parking lot. What now? He was completely clueless about what to do next.

His stomach growled and decided to find a place to eat dinner. He looked at the diner across the street and knew he didn't want to eat there. It was too risky right now to be spotted by Teri or...he hated to even think the name, Mason.

Noah thought he remembered a pizza place a few streets down and got back in his truck. There weren't many customers on a week night, so Noah got seated right away. He was hungry so he ordered a large pepperoni pizza and a beer.

It felt eerie to be sitting in Summer Hill with no one knowing he was here. He kept looking around and wondered if someone who might know him would walk in. They didn't. He was able to eat his pizza without interruption.

After paying, Noah drove back to the motel, he had no where else to go. He wasn't going to hang out in the bar, it was also too risky. He parked his truck and grabbed his left over pizza for later. As he approached his room 107, he noticed a timid dog peaking around the back of his truck.

The dog was just a mutt really, no collar and no owner that Noah could see. Again, he was the only car in the parking lot. It was chilly out and he assumed the dog was hungry, so Noah opened his cardboard box containing his pizza and threw the dog some pepperoni.

The dog slowly inched towards the savory meat and eat it hungrily. Noah decided to throw him a whole piece of pizza and again, the dog ate it. He intended on throwing the last piece of pizza to the dog, but a loud noise coming from down the street spooked him and he took off.

Noah went back inside his motel room and showered. It had been a long, uneasy day. He knew tomorrow would be worse. He would call the Harris's as soon as he woke up and make arrangements to meet. There was no alternative, he had to see them.

He laid in bed while sleep evaded him. He tried flipping through channels and landed on some show about wildlife. He tried to watch, but his thoughts came back to last June. He remembered how he felt last time he spent his first night in this motel.

Noah was feeling a little bit like that now, only now he had history here. It wasn't the unknown that concerned him anymore, it was the known risks he faced. He had a better understanding of what he was walking into but it still left him feeling unsteady.

MASON WAS HAVING DINNER with a girl in the diner. He didn't care that Teri was working, he wasn't going to hide his extracurricular activities anymore. He wasn't going to let the Patterson's run his life any longer.

Even as Teri came to Mason's table to take their order and then again to bring their food, Mason had a smirk on his face that made Teri want to kick him. She knew her job was to be nice to the customers, but Teri hated his guts. The feeling was mutual, but Mason still thought Teri was cute.

The last big scene at the house when the police were called should have been the end of Mason in their family's lives, but Mason still said it wasn't over between them. Kate always felt that she had to watch her back, even in her own hometown. Teri got a creepy feeling when she left after her shift, too.

It was either Mason watching them, or one of his buddies. They were always on edge not knowing when the other shoe, or boot, would fall. Mason was capable of anything, they knew that now. He was dangerous, as dangerous as a viper.

Mason couldn't believe his eyes when he spotted a familiar pick up truck pull into the motel across the street. His chair faced the window and he watched as Noah got out and stood in the parking lot. Even the girl Mason was having dinner with that night asked him if everything was okay when he let out a deep laugh.

"Oh, it's better than okay," Mason replied. "It's like Christmas morning."

Mason watched as Noah went into the motel and then left a little while later, presumably to get something to eat. Mason pulled out his phone and called his buddies to let them know what he just witnessed. He couldn't believe his luck.

The one person who had been a thorn in his side for the last six months, whether he was physically here or not, had just been handed to him on a silver platter. Mason blamed Noah for everything! Right down to the girl he was sitting with.

Mason only had eyes for one girl and Noah made that impossible right now. He still called Kate and texted her but it wasn't the same, it was never the same since Noah came to town. He should have finished the job when he had the rifle in his hands.

Even now, Mason could feel the cold feeling of the Kimber Hunter in his hands and was itching to pull the trigger. The girl opposite Mason was starting to worry about the man who asked her to dinner. They had only met yesterday and she wasn't sure he was mentally stable.

The girl watched Mason react as if he was holding something, a rifle maybe. This made her extremely uncomfortable and she said she had to go. Mason barely heard her as she stood up and ran outside into the night air.

Mason was focused on a different prey. He couldn't believe his good fortune. He was just thankful he was here to see it with his own eyes, he might not have believed anyone else otherwise. He would have just said they were mistaken and maybe not even believed them.

It was like a Christmas present to Mason. He didn't even wait for Noah to return, he didn't have to. Mason paid his bill and left Teri a hefty tip, he was in a generous mood tonight. The little bell on the door rang as Mason went out into the night. He had plans to make.

Teri didn't know what had gone on at Mason's table. She just knew that the girl looked upset when she left and that Mason looked like a kid in a candy store. Their reactions couldn't have been more opposite. Teri didn't know why, she didn't see Noah arrive at the motel or see him when he returned from his dinner.

If Teri had seen Noah that night, she would have at least warned Kate, or even Noah. Noah was back in town and only one person knew it. It was just unfortunate that it was the one person who Noah wanted to avoid at all costs.

Noah remained oblivious to the commotion in the diner. He tried to watch television but he just couldn't relax. Maybe he knew, subconsciously, that he had been spotted. It was probably a good thing that Noah didn't know Mason had watched him earlier.

After fighting sleep long enough, Noah turned off the television and rolled over in bed. It had been a long day but he had a difficult day tomorrow. He tried to breathe deep and relax. His shoulder was aching and he tried to get comfortable.

Sleep finally overtook him in the early hours of the morning. Noah's nightmares had changed over the last few months. The trauma of the home invasion wasn't as prevalent in his dreams, but tonight he did have a restless night for another reason.

Noah dreamt about a pepperoni loving dog who came up to him in a green field. He bent down to pet the dog. The dog was friendly and licked his hand. What the man and dog didn't see was that there was movement in the tall grass. They weren't aware of the deadly viper that was hiding and ready for attack.

Chapter 25

Noah woke up the next morning with a renewed enthusiasm for the task at hand. He tried calling the Harris's but they never answered. He had come to the conclusion after his failed attempts at contacting them that they had probably changed their number. It didn't matter, he knew where they lived.

He gave himself a pep talk in the mirror as he got dressed. He could do this! He wasn't going to chicken out like he had in the past! He would finally deliver Malia's ashes to her parents. Even as he grabbed his keys and stepped outside, the confidence started to waiver.

That was until he spotted a familiar mutt at his motel door.

"Hey there," Noah said to the dog.

He pet the dog for a moment and then put the ashes in the passenger seat of his truck. The dog jumped in, too. Noah, never having a pet before, simply told the dog to get out. The dog just panted and looked at him without moving.

After several attempts of asking the dog to move, he simply made room for him in the seat and shut the door. What harm could it do to bring him along for company on this mission? Noah rolled the window down on the dog's side and he smiled when the animal put his head out the window.

"I need to call you something," Noah said to the dog. "You don't have a collar, so I guess I can just make one up." Noah kept looking from the road to the dog and said, "Pepperoni."

Right on cue, the dog barked. Noah laughed and pet the dog's head. They stopped at a gas station for breakfast. Noah got donuts and a coffee and Pepperoni, or Peppy as he was called, was given a hot dog. He was happy to have the companion, it gave him someone to talk to because Noah was starting to feel nervous again.

They were getting close to the Harris's house. He slowed the truck down as they turned the corner. Noah parked at the same inconspicuous spot he had on the other two occasions when he tried this exact same thing. This time he would be successful.

Noah took a deep breath and actually got out of the truck this time. He came around to the passenger side door and opened it. He took the box that contained Malia's ashes and told the dog to stay.

"I'll be back in a little bit," Noah assured the dog. "Peppy, stay!"

Peppy made no attempt to run, he simple sat on the seat and obeyed his new master. Noah nodded and closed the door. It was all up to him now. Noah turned towards the house and walked very slowly.

He could feel his Glock tucked into the back of his jeans, his constant companion. His head swiveled from left to right, as if he were approaching another dangerous call. As he got closer to the house, he heard noise and movement coming from inside.

Noah was nearly at the front steps when a woman came to the door. Noah stopped, she was about to call for her husband when recognition registered on her face. This was the moment of truth, the moment that had frightened Noah away twice before.

He stepped forward again, cautiously. He knew she saw the box he carried but wasn't sure she would know what it was.

"Hello Mrs. Harris," Noah said.

"Hello Noah," she replied.

"I'm sorry I didn't come sooner, I tried," Noah confessed. "I brought this... uh her, to you."

Noah didn't know what else to say, he just walked up each step slowly, still unsure of what reaction he would eventually get. He nearly fell backwards when her husband came up behind her. Noah stood up tall, trying to portray a confidence he didn't feel.

He had never personally met Bob and Jessie Harris. He had only seen pictures and heard stories of them. He knew they were strict and set in their ways, and that they didn't like Noah.

"Who are you?" Bob demanded.

Noah cleared his throat. "I am Noah Wagner. I was Malia's fiancé."

They both looked at him, unmoving. Noah was too focused on Bob, that he didn't notice Jessie blot at the tears running down her face. Her husband put his arm around his wife and patted her shoulder.

Noah wasn't sure what was happening. Should he just set the box down and leave? The three of them stood silently on the porch. When Jessie finally spoke, Noah nearly flinched at the words that finally broke the silent standoff.

"I'm so glad you came," Malia's mother said. "It's been a year since she died, so it's only fitting that you came now."

To say Noah was surprised was an understatement! Noah was so taken aback when Jessie came forward to give him a hug that he nearly dropped the box he was holding. Instead, he set it on the table between two adirondack chairs and returned her warm embrace.

Noah melted into the hug and felt himself get emotional, too. He didn't know what to expect, but is sure wasn't this. This was acceptance and love. They were giving him a second chance.

Noah looked past Jessie and even saw Bob smile. Was Malia wrong about how they really felt about a mixed race relationship? Noah released Jessie and gestured towards the box.

"I brought her back to you guys. It only felt right that she come home," Noah said.

Jessie brought the tissue back to her tears and nodded her head. "I want to show you something," she said.

Jessie walked down the porch steps and Noah followed. Bob remained where he was, he already knew where she was going. Jessie grabbed Noah's arm, a little unsteady on the uneven grass.

She led him to a large Virginia Pine tree in the backyard. It was tall and old, he could see. Near the tree, Jessie had created a flower garden, complete with a plaque and a bench. It was lovely. He would have to imagine how all of the flowers bloomed in the summer, but the feeling was peaceful.

"I made this in memory of our Malia Ray," her mother said.

Noah sat down on the bench and Jessie sat next to him. They both looked at the plaque and admired the flower garden. But Noah couldn't help struggle with the reality of how nice these people were accepting of him compared to Malia's stories.

"Mrs. Harris, I have to ask you something and I don't want you to take it the wrong way," Noah started.

"What is it?" She asked.

"Well, Malia gave me the impression that you didn't approve of me, of us, of our getting married..."

Jessie put her hand on Noah's knee and patted it. "At first, no," she said. There was a heavy pause that lasted a few seconds. "But then we had to take a good look at ourselves and ask ourselves why."

Noah looked at the woman sitting to his right. She was struggling to articulate exactly what she was feeling. But he waited for her to finish.

"When Bob and I first heard that Malia wanted to move to Pennsylvania, we were hurt. There were plenty of jobs here for her, close to home. We were afraid of how people would treat her, we knew how mean people could be."

Noah nodded and listened.

"When she met you, we tried to talk her out of it, that's true. But when you became engaged, that made us rethink our position." Jessie looked at Noah. "We only wanted her to be happy and if that was with you, it was okay with us."

"Do you know why she still believed you were against the marriage?" Noah asked.

"She stopped communicating with us. I understood why, but we never really had a chance to tell her, to explain that it was okay." Jessie brought the tissue to her eyes. "It was too late."

Noah looked over at the flower garden. He could see rose bushes, Malia's favorite flower. He wanted to picture this place when all of the roses were in full bloom. He could have seen it when he tried coming the last time, but he couldn't do it.

Today, sitting next to Malia's mother in the memorial garden she created, he felt her presence. It was not something he could attempt to describe, it was the medicine he needed to finally move on. It all felt right to be here now.

They sat side by side on the bench for what seemed like hours, but in reality was probably twenty minutes. Noah mentioned needing to go and do something, but Jessie offered him to stay for lunch. He already felt like he had intruded on their day, their lives, enough.

"Thank you so much, but I had better go," Noah said.

Jessie understood, it was hard for him to be here. It was something she wished she could have changed years ago. She hated that her own daughter didn't feel welcomed in her own home but also accepted that she was responsible for that.

She also felt responsible for not being on good terms when her daughter died. Malia died thinking her mother didn't love her enough to be in her life. That Malia wasn't good enough or worthy of being in her parent's lives. Jessie cried for her daughter's forgiveness every night.

It seemed like everyone was blaming themselves for something an evil person did to wreak havoc on all of their lives. Those armed intruders took away so much that night, a life, a future and the possibility of reconciliation.

Noah stood up and the two embraced. It was healing for both of them. Jessie thought she could now arranged a proper memorial service for Malia and asked how long Noah would be in town.

"I honestly don't know," he said.

Jessie nodded and watched him walk back to his truck. She had to admit that she was glad he came. There was a completeness to having Malia's ashes with her at home and she was grateful to Noah for bringing her.

It was not something she ever expected, but now that Malia's ashes were here and tangible, she smiled for the first time in a long time at the memory of her daughter.

As Noah got closer to his truck, he had completely forgotten that he had a passenger. Peppy stuck his head out the open window and waited to be petted. Noah obliged.

"Well, Peppy, I'm glad that's done," he said.

Noah was proud of himself for finally going through with it. He had been so afraid of getting a negative reaction from them that he never even considered that they would he thankful and accepting of him. It blew his mind to think how well it had gone after all. He was sorry that Malia never got to reconcile with them, too.

It took Noah a moment to collect this thoughts. The whole mission took one hour, now what? He knew what he wanted to do, go and see Kate, but he didn't know if he could handle that right now. He put his hands on the wheel and considered his options.

He could go back to the motel, he could go home to Pittsburgh or he could do what his heart was screaming to do and go to the Patterson Ranch. It was a harder decision than he anticipated because he didn't know if he was ready for rejection.

What else could Kate offer him then rejection? He left her after they professed their love for each other. It was the most cowardly thing he could do to the woman he loved. It was a decision that haunted him since July and he wished he had done things differently.

Noah started the engine and put his truck in gear. Suddenly his palms were sweaty and his breath grew shallow. It was not a panic attack, it was Noah finally realizing that the woman he loved was only a short ten minute drive away.

Noah felt his heart pounding in anticipation of seeing her and holding her again. It didn't matter what she said to him when he got there. She could curse him and tell him to go to hell...or she could not. She just might still feel the same way he did right now!

The only way he was going to know for sure was to go there. He hoped she would give him a second chance. Noah drove to the Patterson Ranch on a mission, a new mission. This one was to win back the woman he loved.

His Katie.

Chapter 26

What Noah didn't know when he pulled out in front of the Harris's house was that there was another pick up truck parked further down the road. A truck that belonged to someone who was very interested in Noah and what he was doing.

Mason sat in his truck and waited until Noah returned and drove off. Mason followed him from a safe distance, not wanting to be noticed yet. He didn't know who he was visiting or why he had spent and hour there, he didn't care.

All Mason could think about was how he would make this guy sorry for ever stepping foot back into his town. He would also prevent him from going to the Patterson Ranch, which he knew Noah would try to do eventually.

Mason didn't always suspect there was something going on between them, but he did towards the end. He knew he wasn't crazy for thinking it, even though Kate tried to deny it. To him, it was obvious. He was just too late figuring it out.

Nobody made Mason look like a fool and got away with it. He would make Noah pay. He found a place in the dirt road that was a good spot to accelerate. He was closing the distance between the two trucks.

Noah was in a great mood, he was on the way to see Kate and would apologize for how he left. He looked over at Peppy beside him and smiled. He noticed a truck in his rear view mirror gaining speed, so Noah slowed down to let him pass.

Passing was not what Mason intended. By the time Noah realized who's truck it was, it was already too late. Mason brought his truck up beside Noah and started honking his horn and glaring at him while driving on the other lane. It was reckless and stupid, exactly something Mason would do.

Noah tried to watch the road and also tried to avoid colliding with Mason. Each of them only had a tentative hold on their respective lanes. Mason was laughing and yelling something at Noah and he swerved and corrected his truck. Noah would glance over, but kept his window rolled up.

Mason was accelerating all the while he was driving erratically and honking his horn. Noah knew this was extremely dangerous and it wouldn't take much for both of them to end up on the side of the road and in a ditch. Noah just kept both hands on the wheel and watched the road. Peppy sank further into the passenger seat.

Noah knew Mason wouldn't just give up, it would only end after one of them couldn't drive anymore. They were driving down roads that Noah didn't know, only Mason. This was his town and his backyard, he didn't know where Mason was leading him and he didn't like it.

He needed to find a way of turning in another direction, anywhere but where Mason was going. It was no use, though. Mason was weaving from side to side and actually hit the left side of Noah's truck. It almost made Noah lose control, but he had his hands firmly on the wheel.

Noah was angry. Just for starting this drag race with a police officer was a crime, now he was assaulting one as well. Noah considered taking out his handgun and shooting at his tires, but he knew that would most definitely cause his truck to flip. He didn't want to be the reason Mason got hurt or even died.

This would just have to play out. Mason kept yelling at him from his open window. Noah just wanted him to pull over. He rolled down his window and yelled back.

"Stop your car!" Noah yelled. "Pull over!"

To this, Mason kept laughing. The look in his eyes was cold and dark. He had no intention of slowing down or pulling over, that was clear. Mason had a crazed look in his eyes and Noah wasn't quite sure what to do other than remain in control of his vehicle.

He couldn't pull out his phone to call anyone, he was struggling enough to keep his steering wheel steady. He didn't dare remove one of his hands to dial, even to dial 911. He was on his own.

The speedometer was reaching one hundred. While Noah gripped the wheel, Mason was carelessly swerving in the other lane. Luckily, there weren't any cars attempting to come the other direction. Mason had one hand on the wheel and the other honking the horn.

Peppy had crawled to the small backseat, it was no longer a joy ride for him. Noah tried talking soothing words to him, but it wasn't exactly working. Well, he should be okay, Noah wasn't planning to crash.

Whenever Noah tried slowing down, Mason slammed into the side of his truck. It was obvious he wanted Noah to play by his rules. They were coming up to a fork in the road and at the last minute Noah turned right but Mason was quick to recover. It only took seconds for him to get back to Noah's side. How long was he going to keep this going?

Noah felt the muscles in his neck tense and tighten. His shoulder was throbbing from the stress and pressure of gripping the wheel so tightly. He didn't think he could keep up this speed for much longer and Noah didn't know what damage Mason was doing to his truck.

The dirt road wasn't helping the situation. Dust was creating a cloud that made it extremely difficult to see clearly and rocks were being kicked up left and right. Mason was in control and they both knew it.

These back roads were dense and thick with trees all around them. He was sure that if they both crashed it would take days to discover the accident scene. This isn't how Noah wanted things to end. He finally felt his life coming together, he wanted a second chance with Katie.

Kate's face flashed before his eyes, he needed to get to Katie. She needed to know that he was sorry, that he made a huge mistake by leaving. Noah needed her to know how much he missed her and loved her. He needed to get to the ranch.

He hated Mason for creating this situation and keeping him from Katie. He must have seen him arrive into town or someone told him. Noah had tried to be discrete in where he went and who saw him. Apparently it wasn't enough. Mason found out, Mason always found out.

Mason Fisher was a menace to society and Noah wanted the opportunity to put him away for good. Noah prayed as their speed accelerated to one hundred and ten miles per hour. He prayed that he survived this day and could put his past behind him once and for all.

Noah didn't know where they were but it was far away with dense vegetation. There were pine trees in all directions except straight ahead, that was more dirt road. Mason was still taunting him and honking. Noah didn't know how to get out of this mess and simply maintained control of his truck.

He glanced down at the speedometer, one hundred and twenty. Just then, two deer jumped out of the forest. Noah, who had his eyes on the road ahead saw them. Both Noah and the deer stared at each other in horror as Noah slammed on his breaks.

Noah's tires skidded and slid on the dirt and gravel but finally came to a dusty stop. Mason wasn't looking ahead, he was watching

Noah most of the time. Mason was enjoying this game of cat and mouse too much to think anything bad would happen, at least not to him.

Mason hit the accelerator while Noah had hit the breaks. Noah could still hear him laughing right up until the moment he followed Noah's horrified look and saw the deer. It was too late. Mason swerved to avoid a collision but it was too hard and too fast.

Noah watched as if everything happened in slow motion. Mason's truck slid on the gravel and hit the ditch which caused the truck to be airborne for a minute. When it finally hit the ground it rolled a few times before resting upside down in the opposite ditch.

It took Noah a moment to comprehend what had just happened right in front of him. He actually touched his chest and then looked back at Peppy to make sure he wasn't dreaming. They were alive and unharmed. His next thought was Mason.

There wasn't any movement coming from the truck, he was either unconscious or dead. Noah's training took over and he rushed in to help the injured man. When Noah jumped out of the truck, he pulled out his phone. He wasn't getting any signal and he cursed Mason for taking him so far into the forest.

Next, he focused on the man in the truck. He went to the driver's side and looked inside. He saw blood everywhere which made him check for a pulse. It was faint, but it was there. He tried his phone again, still no luck.

If this man was going to survive, he had to get him out of this mangled truck and into his. He wasn't even sure where they were, but he thought he could backtrack good enough to find his way into town. Noah ran his hands through his hair, he wasn't sure how he was going to get this guy into his truck. Mason was larger and taller than Noah, it would take everything he had.

Noah struggled to get the door open. It was too crushed to open. Then he went to the passenger's side door. He was able to get it open enough to slide inside. Noah wished he could make a call for the police, ambulance and paramedics to use the jaws of life to extract him. It was just Noah.

He didn't know if Mason had any broken bones, most likely there were, but he couldn't worry about that. If he left him here he would surely die. Broken bones could heal, death was permanent. He could attest to that. Noah looked around for anything to help him extract Mason from the cab of the truck and then saw Mason's pocket knife.

Noah cut the seatbelt and pulled his upper body with all of his might. It was cramped quarters inside the cab but Noah wouldn't give up. As much as Noah hated this man, he was still a person. He would do everything he could to get him to the hospital.

It took all of Noah's strength to get him out inch by inch. The pain in Noah's shoulder was excruciating but he kept pulling harder. He was nearly out of the cab of the truck when Noah collapsed from exhaustion. He was sweating and panting, even though it was probably forty degrees, but he wouldn't stop now.

Noah took a deep breath and held it as he gave one more big pull with his arms under Mason's upper body. It was just enough, he was finally free of the truck. It wasn't over yet, now he had to get him into the back of his truck.

Noah's shoulder was screaming in pain. He even wondered if he had reopened his own wound because there was blood all over him until he realized it was all Mason's blood. Noah knew it was taking too long. He needed to get this man to the hospital as soon as possible.

With a superhuman strength that came out of nowhere, Noah bent his knees and pulled letting out a scream as he did it. He managed to drag Mason all the way to his truck which looked like a mile away. In reality, it was probably fifty yards. At Noah's truck, he brought Mason's body over his good shoulder and loaded him into the bed of his truck.

Noah took off his coat and laid it over Mason. If he died now, it wouldn't be from frostbite. Exhausted and in pain, Noah climbed in the driver's seat and made a u-turn. Satisfied that everything was okay, Peppy emerged from his hiding place and took his spot up front.

Noah wasn't so sure everything was okay, but he certainly tried his best. He drove as fast as he could back the way they came keeping the unconscious Mason in mind laying in the back of his truck. As he got into town he followed the signs to the hospital. Noah pulled right up to the Emergency Room doors and went in yelling for help.

The name Mason Fisher was at least well known enough to get quick and efficient care and attention. Noah's job was done, there was nothing else he could do to save that man that he hadn't already done. Satisfied that he was now in capable hands, Noah returned to his truck and he and Peppy fell asleep in the hospital parking lot.

Chapter 27

Mason was immediately taken into surgery. Noah tried to give an accurate account of what happened when the doctors and nurses asked. What he didn't say was that they were mortal enemies and Mason really wanted it to be Noah being wheeled into surgery instead.

Noah did consider himself very lucky. He let the nurses know he was outside in the beat up truck sleeping with his dog if they needed him. They didn't know what to say to that and simply nodded in acknowledgment. Noah didn't know why he felt the need to stay, but it just felt like the right thing to do.

As news of Mason's accident spread, more people started arriving at the hospital. Kate was still listed as Mason's emergency contact number, so she was surprised when she got the call to come down to the hospital to sign some paperwork.

She tried to explain that they were no longer together, but they said until Mason changed the contact number, himself, she was it. Kate just rolled her eyes and signed the paperwork allowing them to do whatever they needed to do. She asked how bad it was and the nurse simply shook her head.

The nurse did tell Kate that it was a good thing his friend saw the accident and brought him in when he did. If Mason had waited any longer to get to the hospital he might not have survived. He wasn't out of the woods, yet, there was still a possibility that they may lose him, but the doctors are doing their best.

"He's lucky to have a friend who cares so much," the nurse added. Kate was confused. "Friend?"

"Yes, the gentleman said he'd be out in the beat up truck with his dog taking a nap if we needed him. He was really very sweet," the nurse replied.

Kate didn't know who they were describing but Mason didn't have any sweet friends and she didn't know anyone with a dog or a beat up truck. Still wondering who this friend was, Kate went outside to thank the man in person, even though Mason wasn't on the top of her prayer list.

She saw the beat up pick up truck, it was hard to miss. She wondered what the real story was behind the accident and hoped Mason's friend could shed some light. A cute little mutt poked his head out of the partially opened window and Kate scratched his head.

Kate went around to the driver's side window and knocked on it. She tried to peer inside, but all she saw was a jacket pulled up over the man's head. Apparently he was trying to shield his face from the sun in order to sleep.

The knock startled the man and the jacket fell to the front. Noah was looking into the startled face of Kate. Kate's eyes widened when she realized who this 'friend' really was. Noah opened the door, put on his coat and stood in front of Kate for the first time in nearly five months.

Neither one of them knew what to say. They half smiled at the sight of each other, then the confusion returned to Kate's features.

"What happened?" She asked. "What are you doing here?"

They were both cold and Noah knew his explanation would take a while. He closed the door and led Kate back into the warmth of the hospital waiting room. They found a quiet corner with empty chairs and they sat next to each other. Noah couldn't believe she was here, with him.

"First of all, I didn't mean for any of this to happen," Noah started. "I didn't come back for him."

"Who did you come back for?" Kate asked. It was a loaded question and they both knew it.

Noah thought it was best to start at the beginning. He told Kate the story of being back home and feeling so guilty about how he left things here, he had never even taken Malia's ashes to her parents. He also mentioned that he couldn't stop thinking about her. Then when he got shot again...

"Wait, what? You were shot again?" Kate asked.

"Yes, it was while on a call about an armed robbery," Noah replied. "Same shoulder, too."

Kate looked at him and then to his shoulder. He was covered in dried blood but her first instinct was to touch his shoulder. Noah watched her face the entire time. She looked sad and he wanted to reassure her that he was okay. Kate gently touched his wounded shoulder and Noah closed his eyes.

"It hurts a little, especially after lifting and carrying Mason for the last two hours," Noah said.

"Yes, about that...can we fast forward to where you are here and saving Mason's life?"

Noah laughed. "Okay, I decided I needed to do what I failed to do before. I finally took Malia's ashes to her family. It went better than expected and then I realized I needed to see you. That's where I was headed until Mason wanted to race."

Kate covered her mouth, she had no idea that was what happened. "But the nurse said you found him."

"No, he was racing me, yelling, honking and trying to run me off the road. We were going in a different direction than towards town. I didn't know where we were, my phone had no signal and a deer jumped out in front of us while we were doing one hundred and twenty miles per hour. I stopped, he didn't."

Kate gasped at the real story as Noah recounted every horrific detail. She scooted over and gave him a hug. Noah never felt anything more wonderful in his life. He melted into her embrace and she felt tears welling up in her eyes.

The realization hit her that it could have been Noah being wheeled into surgery just now instead of Mason and it made her never want to let him go again. She wouldn't have even known if Noah had been injured or dead laying in a ditch because she knew Mason would have covered it up. She knew it as sure as she knew her own name.

"Look, I'm sorry if my being here is hard for you, I can go back home right away if that's better," Noah said.

Kate put her hands on Noah's face and made him look directly into her eyes. "I never want you to leave me again. Do you hear that Noah Wagner?"

Noah smiled. "I hear it, but what about Mason?"

"Right after you left I ended things with him once and for all. It's over," Kate said.

"Not for him," Noah replied. "Not really. This isn't something someone does who doesn't care."

"This wasn't about me," Kate said.

She promised to talk to him as soon as he was well enough. She didn't want to admit that this behavior from him scared her. She had to get it through his thick head that it was over and he needed to let her live her own life. These kinds of stunts had to stop.

"One more question," Kate said. "Who's dog is that?"

Noah laughed. "Mine. His name is Pepperoni."

They both laughed and caught each other up on what's been going on in their lives. It was easy and natural to talk with Kate as if the last five months faded away. Kate said there was so much to show him, she couldn't wait until they got back to the ranch.

Their conversation was interrupted when Teri and Henry walked into the waiting room. They looked around for their sister and screamed with delight when they saw her with Noah. They both ran over and gave him a hug.

Noah winced when they squeezed his shoulder too hard and said he would explain everything later. Henry said they had just come back from the crash site.

"Dude, he was lucky you were there! I wouldn't think anyone could survive that twisted metal," Henry said.

Teri agreed and Kate remained quiet. She didn't think she ever wanted to see it, just thinking that it could have been Noah made her nauseous. Mostly because if the roles were reversed, would Mason put forth as much effort to get Noah out and to a hospital? She really didn't think so and that made her shiver.

Mason had wanted revenge so badly he was willing to die for it, that was just sad. Kate would tell the doctors to call her as soon as he woke up, they had a lot of things to discuss in person. Mason was going to listen and hear her this time. It ended now.

Teri and Henry were showing pictures of the wreck to Noah. He hadn't really looked at it, so it really was amazing that anyone survived that, if he survived at all. They also couldn't believe that one person could get him out and into his own truck alone.

Noah chalked it up to adrenaline. People did amazing things when adrenaline kicked in. For Noah, it was knowing he would live to see Kate again, that's what gave him the inner strength and physical ability to get it done. He was still sore and in pain, but knowing he did the right thing was worth it.

Would Mason have done the same for him? He would like to think so, but really he wasn't so sure. Why would he have chosen to race in the first place? He wanted a fatal outcome, he just never imagined it could have been him that would be fighting for his life right now.

Kate suggested that they all go home. Noah said he wanted to stay and make sure Mason got out of surgery okay first. Kate thought he was joking and had laughed. But when Noah didn't laugh, she realized he was serious.

"It's okay, the doctors will call me when he gets out," Kate assured him.

"Still, I think I'll wait. You can go." Noah replied.

Kate wasn't sure if this was a ruse to get him alone and smother him with a pillow. Again, she laughed. Noah was serious. Even when his enemy was injured or dying, he wanted the best for him. Kate had to stop and look at the man sitting beside her, she didn't think she could love him more than she did right now.

"I'll wait with you," Kate said.

Noah took her hand and she laid her head on his good shoulder. Noah knew she was it for him. He never wanted to leave her side again. He would do anything to protect her, even have a very harsh conversation with Mason when he woke up so that he never did anything to hurt them again.

They closed their eyes and leaned their heads back against the wall. They stayed like that for hours. Teri and Henry had left already. Noah had asked them to take Peppy home with them and they were happy to do it.

Kate was afraid to let go of Noah's hand. She imagined that it was a helium balloon that would float away and never return if she loosened her grip. Noah had a way of coming and going at a moments notice or no notice at all and she wasn't willing to take that chance. Never again.

She wanted him to stay, she had even said it, but he didn't give her an answer. Kate wasn't going to beg, but she secretly wished he wanted it as much as she did. Noah had a lot of things to work through and she didn't want to make it any harder on him.

If Noah stayed, she wanted it to be because he wanted to, not because she asked him to. She never let herself dream about this day happening, that he would come back and be sitting next to her, but here he was.

Noah's return still concerned her because he obviously had been back in Summer Hill for a couple of days and never once tried to call her. In fact, he almost died just miles from her home and she would never have known until it was too late.

When Noah opened his eyes after finally dozing off for a short time, he thought he was still dreaming. He looked over and saw Kate sleeping on the chair next to him. Even after feeling the weight of her head on his shoulder, he couldn't be sure it wasn't a dream.

Noah knew how vivid dreams could be and he needed to be sure this was real. He leaned over and kissed the top of Kate's head. It was real. He still smelled the faint scent of lavender. He told himself he would make it up to her, after all of the worry and time apart, he would be better. He wanted her to give him another chance.

He knew she wanted more answers and he would try to give them. Later, he thought. Now was not the time for that kind of deep and emotional conversation. Now was just their reunion. It might have be awkward and strange to meet again under these circumstances, but he was glad Kate was here by his side.

Kate and Noah had been waiting for hours for the doctors to give them any news. Noah knew his injuries were extensive and he wasn't even sure he would survive the night. Still, they waited. He was sure that to everyone else in the waiting room, they looked like any other couple worried about their friend.

Friend was not the word either of them would use to describe Mason Fisher.

Chapter 28

When Noah stretched, the movement woke up Kate. It took them both a minute to recall where they were. Oh, yes, the hospital. Noah tried to stand up but every muscle in his body screamed with pain. He sat back down and rubbed his left shoulder.

"Do you want some coffee?" Kate asked.

"Sure," Noah replied. "I'll go get it."

Kate smiled. "No, you rest. I wasn't the one who carried a two hundred and fifty pound man across a football field."

Noah was about to object, but secretly he was glad to remain sitting. He wasn't sure he could even make the trek down to the cafeteria without collapsing. He had never felt this exhausted before.

Kate returned twenty minutes later with two hot coffees and two blueberry muffins.

"Here," she said, handing him one of each. "You'll feel better after you've had something in your stomach."

Amazingly enough, he did. Maybe it was the power of suggestion or maybe he just remembered he hadn't eaten anything since the donuts with Peppy. A muffin and coffee would have to do for now. They ate their breakfast without many words.

Kate was still trying to comprehend the fact that Noah was here, sitting beside her. She hadn't heard a word from him in five months and now he was in Summer Hill. She watched him eat and tried to read his face.

He no longer looked like a man burdened with trauma and nightmares, although she was sure they were still in there somewhere, dormant. Kate had to admit that he looked...happy. Was he happy to be here with her? He never did say how long he was staying.

Kate decided to let things play out organically. She knew Noah would open up about his plans when he was ready. She was on Noah's time frame. She wouldn't push, she would just enjoy the moment with him.

"You know," Kate started, hesitantly. "I had wanted to tell you that we had a corn maze in the fall and it was a big success."

"Why didn't you?" Noah asked.

"Well, I wasn't sure if you wanted to hear from me."

Noah paused and closed his eyes. He was feeling a wave of guilt and had to get past it. It would take him a long time to build up trust with Kate again. He had tried to forget about Summer Hill, the ranch and her. Now he regretted leaving at all.

"I'm so sorry you felt that way," Noah replied. There was so much more he wanted, needed, to say but not here. "So tell me about it."

Kate told Noah all about the crowds that came for weeks while the maze was open. They sold pies and cakes and everyone had a great time. It was a huge boost to their ranch. Kate went on to explain their plans for expansion next year.

"It is all thanks to you," Kate said.

"No, Katie, you did all the work," Noah replied. "That's why it was a success."

There was more silence as they were each in their own thoughts. Finally, Noah got up the courage to ask something he had wanted to since he saw her yesterday. A question he was afraid to hear the answer to.

"So, are you and Mason still..."

Without any hesitation, Kate replied, "No!"

Noah nodded his head and took another sip of his coffee. He thought that might be the answer, but he had to ask, to be sure.

"Do you think I could stay in your cottage again?"

Kate's face lit up with joy. "Yes and no," she said and then smiled.

Noah smiled but was confused. There was obviously something she wasn't sharing with him and he waited until she finished.

Kate laughed. "Yes, you can stay at the ranch, of course. But not in the cottage, there are other people in it."

It took just a moment to realize what Kate meant. "You rented it out?"

"Yes, That has been another huge success!" Kate said, nearly jumping out of her seat. "I got it all neat and tidy and then listed it online and we were shocked when we started booking reservations right away."

"I'm not. I told you that was an easy decision," Noah replied. "You had a gold mine there and you didn't even recognize it." Noah reached out and took her hand. "So...where would I stay?"

"Well, we have an extra bedroom since Teri moved out and got her own place," Kate answered. "Or..."

Kate and Noah looked into each other's eyes. A hospital waiting room was not the romantic setting Noah envisioned for their first kiss after being reunited, but it would have to do.

Noah put his hand on Kate's cheek and kissed her. It was not long or passionate, but it was enough to convey Noah's feelings. He would stay with her.

"So, how long are you planning to stay?" She asked.

Noah still didn't really know how to answer that. He didn't exactly have a plan. He would need a job and he wasn't exactly sure the offer to stay at the ranch was indefinite. He had to be honest with Katie.

"Well, I'm not sure. I want to stay for a long time, but I would need to see if I could find work here," Noah said. "We can discuss this all later. I will be here for a while."

Kate nodded, satisfied. She knew that if he stayed long enough, she could persuade him to stay permanently. Noah just tried to be as truthful as he could. He just didn't know.

They both jumped when Noah's phone started ringing. He quickly stood up and brought it out of his pocket to see who was calling. It was Mrs. Harris. Noah walked outside to take the call.

"Hello, Noah?" Jessie asked.

"Yes, hello, Mrs. Harris."

"I made arrangements for a memorial service on Sunday for Malia. I wanted to invite you, if you would like to attend," She said.

That was three days from now. "I would love to, thank you Mrs. Harris."

Noah stood out in the crisp morning air. Well, he knew he was staying at least three days, that was a start. He knew he had to tell Kate about the memorial service, but that could wait. He was on shaky ground with her at the moment and didn't want to bring up Malia just yet.

He stayed outside for a moment considering his future. He really did wanted to stay here forever, he just didn't know if he would be satisfied here. He loved Kate, that was the easy part. What would he do here? He didn't want to just work on fences, there had to be more to it.

Noah walked over to his truck. He hadn't really seen all of the damages to it yet. He took a walk slowly around the entire truck. It was unrecognizable. It made him mad to think that Mason did this, but then he thought about Mason's truck...and Mason.

Noah was alive and well, that was something to be very thankful for. He could always get a new truck, it didn't matter as much as his life. He smiled at the irony of sitting overnight waiting to hear whether the man who tried to kill him, twice, was going to make it or not.

He returned to the waiting room and saw that Kate was on her phone. As Noah sat down next to her, she explained that it was Teri telling her that Henry was on his way with some food.

"Listen, why don't you go home with Henry," Noah suggested. "I'm okay to wait here and call you with any changes."

Kate shook her head. "No, I'm not going anywhere." They kissed, again.

Henry entered the waiting room with drinks and sandwiches. They decided to all walk down to the cafeteria where they would be more comfortable. Noah's weak legs felt better, at least he knew he could make it that far without collapsing.

Henry produced ham and cheese sandwiches, chips and soda. As they ate, Noah asked Henry to tell him more about his studio experience. Noah was eager to get caught up on everything that has been happening with the Patterson family since he left.

"How did you know about that?" Kate asked.

"Henry told me when I texted him," Noah replied.

It wasn't until Kate's face dropped that he realized his mistake. He had reached out to Henry but not to her. Noah tried to explain that he was too afraid to contact her. He thought she and Mason were still together and he didn't want to cause any more complications.

She nodded in agreement but Noah wasn't convinced that she meant it. He knew this fact hurt her and he felt guilty again. He should have had the courage to reach out to Kate, he promised himself he would be better. She deserved better.

Kate couldn't believe his lame excuses. How could he say he loved her and then be afraid to text her? He felt comfortable enough to reach out to her brother but not her. It did make her question him a little. Was he really willing to try to make it work here with her?

Henry tried to ignore the looks between Noah and his sister and went on to explain what a great experience he had recording his demo. The staff were so friendly and willing to help him any way they could. He recorded two of his own songs and it felt great to hear them when they were finished. He almost felt like he could make a future in music.

Noah was encouraging to Henry. He could see how Henry's face lit up when he talked about his music. Everyone should be that invested in their future. Noah didn't feel that spark, yet. He hoped he would soon.

The whole time they sat in the cafeteria and visited with Henry, Kate kept looking around. Noah suspected she was looking for any doctors that might be looking for them. He wondered if her concern was more than just whether he lived or died. Did she still have feelings for him?

Noah wasn't going to bring it up, not now. He wasn't sure he wanted to know the real answer anyway. It was just nice to be sitting and hearing Henry talk so animatedly about his budding music career.

"That's why I don't want to go to college," Henry said.

This statement caught Kate's attention and brought it back to their little table. "What?"

"I don't want to," he repeated. "I know I haven't said anything to mom or dad, yet, but that's my decision."

"Oh yes you are!" Kate replied.

Noah listened to the siblings argue for a little while before interrupting. "Perhaps this isn't the correct setting for this kind of conversation. Henry, maybe you should talk to your parents about it first. There are actual colleges who could help you with your music career, not take you away from it."

Kate was thankful for Noah's help and nodded her head. "Yes, we will discuss this later, that's for sure."

"Teri didn't go to college," Henry said, wanting the last word.

"Teri has also bounced from job to job without a stable future ahead of her," Kate replied. She felt bad for throwing her sister under the bus like that, but it was true. Teri might have a steady income and change jobs each year, but that wasn't a sustainable future. At least that's what she kept telling Teri.

Kate didn't like the way this conversation was going. "We will discuss this later," she said to Henry.

Henry took the cue to remain silent. Noah nodded to him, trying to convey that it was in his best interest to listen to his eldest sister right now. Noah knew that some battles were better to be put off until you had allies in your corner.

Noah knew he had to talk to Kate's parents, too. First, he needed to apologize for how he left in July. He knew that couldn't have made a very good impression on them, on the whole family as a matter of fact. He never said a proper goodbye and he still felt bad about it.

Next, he wanted to congratulate them on creating a successful business venture by implementing some of his ideas. He wouldn't take credit, of course, but he still wanted to hear more about them. It was exciting to think of all the new changes that would be coming to the Patterson Ranch.

Thirdly, he needed to let Kate's parents know how desperately in love he was with their daughter. He had to confess that his feelings started while he was staying with them last summer and have only grown since then.

Actually, Noah couldn't wait to tell them!

Chapter 29

When Mason first woke up, he wasn't exactly sure where he was and why he was there. He knew he was hooked up to several machines and that he couldn't move. Beyond that, he was at a complete loss. He looked around for anyone who might be in the room who could answer his questions, but no one was there.

He didn't think he was dead, he wouldn't be in this much pain if he was. He could tell the sun was setting outside his window, but it gave no clue as to what day it was. Mason wondered how long he had been in here. Was anyone looking for him?

He tried to remember what happened to him. He knew it couldn't have been good if this was the end result. He concentrated as hard as he could but all he could remember was Noah. That couldn't be right, Noah left town months ago. Why would Noah be his last memory?

Mason looked for a call button for the nurse but even his neck's range of motion was limited. How bad was he? He could see that one of his legs was in a cast as well as one of his arms. Well, that would definitely put a damper on his lifestyle, he thought.

Mason would just have to wait until someone came to check on him. In the meantime, he tried focusing on the accident that put him here and wondered how many people were hurt. It had to be massive. Every time he thought he saw a glimpse of something, it still came back to Noah.

Perhaps he was hallucinating. He was sure the pain medicine he was on was strong, that had to account for his visions of Noah. Mason wanted to sit up, but that was impossible. He realized he couldn't do anything without help.

Mason was vulnerable and it was not a position he liked or tolerated. It was part of the reason he hated Noah so much from the beginning. Noah was being welcomed and accepted on his own turf, the Patterson Ranch.

It irked him that his own girlfriend preferred to spend time with Noah instead of him. How this stranger could walk right into town and get everyone on his side was what angered him every time Mason saw him or even thought about him. Why didn't they appreciate him and everything he did for them?

He had to admit he took the whole target practice and competition to an extreme, but he was only trying to see what Noah would do. He wouldn't have really shot the guy, he didn't think so anyway. He just wanted to scare him and get the truth about why he was really there.

Being tough was the only way Mason knew how to be. After his mother died when he was young, his father wasn't home much. He would hang out in bars and Mason believed his father even forgot he had a son. Mason had to learn to fend for himself at such a young age.

It was a skill that served him well in life, it got him to where he was today. Mason thought about that for a minute. Where was he in life, exactly? He lost his girlfriend, he hated his job and he had no one who cared enough to be by his side when he was messed up and in the hospital.

Mason was a thirty year old man without anyone who really cared about him. He was suddenly left with an overwhelming feeling of sadness. He wished a doctor or a nurse would come soon. He didn't like that he was spiraling into a hole of depression right here in this dark and empty room.

He had told himself he was happy, even believed it when he was hanging out with friends or bringing different girls back to his house. He could almost convince himself he had everything he ever dreamed of. Almost.

Today, he wasn't even close to believing it. Mason didn't know if he could ever change, but maybe he should try it. He lost Kate, he knew that much, but why did he still have such a heavy grudge on Noah? Was he jealous?

Mason was done trying to analyze his life's choices. He was sleepy and closed his eyes. A nurse had walked by, wondering when her patient would finally open his eyes and when she looked in the window on the door, saw he was still unconscious and kept walking.

AFTER TALKING WITH Mason's nurse, Kate and Noah agreed to go home. The nurse said he was still unconscious and sometimes these things took time. It had already been twenty-four hours and there wasn't any change. There was no reason for them to stay at the hospital.

Kate was glad when Noah finally conceded. She wasn't sure why he was so firm on staying in the first place, but maybe that was the police officer in him. Either way, it wasn't good for him to stay in the waiting room any longer. She wanted to take him home.

They got in Noah's truck and headed towards the ranch. Kate was eager to show him everything they had done to the place since he was there last. Noah was excited, too. The ranch represented a happy time for him, except for that one night when Mason tried to kill him.

Noah missed the open fields, the horses and the waterfall the most. He had become a pretty good rider while he worked there if he had to say so himself. The ride through town was peaceful. He had Kate next to him and it felt right. He had waited for this moment for months.

Kate looked over at Noah and smiled. When their eyes met, Noah took her hand. He wanted to be there for her always. The ride back to the ranch didn't take long. He passed the motel, the diner and the bar before turning off towards the house.

Pulling into the gravel driveway, Noah felt at home. He couldn't describe out loud how he felt driving up to the house and parking. He squeezed Kate's hand before releasing it and got out of the truck. They walked up the front steps together and into their future.

Kate watched his reaction as he slowly walked around the house. She didn't think much inside has changed but to him everything looked more vivid. He would get the chance to start over and it opened his eyes to the possibilities. Noah would touch things as he passed them, still not believing he was actually here.

They walked from room to room as if Kate was giving a tour of some museum. Lorna was sitting at the kitchen table doing homework when they entered the room. Lorna gasped at the sight of Noah and jumped up to give him a hug.

Noah was encouraged by her enthusiasm. Maybe other members of the family will feel the same. He didn't see anyone else, though. He would have to face Clayton later.

"I'll show you where you'll be staying," Kate said.

Noah stepped aside to let her lead the way. He had never been to the second floor before. This was all new to him. Kate turned left and went down a hall and then turned left again. Her room faced towards the barn and fields.

Noah took a cautious step inside, silently asking if it was really okay. Kate laughed.

"Come in, Noah. I'm not going to bite," Kate said.

"Are you sure your parents will be okay with this arrangement?" Noah asked.

"I'm twenty-five years old and practically run this place," Kate assured him. "They will be fine."

Noah had to take her word for it, for now. She did offer the other room, though. It would give them each more space, if that was his concern. Actually, he would rather have the separate room. It just didn't feel right to stay in Kate's room, even if she did run the place.

He wanted to make a good impression on her parents and he was sure that sleeping with their daughter, in her bed would not do that. Reluctantly, Kate gave in, for now. She helped him carry the few belongings he brought into the spare bedroom.

Noah started unpacking a few items when Kate remembered something. "I'll be right back," she said.

Curious, Noah stopped and sat on the bed. Kate returned just as suddenly as she had left and handed him a picture frame. "This is for you," she explained. "Well, actually, it's yours. You left it here by accident in July. I found it under your bed in the cottage."

Noah took the framed photo and stared at the very familiar image. It was him and Malia in Niagara Falls. The picture didn't make him cry like it used to. He was sad, of course, but it was different. He was different.

Noah looked at the picture and recalled the memories of that day, not the heartache it brought back. "Thank you," he said and set it down on the table. "I hope to make our own happy memories now."

"You know," Kate started, "when you talked about Malia, I never actually saw her picture until that day you left. You said she was from Summer Hill and I never really thought much about it but it was Teri who remembered her."

"Remembered her?" Noah asked.

"She used to be our babysitter. It was a long time ago, I didn't recognize her from the photo, but Teri did. It was probably fifteen years ago. Lorna wasn't born yet and Henry was only two. We have so many great memories of her. She was fun."

"Yes, she was," Noah agreed. "Small world isn't it."

"I guess so, at least it's a small town," Kate said with a laugh.

"The Harris family is actually having a memorial service for her in a couple days. They were happy that I brought her ashes to them. It wasn't the reaction I expected, but then it seems like most things aren't."

"I'm so happy for you," Kate said. "Do you think I could come with you? I'd love to pay my respects as well."

"Of course." Noah said.

They kissed and hugged and thought about endings and beginnings. Kate thought that Malia, in some weird way, brought Noah to her. If he hadn't been trying so hard to return her ashes to her family, he never would have come into her life.

Noah had so many things to be thankful for, he didn't want to dwell on the sadness any longer. They heard talking and commotion downstairs and they both went down to see. Just as they were entering the kitchen, Clayton and Ashley shouted with joy at seeing Noah.

Noah, however, couldn't believe his eyes. Clayton was actually walking! "Mr. Patterson, sir, what have you been up to?"

Everyone laughed. "You can see what I've been busy doing!" Clayton replied.

Noah went over and gave the man a hug, both now the same height. It was wonderful to see and Noah was eager to hear the story. Clayton and Ashley both told how, even though he was stubborn, he actually followed the exercises his physical therapist gave him to do.

More laughter as Clayton walked around the kitchen. His steps were slow and stiff, but Noah knew that with practice, he could out run them all one day. Everyone had a big smile as they recounted the last few months.

Noah would not take any praise for how business had turned around, he knew it was all because of the family's hard work and determination to not let the ranch fail. It was a wonderful reunion in the warm kitchen. Noah was relieved that they were happy to see him and not wanting to throw him out the door.

Ashley had made lunch that afternoon, pot roast. Noah felt so welcome sitting around the kitchen table with the whole family, minus Teri, and talking about what was going on in all of their lives. It felt just like last summer.

His memories of last summer had to be some of the happiest of his life. He didn't even think anything else could top it, to be honest. Life was good. Life was perfect.

Noah didn't think it could get any better, or worse, until Clayton asked a question about a very touchy subject.

"So, Noah, where are you staying?" Clayton asked.

Chapter 30

The Pattersons were fine with Noah staying in the spare bedroom. It would be nice to have a police officer under their roof. Noah apologized to the family for how he left last summer and all of the trouble he caused. He hated how he left and wanted to make it up to them.

"Nonsense!" Clayton said. "It was all Mason's fault with that stupid target shooting and then he beat you to a pulp. We don't blame you at all. We are glad to be rid of him once and for all. In fact, we heard he was in a bad accident and was on the brink of death. Death would be too nice for the likes of him."

Noah was a little taken aback by Clayton's harsh words, but he understood that they had put up with the man a lot longer than he had. Noah, however, had the uncomfortable task of explaining that he was the other vehicle involved in that accident but he managed to walk away, Mason didn't.

Clayton listened carefully as Noah gave a detailed account of the whole morning. It just made him more mad than before. "It could have been you!"

"Yes, sir, it could have but it wasn't," Noah reassured him. "I just had the better sense to watch where I was going, that's all."

"No, that's not all. You have better sense, period." Kate replied.

They talked a little more about Mason and what it meant for them. Hopefully he would stay away and leave them alone once and for all. Kate hoped so, too. They finished lunch and Kate looked at Noah.

"I want to show you something," she said.

They left the table and went out to the barn. Noah almost didn't recognize the foal. She was bigger and could easily keep up with the older horses.

"Her name's Marigold," Kate said.

Just then Noah's new mutt came running across the field and jumped right up on Noah. Noah gave him a scratch behind the ears and let him go back to running.

"Lot's of new animals around here, now," Noah said.

"Well, I think Pepper will fit in quite nicely," Kate said.

"Pepper? His name is Pepperoni or he likes Peppy, too," Noah corrected her.

"No, it's Pepper." They laughed and saddled up horses to take out for a ride. "As cute as Marigold is, she was not actually what I wanted to show you."

Kate took Noah to see the corn field. It was where his vision for a corn maze came to fruition. Even though it was long past, Noah could still get an idea of what it was like. He praised her for following through with it, with all of it. The ranch had changed but it was all for the better.

When they had passed the cottage, he had seen the happy couple who were renting it. They were on their honeymoon. It was a blessing that renting out the cottage was such a big hit. It was easy and sustainable for them to continue indefinitely.

Kate tried to take out her phone to show Noah pictures of the corn maze when it was up and running, but she panicked when she realized she left it back at the house.

"Meet me at the waterfall," She called out to Noah as she galloped away.

Noah knew the way. He rode slowly and even closed his eyes. He missed this, the country air, even though it was crisp and cool, was welcomed. He listened to the birds who bravely stayed for the winter. He was never as calm as he was here. It felt like home.

Noah made it to the waterfall and tied up his horse. He walked to the edge of the water and waited, the memories coming back to him as he stood listening. The water sprayed him and it felt like icicles, but he didn't move. It was one more reminder that he was here and he was alive.

Here was were Noah lost all inhibition with Kate. It was at this waterfall were she coaxed him to come in the water and he willingly stripped down to his briefs. He trusted her then and he still did now. This would always be their spot, the waterfall.

Noah heard Kate approaching and turned to her. She got off her horse in one swift motion and was at Noah's side in seconds. She ran into his open embrace and they kissed. There were no witnesses here, no prying eyes, just the two of them. If it was warmer they probably would have gone into the water.

Instead, they kissed with a passion that had been building up for months. Since the night they made love in the cottage, Kate had dreamed of this moment. She imagined holding him in her arms again and kissing him until morning.

Kate felt herself dissolving into Noah, they were becoming one person. She had never felt like this with anyone before. Never with Mason. This was love, even more than that, this was needing, becoming, and evolving. She was sinking deeper into his arms, into his soul.

Noah wanted to explain how he felt about Katie, but his body was doing it for him. He wanted her so badly but it was too cold to make love out here. For now, this was enough. Noah was breathing in everything about her. He would never be able to get enough of her.

These feelings took ahold of Noah and it was almost too much to bear. They fell to the frozen ground and the world melt away. Their pasts were erased, only their futures were important. It was as if the weight of a snowflake could crush Noah now, he was open and vulnerable.

They were no longer separate people. There was no end and no beginning. Out of breath, they looked at each other, eyes so intent on the other, they didn't even recall where they were. Oh, yes, they were at the waterfall.

Neither one of them were concerned with time. They didn't know how much time had passed until the sun started setting. Noah didn't want to leave but he knew Kate was cold. She tried to deny it but he knew it and didn't want her to get sick. Their parting kiss would have to last them until they were alone again.

Reluctantly, they got back on their horses and headed home. Noah's home. He would be staying in the main house now, with Kate. At the barn, they got the horses settled back into their pens and they watched as Pepper ran all through the fields. He liked his new home, too.

"You know, we never really talked about the day you left," Kate said.

Noah gestured to some chairs along the wall and they sat down. "I know, I've been avoiding it."

"I was really hurt when you just left without saying goodbye. The note didn't count, it only made it worse. How could you leave someone you said you loved?" Kate was near tears.

"I'm so sorry. I will say that everyday, one hundred times a day if that's what it takes. I should have said something." Noah replied. "I just thought that I had brought too much trouble to you and your family and I needed to get away, get back to my old life."

"Well, how did that work out for you?" Kate asked.

"Don't you see me sitting in front of you? That's how it worked out. It all brought me back to you, Katie. No matter where I go or what I do, I will always come back to you," Noah replied.

"I was devastated, Noah," Kate whispered. "You left me alone with Mason."

The mention of his name still made him upset. Noah clenched his jaw and fists as if his name alone would manifest him in this barn. Noah might never forgive himself, but he certainly would never forgive Mason.

"I'm sorry, Katie. If I could take it all back, I would," Noah said, defeated. He didn't know what else he could say to make her believe him. "I will try everyday to make it up to you."

Kate knew he would try. "Let's go inside. I'm cold," she said.

They walked hand in hand into the house. The kitchen was warm and inviting and the smell of apple pie welcomed them home. They had fresh apple pie, hot from the oven, and hot chocolate at the kitchen table.

The house was quiet. They might not be alone in the house, but to them, they were the only ones here. That is until Lorna came into the kitchen. She looked at Kate and Noah.

"Christmas break starts next week," Lorna announced. "When are we getting a tree?"

Noah looked around, it was true, there weren't any Christmas decorations at all. Kate tried to explain that they were just so busy lately and some things, like Christmas were taking a back seat right now.

"Christmas takes a back seat for no one," Noah replied. "We will get a tree tomorrow!"

Lorna was happy that this oversight would be correctly quickly. She was not going to risk skipping over Christmas entirely and then not getting any presents. That was not an option. Noah offered the use of his pick up truck and said he would find out where to go later.

Kate laughed as she listened to Noah talk about the simple things of picking out a Christmas tree. She couldn't wait for him to celebrate all the holidays here with her. Their future started now.

After finishing their pie, they went into the living room to watch television. Kate found a sappy Christmas movie on and insisted they would watch the whole thing. Noah did not protest. He wouldn't have it any other way.

Henry came home from a gig and joined them. He had confessed to his parents about sneaking out and playing in the bar at night for tips. They grounded him but then helped him find alternatives. Turns out Teri mentioned it to the owner of the diner and they loved the idea of having Henry perform on the weekends.

It didn't involve drunk people, his sister was there, and he could come and go out the front door at a decent hour. Henry was happy with the compromise, too. Especially on school nights. He still got decent tips and saved it all.

It was a nice evening to just sit around as a family. It would take some getting used to having Noah around, especially in the main house. Even Noah felt like an intruder because he never even spent a night in there.

Henry made popcorn and joined them in the living room. For Henry it was like having his big brother back. He and Noah had bonded over the summer and it was good to have him back. He just hoped he would stay.

Henry knew the accident had probably shaken him up. He may not have even hit him how he had just dodged a fatal crash. They weren't even sure if Mason would survive. Kate hadn't gotten a call back from the hospital, so he must be hanging on for now.

Henry watched Noah and his sister interact. They looked happy. So many things about Noah had come to light right before he left. He was a cop, he suffered from the trauma of being shot during a home invasion and his fiancé died next to him.

How he even came out from that and lived to tell the tale was amazing. Now to find out he was shot again, well that was nothing short of a miracle. Henry would definitely like having Noah around and prayed that he stayed. He didn't think anything else could scare him away now.

Henry was tired and decided to let them have the living room to themselves. He said goodnight and went up to bed, still letting it sink in that Noah was back.

Kate cuddled in closer to Noah's shoulder, the good shoulder. She had offered to bring him more pain medicine, but he refused. Noah insisted he could handle it.

Noah had never felt more alive. He had the love of his life next to him and was never letting her go. He had to admit that Mason was on his mind non-stop and was eager to hear when or if he woke up. He and Mason were going to have a very serious talk.

When Kate yawned, Noah did, too. It was late and it had been a long day. It would be nice to finally sleep in an actual bed, rather than the hospital waiting room tonight. After Kate turned off the television and then the lights, she took Noah's hand.

"Let's go to bed," Kate whispered.

Chapter 31

Before heading out to find the perfect Christmas tree, Noah made sure to invite everyone. Clayton and Ashley declined, saying they would enjoy a quiet house to actually get things done for a change. That just left the siblings. Teri was working so that left her out, too.

Henry was hesitant, but said he'd be willing to brave the cold and snow to make sure we got the right one. Lorna was thrilled, practically running out of the house and into the truck before everyone else could even get out the door.

Kate led the way. Noah drove them a few miles away where she said they had a large selection on the back side of their property. They planted new pine trees every year so she knew there would always be an ample supply each Christmas.

Pepper came along, too. He was fitting right in. For a family who never really had any pets besides horses, chickens or pigs, Noah was surprised how much they loved Pepper, who always wanted the window seat.

Now that Lorna had brought it to everyone's attention that Christmas was only two weeks away, Kate was suddenly in the Christmas mood all day. She tried getting everyone to sing Christmas carols, but Noah and Henry just looked at each other, not willing to give in. Lorna, on the other hand, sang at the top of her lungs along with Kate.

Noah had to admit to himself that he loved every minute of it. He wouldn't sing, but he smiled and hummed a few times. Noah didn't grow up with a big family. They didn't even go and cut down real trees. His mother had the same artificial one they used year after year stored in the garage.

He could almost forget all of his troubles when he was this happy. He never said anything to Kate, but he was still concerned about Mason. They hadn't heard anything from the hospital, which meant he still hadn't woken up. It also meant he was still alive.

When they arrived at the site Kate directed them to, they all got out and started looking for the perfect tree. Noah carried the chainsaw and followed. All of the kids split up and went in their own directions, determined to be the one to find it.

One would call the rest over to see their selection and the others would quickly vote it down. It started as serious selections, and then they all made a joke of it, calling the others to see the sickliest and scrawniest tree in the entire state of Virginia.

The laughter made all the extra walking back and forth worth it. They were all cold, but no one felt it. The warmth they felt carried them on until they ultimately found the perfect tree for their home.

It was Lorna who finally discovered the hidden gem. It was the right size and shape and everyone agreed on it. Noah started the chainsaw and it came down in one swift motion. They all dragged it back to the truck with a renewed spirit. Pepper didn't want to leave just yet and continued to jump and play in the snow.

When everyone was finally back in the truck, they headed home. The merriment continued as they pulled their tree up the front steps and into the living room. Clayton and Ashley complimented the group on their selection and their mother already had boxes of decorations brought in from the garage.

The rest of the day was spent hanging lights and placing ornaments all around the tree. They hung stockings, garland and even found the old nativity that they used every year under the tree. It was magical. Noah helped Henry put lights on the front porch and couldn't wait to turn them on tonight.

Ashley brought in hot cocoa for everyone as they sat and admired all of their hard work. Christmas had arrived. Noah thanked them for allowing him to be a part of their family traditions and also thanked Lorna for reminding them to get into the Christmas spirit.

"We feel like you are family," Ashley replied.

It was sweet of her to say, but Noah knew he wasn't true. He may not be a stranger, but he was still new to them. They were all still learning a lot about each other. Pepper, oblivious to the chaos and drama all around him, laid by the fire and called this house his home, too.

It was almost dinner time and everyone could smell the delicious aroma coming from the kitchen. Everyone gathered at the kitchen table to eat. Clayton had made steaks. Noah said it was the best steak he had ever eaten and everyone agreed.

Henry mentioned that his music teacher had a friend who worked at a local radio station nearby. He was going to give them a copy of his demo and put in a good word for him. Noah had to admit that there were advantages to such a small town, it just might work.

Chances are that someone knew somebody who could help with something. It was inevitable. In Pittsburgh it would have been much more difficult for a senior in high school to get played on a radio station, no matter how small it might be.

Here, it was possible. They all said they would tune in to listen for it. Henry laughed but he was also optimistic. He really wanted it to happen so that he could prove to his family he had the talent and drive to do it.

Henry excused himself after dinner, he was working on something new and wanted to get back to it after being out all day.

Kate wanted to go and check on the horses, so Noah went with her to the barn. It would give them a chance to finally be alone today.

Little Marigold was getting bigger and stronger. Kate made sure they all had enough hay and blankets. She loved just sitting on the bench and talking to them. Now she had Noah beside her. Even after only a day or so of having him back, it felt natural.

They talked a lot about the upcoming Christmas season. Maybe next year, when they had more time to prepare, they could actually do the sleigh rides or ice skating, something to draw people in during the winter.

Noah loved seeing Kate so excited about the ranch. She lived and breathed the Patterson Ranch, it was in her blood. Noah was slowly feeling the same fire just being near Kate, it was contagious. He knew there was nothing they couldn't do together.

Kate's phone rang and she walked towards the door to take the call. Noah stood up, too, and gave Daisy the carrot he had brought from the kitchen. He glanced and Kate and it looked like she was getting bad or upsetting news. He waited for her to return to ask.

Kate mostly listened while the caller talked. Kate made a few responses during the conversation, but it was mostly one sided. Noah was getting more curious the longer the call lasted.

Finally, Kate hung up and came to Noah. "It was the hospital. Mason is awake but they are keeping him in ICU overnight. His injuries were pretty extensive, collapsed lung, concussion and several broken bones," Kate said.

Noah nodded his head. He knew it was bad. Mason was lucky he survived.

"The doctor said that we can come visit him tomorrow morning," Kate continued. She looked at Noah. "And he said to thank his friend, again, for bringing him in so quickly. It saved his life."

Noah ran a hand through his hair and took a deep breath and then exhaled slowly. Kate knew he didn't want to be called Mason's friend, but for the doctor, it was an honest mistake. Noah still wrestled with the thought of saving his enemy.

"Listen, I know what you did was hard, but it just proves what a wonderful man you are. It's why I love you so much," Kate responded.

"I was only doing my job, Katie," Noah replied. "After what he put me through, I still couldn't just walk away, no matter how easy that would have been."

Kate knew it was true, he would never have just walked away, even when his worst enemy was in need. She could only imagine how difficult it was for him to walk over, risk his own life and save Mason.

"I can go alone, if you don't want to go," Noah said.

"No, I'm going. We have some things to set straight," Kate replied.

Noah would not miss this opportunity, either. He knew Kate wanted to tell him to go to hell, and so did he. He needed to hear it and really listen to the words. Mason would probably be mad that his diabolical plan didn't work out, but Noah didn't care. He might be walking into a hornet's nest after just kicking it off a tree.

He was so tired of waisting time and energy on Mason Fisher. He wished he would just leave them alone and get out of their lives for good. Noah took Kate's hand and they returned to the house. First they walked to the front porch to admire their handiwork.

The twinkling white lights were beautiful. They looked like stars that fell right out of the sky and onto their porch. Noah gave Kate a big hug and they stood like that watching the lights for a minute. It almost scared him how happy he was.

Kate kissed him and they walked up the steps and into the living room. The Christmas tree all lit up in the dark room was spectacular.

Noah was most struck by the fresh smell of pine. His house never smelled like a fresh cut tree before and it was a sensory overload.

The smell and the lights combined made Noah want to just sit and admire it all. The warm feeling he felt in this room had nothing to do with the fireplace, it was the people. Kate turned on some old Christmas music featuring singers that have long since passed and they danced. With the string lights and fire as their backdrop, they closed their eyes and slow danced to the soft music.

They were making new memories and it was emotional for both of them. Noah had never had such a peaceful and calm holiday season before. He had always been so busy, he never took the time to appreciate the small things. Never like this.

Kate never had this feeling with Mason, either. Mason would never had just sat on the couch and watched the Christmas tree with music playing lightly in the background. This was the feeling of the season for her. He would never have danced in the firelight, either.

It wasn't until Lorna came in and turned on the television, that they were reminded that they weren't completely alone. To her credit, Lorna did apologize for interrupting their moment, but it didn't stop her from watching television.

Instead, Noah and Kate went into the kitchen to see if there was any dessert. There was always dessert. Her mother was sitting at the table eating a piece of sweet potato pie when they walked in. They both took a slice of pie and joined her at the table.

"We heard from the hospital," Kate said. "Mason woke up tonight and we can visit him tomorrow."

Ashley simply ate her pie and nodded her head. She had to admit to herself she was surprised he made it out of surgery, but then again, of course he did! It was Mason Fisher, he always got his way. She had no intention of visiting the man, though. She never wanted to see Mason again.

Ashley let them know that they have been taking reservations non-stop for the cottage. They had bookings going as far out as next summer. It was all thanks to Noah. It was the best thing they could have done.

Noah didn't like taking the credit, but he did to make her happy. Ashley didn't know why they never thought of it before. The guests loved taking the horses out or just going for a hike. The summer would be nice with the lake and the waterfall.

At mention of the waterfall, Kate and Noah exchanged a look. Ashley got up to leave and briefly looked back before retiring for the night.

"Turn the lights off, please," Ashley said.

"We will," Kate said, looking at Noah with a smile.

Chapter 32

On the way to the hospital, Noah felt a little uneasy. Kate fidgeted in her seat which led him to believe that she was, too. It was an unpleasant thing they were doing, confronting a person who created so much pain for both of them, but definitely necessary.

Mason Fisher had to be told off once and for all. By the time Noah left the hospital, he had to be absolutely sure that Mason understood that he must leave them alone or suffer the consequences of his actions. Noah would make it as crystal clear as possible.

Noah and Kate were quiet on the ten minute drive to the hospital. They walked up to the room they were told he was in and nerves got the best of Kate when they got to the door. They looked in the little window and saw Mason sitting up in his bed. He was awake.

Noah told her to take some deep breaths and let them out slowly. She could do this, she was in control. Kate walked in the room followed by Noah. They hesitated by the door before slowly walking to the two chairs on the side of the room.

Mason was more than a little surprised to see them both walk in his room. He didn't even know Noah was back in town, but it did confirm his dreams were more real than he realized. Maybe they were all real. He wasn't really expecting any visitors, so this was a complete surprise.

"Hello," Kate said as she pulled a chair closer.

Noah followed her lead and brought the other chair next to hers.

"Hello," Mason replied, looking from one to the other.

"Well, you're looking better than you did when I brought you in here," Noah said.

Mason looked genuinely confused at Noah's statement and stared at him for a moment. "What do you mean that you brought me in here?" Mason asked.

"Don't you remember that day? What happened?" Noah asked, surprised.

Mason shook his head. "I've had dreams and bits of pieces would come into my head, but I didn't believe them. I thought I was just imagining things, especially when your face came to mind."

Kate looked hard at Mason. "Mason, this man saved your life. Even after everything you did to him!"

Mason was still foggy on the details but was starting to put pieces of the accident together in his head. So, those dreams were reality, he told himself. The visions of racing and seeing Noah beside him. Then swerving and crashing and Noah carrying him. It was all true. He caused this.

Mason needed a moment to let it all sink in. It was hard to believe everything Kate and Noah were telling him about the accident. The doctors and nurses were telling him he crashed and someone found him, now he's learning that he caused it. It was all too much for him.

Mason took a moment to wipe at his eyes. He was getting emotional. Kate and Noah looked at each other and then just let Mason cope with his own demons. No one spoke while Mason relived what he thought was just a dream. It was real, all of it.

"I have been remembering some things, but I had no idea it all really happened," Mason started. "I remember waiting in my truck and then following you," he said, gesturing to Noah. "Then something, a deer, was it? He came out of nowhere and then all of a sudden I was in pain, lots of pain."

Noah simply nodded his head and let him work through that day on his own.

"Then someone pulled me out," Mason said, looking at Noah. "It was you?"

"Yes," Noah replied.

Mason was quiet and nodded his head. "Why?"

Noah wasn't prepared for that question. He had asked himself that question over the last two days and his only response was that it was his job. But it was more than that. Noah believed in good over evil. He believed that the good in us would always come out on top. He believed in second chances.

"Because it was the right thing to do," Noah replied.

Mason let the tears run down his face. He made no attempt to wipe them away. Even he was not expecting the reaction he was having to Noah's answer. Mason looked from Kate to Noah. These two people had been a source of hurt and revenge for months or years as the case may be and they were now bringing him to tears.

"I'm sorry." Mason said softly.

The words hung in the cold and sterile room like an alarm that wouldn't turn off. The words were numbing and emotional. They said more than any book could convey. They were heartfelt and sincere, Noah could tell. Mason was sorry.

Kate, who had known this man for years, had never heard those words come from those lips before. She was dumbfounded. It took her a few minutes to comprehend that they even came from Mason Fisher. She watched him break down and melt right in front of her.

Noah never expected it, either. He thought Mason would put up a fight, be the same maniacal, stubborn man who had tormented him since last summer. Noah was prepared to tell him to leave them alone, he never planned for this, an apology.

"Mason, there's something I want you to understand," Kate started. "Noah and I are together." Kate waited for any argument or threat, none came. "And I need you to leave us alone. That means me, Noah and my whole family. Do you understand?"

Mason's tears kept falling as he nodded his head. He understood, loud and clear. He never fully understood until this very moment how much he really cared about Kate, cared enough to let her go.

Noah, however, wanted him to say it. "Mason, this will all end today. Everything. The following, the racing, the shooting and the threats. To me and to Kate. Everything. I need you to say that you hear me."

"I do and I will stop," Mason said quietly. "I promise."

The three of them sat in silence. Kate leaned back in her chair and exhaled. Noah wiped his hands on his jeans. Everyone had been so tense that they could finally relax and breath. The beast had been slayed or so they hoped.

There really was nothing more to say. Kate and Noah both stood up and walked towards the door. Noah stopped and turned around. "If there's anything you need, call. You have a long road of recovery ahead of you, man. It's going to be hard, I'm not gonna lie."

Noah knew a thing or two about being injured, not to that extent, but he knew it wouldn't be easy. Mason was so overwhelmed by the sincerity in Noah's words, he could only nod his head in acknowledgment.

Noah nodded back and he and Kate left the room. Kate couldn't believe how generous Noah's last comment was. She had never experience that kind of selflessness in her life. Noah put his arm around her and they went down the elevator to his truck.

They left the hospital with a renewed sense of calm. It was amazing how much weight was lifted off of Noah's shoulders. He could have sworn the pain and ache in his left shoulder went away the moment they left the hospital.

Kate was still in a state of disbelieve. Did that really happen? Did Mason Fisher just apologize for everything? It was much more than she ever could have hoped for. She felt as light as a feather and didn't want to go home right away. Maybe they could give Mason Fisher another chance at being a decent human being.

"Let's have a real date," Kate said.

Noah smiled. "Sure, where do you want to go?"

"The diner," Kate replied. "I want to sit at a table and have dinner with you, in public!"

It was simple yet symbolic. There was no one watching who would go back and report her for being out with another man. There was no threat of retaliation anymore. There wasn't anyone watching or caring any longer. There was no more Mason in their lives.

It felt good to park in front of the little diner and walk inside hand in hand. The little bell rang on the door to announce their arrival to everyone. There were still looks, stares and whispers but they didn't care. They walked up to the counter and sat down.

Teri came over and smiled. They looked happy. Teri knew something must have happened but she would never have guessed what it was. She would call her sister later and get the scoop. For now, they ordered the meatloaf and waited for their coffee cups to be filled.

It was like any normal date, only it wasn't. Kate was with Noah. They could go and do anything they wanted whenever they wanted. For months they lived under the umbrella of threats of violence, now it was acceptance of their relationship.

They sipped their coffee and talked about tomorrow. Tomorrow was Malia's memorial service. It would be a nice day, too. Noah was happy that Kate was coming. It felt right that she should be there. Malia and Kate knew each other longer than Noah did.

It wasn't very busy in the diner, so Teri was able to stay and talk. It was nice to catch up with her. Now that she had her own place, it was more difficult to do. Noah told her she needed to come and see the Christmas tree and all of the decorations. It was a real life winter wonderland.

Teri couldn't believe that Noah got Kate to slow down enough to even attempt any holiday decorations or holiday spirit, no one had ever been able to do that before. Kate gave Noah all of the credit. Life was worth living, not just going from one task to the other.

If you didn't take the time to look around, you might just hit a deer. Noah knew all too well the need to slow down and take the time to observe what was going on around him. In fact, Noah noticed two police officers having dinner in the corner. He had an idea.

Noah gave Teri his credit card and said he wanted to pay for their meals. Teri winked at him and did just that. It wasn't until he and Kate were halfway through their own dinner when he felt a tap on his shoulder. It was the police officers.

"Thank you, sir," one of the officers said. "That doesn't happen too often and I would be remiss if I didn't acknowledge the kind gesture."

"No, thank you," Noah replied. "I'm an officer myself and I just wanted to thank you for your service to the community. You put your lives at risk everyday and I just wanted to say thank you."

"I'm sorry, but I don't recognize you, are you an officer around here?" He asked.

"No, I'm from Pittsburgh," Noah said and then looked at Kate. " But I've just recently moved down here."

"Well, if you're ever looking for a job, you can come talk to us. We're right down the street and we'd be happy to have more police officers in Summer Hill," the officer said.

Noah thanked them for the offer and said he would come talk to them later. Kate couldn't believe it, neither could Noah. He could continue the job he loved in his new home. It was something he didn't have to decide right now. He was on a date.

Teri came back and asked if they wanted dessert. Kate said she wanted a hot fudge sundae. They ordered one big hot fudge sundae and split it. They looked and felt like a couple of teenagers again. They laughed and listened as Teri told then all of the local town gossip.

Teri refilled their coffee a few times as they lingered and delayed going home. They wanted their first date to last as long as possible. Forever would be nice. It was dark when they finally left the diner. They turned back to remind Teri to come by the house soon.

On the ride back home, Noah listened as Kate quietly sang a Christmas song. He even hummed along. They passed houses that were all lit up for the holidays and it was a great feeling to be there with Kate. It was like a dream come true after months of thinking it wouldn't.

When they pulled up to their own house, it still struck them how beautiful it was all lit up and decorated. They sat in the truck a little while longer to just absorb it all. Kate slid over and kissed Noah. He kissed her back. They stayed like that in his truck until it got too cold.

"Let's go inside," Noah said. "I can think of somewhere that's warmer where we can continue this." Noah smiled at her, thinking how lucky he was to be sitting here beside her.

"What exactly are you trying to say?" Kate asked with a smile.

"I think I would rather show you," Noah replied as they entered the house and went to Kate's room.

Chapter 33

Jessie and Bob Harris hadn't given themselves very much time to arrange Malia's memorial service, but it didn't matter to them. They were just so happy to have her back home. If they were truly honest, they would have just had a small service in their backyard with only the birds and squirrels in attendance.

A small service didn't seem right, though. They wanted all of their family and friends to remember their daughter with a proper Church service and then reception at home in her garden. That felt more fitting, even though it was over a year since she died. She was home.

Jessie was quick to invite everyone she knew would want to be there and that included Noah. Noah wasn't the enemy, she knew that now. Malia had loved him and he loved her. They would finally accept him and move on. Life was too short to worry about things that were insignificant.

Bob was dressed in a suit. He didn't remember the last time he had worn it. Every time he thought about complaining about this or that, a tie or stiff shoes, he remembered the reason for the day. It always made him quiet, again. Bob missed his daughter terribly. Things were never the same around here since she left.

Jessie had a black dress that she kept for special occasions. Well, this was definitely one of them. When she looked at herself in the mirror, she got very emotional. Parents shouldn't be burying their children, but here we were. Jessie added a string of pearls, looked in the mirror again and went down the stairs.

Jessie smiled when she saw Bob. He really did not like getting all dressed up, but he looked handsome in his dark suit. Jessie came over to him, adjusted his tie and gave him a quick kiss. This was the moment they had waited for and dreaded at the same time.

It was almost time to leave for the Church, but Jessie wanted to look around the kitchen one last time. It all looked perfect. Malia would have loved it.

Family, friends and neighbors had been bringing covered dishes and desserts by all day yesterday and today. She made sure everything looked good and was ready for when they came back to the house for the reception.

She had Malia's high school graduation picture on the sideboard in the dining room. It was the last formal picture she had of her. Malia's smile could light up a room, just like today. Jessie regretted all of the waisted years that their arguing created. It was so unnecessary.

Bob reminded her of the time and they went out to the car to leave. Jessie had the decorated wooden box that contained Malia's ashes on her lap. She couldn't stop caressing the carvings on the side of the box. Her baby.

At the Church, they were surprised to see so many people. At first, she thought there was some kind of mix up in the dates. Surely they were interrupting a wedding or something. Jessie gazed at the faces as they parked their car and walked towards the Church.

No, she knew these people. They were all here for Malia Ray. Jessie was emotional as she grabbed Bob's arm and they walked up the front steps, stopping along the way to greet people and give hugs. Most came up to her and Bob to offer condolences, but some simply nodded their heads and waved.

There would be time enough later to properly thank everyone for coming out today. They wanted to keep the service on schedule, so they went inside and took their seats. All the other guests followed them inside and waited for the memorial service to begin.

Noah and Kate arrived right before the Harris's got to the Church. The whole Patterson family wanted to come, so they had to come in several cars. Clayton struggled going up the front steps, but he did it. Ashley was by his side followed by Teri, Henry and Lorna.

The Pattersons remembered their friendly and outgoing babysitter who was always willing to come, even on short notice. They knew she had strict parents, but they thought they were strict, too. They liked the Harris's.

They filled in the pews and waited quietly for the music to start. People were still slowly filing in, so it took a few extra minutes. Noah felt a tapping on his shoulder as a man sat behind him in the pew. He was startled and turned around.

It was Steven. Noah's confusion suddenly turned to joy as he stood up and shook hands with his former partner. He had mentioned going to Malia's memorial service and had casually said the day and time in case he was interested. Apparently, he was.

Steven told Noah he wouldn't have missed it. He loved Malia, too. It was like she was already a part of the extended family. This unexpected encounter left Noah feeling emotional. He would never have guessed how many people Malia had touched but looking around the crowded Church, he was beginning to understand.

Kate simply smiled and said hello to Steven. There would be time for formal introductions later. Steven, however, already knew who Kate was because Noah wouldn't stop talking about her when he was back home in Pittsburgh.

Even the phone conversations they have had since, would always come back to Kate. There were other things that needed to be discussed, Steven thought, but it could wait. Right now they were remembering the woman he thought would be Noah's wife.

How quickly life changes and demands that you adapt or be forever lost. Noah was engaged once, Steven assumed he would be best man at a wedding by now instead of at a memorial service for the same woman. Life just didn't work out sometimes.

It looked like most of the people had finally come in and found a seat. The music started and the service began. It lasted about thirty minutes and was filled with song and praise for the wonderful person Malia was. Her life may have ended too soon, but to look out at the crowd, you couldn't help but be touched by the amount of people who loved her.

When the service ended, everyone filed out of the Church and followed the directions to the Harris's home. Noah knew the way. He was one of the first people to arrive and had a few moments with Jessie and Bob alone before everyone else arrived.

They thanked him, again, for the courage to come and bring their little girl home. He insisted it wasn't courage, since he had failed twice before, but he was happy to do it.

"No, son," Bob told him. "Courage is knowing that the task ahead of you is hard, but you choose to do it anyway." Bob patted him on the shoulder and smiled.

At that moment, Noah knew that he would always come back here to visit. He would make sure that if there was anything they needed, Noah would be there for them.

When Steven arrived, they could give a proper greeting and hug. It was good to see his old partner and introduce him to Kate. Kate was warm and friendly to Steven and he knew exactly what Noah saw in her. She had a calm demeanor and welcomed him to Summer Hill.

"Thank you," Steven replied. "Actually, Noah, there's something I need to tell you." He glanced at Kate, not sure how to get Noah alone.

Kate took the hint and said she wanted to go see Mrs. Harris anyway.

"It sounds serious, Steven. What is it?" Noah asked when they were alone.

"It's about your case, the home invasion."

Noah's face reflected the seriousness of the conversation. He had tried putting all of that trauma behind him and thought he actually had some success, until today.

"What now?" Noah asked.

"Well, the detectives had followed several leads and they were able to connect similar home invasions with violent and deadly attacks," Steven said.

"And?"

"They were finally able to put names to the unknown faces."

"And?" Noah was getting impatient.

"They caught them, Noah."

The relief Noah felt was both immediate and visible. He could feel tears welling up in his eyes and his chin was starting to quiver. It was vindication for all that they had suffered, Malia would have been so relieved that they were caught.

"So what now? Are they pleading guilty?" Noah asked, impatient for more information.

"Well, as you know, these things take time. They are saying not guilty, of course, so if it goes to trial, you will be called as a witness," Steven said.

"Gladly!" Noah replied. "Just tell me when and where and I will be there."

Now that Steven had gotten business out of the way, they could relax a little bit more. Noah introduced him to the whole Patterson family and they were so happy to meet a friend of Noah's, especially Teri.

Teri winked and flirted her way to Steven's side in no time. She flattered Steven by saying she was excited to meet Noah's handsome partner. Even asked if he brought his uniform with him.

Jessie couldn't believe that the whole Patterson family had come to the memorial service. Malia was only a teenager when she was allowed to babysit them. In fact, she was only allowed to babysit for certain families, families they knew and trusted would look out for their daughter.

Bob and Jessie knew the Pattersons were good people, maybe even the best ones in Summer Hill. They thanked them all for coming and said they were welcome anytime. She showed them her garden in the back and invited them to sit and stay awhile.

Kate loved Jessie's garden. She thought she might like to continue the idea on their own ranch. It would be easy to create their own memorial garden for the friends and family they've lost over the years. Kate liked the idea of a permanent reminder to come and reflect when you needed a moment of peace.

Noah still found himself surveying the crowd for Mason, even though he knew the man was still in the hospital recovering. With a leg and an arm in a cast, he wouldn't be able to get around easily anyway. Still, the ghost of that man may leave Noah always scanning crowds.

Noah never felt guilty about carrying his Glock 17 in his belt everywhere he went, it was part of him. He knew, without a doubt, that Steven would have his on him, too. He walked over to Steven and asked how long he could stay.

"I'm afraid I have to get back," Steven replied. "I only have the one day off."

"You're driving back tonight?" Noah asked.

Steven confirmed that he was. It was important enough to come down to Virginia, even though he knew he had to do it in a day. He wouldn't have missed it. Noah hugged him and thanked him, again, for coming.

He told Steven that next time he had to agree to stay longer. He wanted to show him the ranch and take him out on the horses.

Steven promised he would plan a proper trip next time. Noah would look forward to it.

As the evening approached, guests were saying their goodbyes to Jessie and Bob. They had thrown together a fantastic memorial service in such a short time. It was a wonderful tribute to an amazing woman. Jessie was sad to see it all end, but she was exhausted.

Noah and the entire Patterson family said good bye as well. They promised that they would each come by and check on them from time to time. Jessie said they were always welcome there and that they could visit the memorial garden any time they wished.

Steven headed home and Teri even managed to get a kiss. Noah smiled when he thought about how she had tried that on him when he first arrived in Summer Hill. Time will only tell if Steven really comes back to see him or Teri.

At the ranch, Noah changed clothes and went out to the barn. He no longer had the nightmares that tormented him at night. And with Steven's news that they finally caught the murderers, he was starting to feel whole again. It would just take time and he had plenty of that.

He had to admit that part of that was because he put in the work, but another part was Kate. Noah fed Daisy a carrot he swiped from the kitchen and stroked the soft hair between Daisy's eyes. Today had been a day of reflection for Noah.

He thought about his life before, with Malia, and the one he now had with Katie. They couldn't be more different, he wasn't comparing them really, he was thinking about how he had changed. He was a better man for loving these two women.

Chapter 34

Over the next week, Noah fell into a comfortable routine at the ranch. He loved working with his hands and following Clayton around during the day. He was learning a lot and it was satisfying to see how he made a difference.

But was it enough? Noah was missing his place in the community. He liked getting to know the citizens and making a difference for everyone, not just him. He decided to go to the Summer Hill police station and see if they still were looking for another police officer.

They would be happy to have Noah join the Summer Hill police force and wondered when he wanted to start. He admitted that he had to tell Kate first, but could possibly be ready by the first of the year. They would be eagerly waiting to hear back from him.

Noah wasn't sure how Kate would react to the idea of him being a police officer, again. He already had two bullet holes in him, would he be so lucky a third time? He would never be able to answer that question, no matter who asked it.

It was just something that was missing in Noah's life. He felt like he had everything he ever wanted, but he liked wearing the uniform and protecting and serving the community. It wasn't just a job, it was a calling. He would have to break it to Kate nicely, maybe on another date.

It was nearly Christmas and he still had lots of shopping to do. He had actually put a lot of thought into Kate's gift for a while now, but never could find just the right thing, until now. The idea finally hit him and he had to get to work on it.

Noah took full advantage of being alone on an errand and would now get things done that he couldn't if Kate was with him. He had told her he had needed dog food, so that was his first errand. The police station was a secret one. His third one would be his best secret yet.

Kate was busy at home. Today was Christmas cookie day. It was a tradition that had been going on for decades. The family picked one day to make sugar cookie cut outs and then mix bowls of brightly colored icing. The rest of the afternoon was icing and decorating the mountains of cookies to eat and give away.

It could last all day long, depending on how many helpers could be wrangled up. Today was Kate, Teri, Henry and Lorna. Their parents would help out when they had time and Noah promised to help when he got home.

Kate only knew Noah had an errand to run, but he sure was taking his time buying dog food. Maybe he suspected how much work and mess cookie day was and decided to stay away. No, that wasn't like Noah. He would come whenever he was done, she was sure of it.

Cookies were mixed, rolled and cut into various shapes and then baked. That process was done by assembly line and went pretty smoothly until some were either left in the oven too long or snowmen started looking like candy canes.

No one criticized each others creations, that was the rule. Each cookie that was made could come out looking like anything they wished, preferably something Christmasy. There was no cookie shaming allowed. They were made with love and that was all that mattered.

Kate looked at all the cookies that had already been completed. She smiled at all of the Santas, stockings and Christmas tree cookies.

Some trees were pink, others red and a few were green. She loved them all.

When Noah finally arrived, he pitched in as best he could. He had never done anything like this before and didn't know where to start. Cookies were bought, not made, in his house. He watched the careful instructions that Lorna gave him and then he tried his best.

Everyone laughed as he ended up with more icing on his hands than on the cookie. The laughter grew louder as he touched a finger full of green icing to Kate's nose. Of course that only called for retaliation. Soon everyone was trying to cover each other in colorful dabs of icing.

Finally, Kate had to ban Noah from cookie duty. He was okay with that. Clayton was going to show him how to change horse shoes today and that actually sounded like more fun than lathering a cookie in frosting.

As Noah walked to the barn, Kate watched him. She couldn't believe she was so lucky to find such a great guy who was willing to love the ranch as much as she did. After making everyone clean up their messes, they got back to work on the rest of the cookies.

Noah watched Clayton intensely and tried to remember each and every step that he was told. Clayton let him watch a few times and then handed Noah the tools. After changing the horse's shoe, Clayton called it a success.

"You only need a little more practice," Clayton said. "That's all."

Noah knew it would take more than just a little practice to be as good and as efficient as Clayton, but that was normal. He had been doing it his whole life. Noah had only done it for one day. Noah hoped he had the rest of his life to practice.

Which led him to a pressing matter Noah wanted to discuss with Clayton. This was not easy to bring up and it actually made his palms sweat a little, but he had to do it. Now was the time.

"Clayton," Noah said, "I need to talk to you about something."

THE NEXT DAY, KATE said she needed to pick up a few more gifts for her siblings and asked Noah if he wouldn't mind driving to the next town over. It was bigger and they had a mall she wanted to visit.

Noah was more than happy to take her anywhere and they headed out of town that morning with a plan to finish their Christmas shopping list. Christmas was only a few days away and everyone was feeling the excitement, even Noah.

As they drove out of Summer Hill, Kate scanned the radio stations for another local station that was playing Christmas music. When Kate screamed, Noah nearly veered off the road thinking something happened to her.

"It's Henry's song!" Kate shouted. "They're actually playing Henry's song!"

Kate had stumbled upon a local radio station in the next town that played local and little known artists. It was a great start for singers and bands who just wanted to put their music out there, the perfect platform for Henry.

Kate blasted the radio and they listened to Henry's voice coming over the airwaves. It was a special moment and Kate called Henry to tell him. Henry was ecstatic and Kate said she was so proud of him. Noah was, too.

When they pulled into the mall parking lot, they realized that everyone in the whole county must have had the same idea as them. They circled the lot a couple of times before finding one near the back. They wouldn't let the crowds deter them from having a successful shopping day.

Moving swiftly from store to store, Kate found things for her parents and siblings without any trouble. This mall had such a wide variety of stores, more than anything they could find back home.

They found Lorna the new video game she wanted. Henry was getting new guitar strings and headphones.

Teri said she had wanted luggage and they found a three-piece set on sale. Things were going well. Noah asked her what she wanted and Kate said that she had everything she wanted right here. They kissed in the middle of the mall and then continued shopping.

Kate asked what Noah wanted and he thought about saying the same sappy answer, but it was true. He didn't need anything, except maybe a new cowboy hat. Kate's face lit up when he actually gave a tangible answer.

Kate knew exactly where the western wear store was and had him pick it out. Noah chose a black one and tried it on. Kate had to admit he looked really good in the hat. She might just have to let him wear it now.

They stopped and had lunch in the food court. There were so many more choices than back at home, so they each chose something different and shared. A little worn out from battling all of the crowds from shopping, they only had a few more items to get before they could leave.

Noah enjoyed being away from the ranch and so did Kate. They didn't often have the opportunity to get away but the winter offered them more chances. Things were slower and the holidays gave them a reason to shop.

Kate couldn't believe that he had only been back in town a few weeks because it felt like he had never left. All the drama and turmoil that they suffered in between had started to melt away, at least for her. She wasn't really sure how Noah felt about living in the same town as Mason, he never brought it up after seeing him in the hospital. She was pretty sure he wasn't a threat any longer, but she had thought that about him before.

Kate had heard that Mason was released from the hospital and was recovering at home. He wasn't able to work at the car dealership for the moment, but maybe he could work from home or something. She had no idea what his future plans were. All she knew was that Mason didn't mean anything to her any more.

Noah spotted a pet store and said they had to go in. He bought Pepper the largest bone he could find. Even his new dog needed to feel the Christmas spirit this time of year. Kate was beginning to love the dog, too. It was nice having him around and Pepper would be put to work chasing crows when the corn starts growing next spring.

They sat down one more time to have a coffee before they left the mall. It was so magical to be in the middle of all the families out shopping and they absorbed the cheerful atmosphere. There were kids waiting in line to have their pictures taken with Santa Claus and the kids were thrilled when it was their turn.

Kate had never thought about having kids before. She looked at Noah and wondered if he would ever want kids. It was something they had never really discussed, they weren't even in a relationship until a few weeks ago. She didn't want to scare him away, so that conversation might have to wait.

People watching was actually very entertaining. There were crying babies and frustrated adults mixed in with the happy couples and then the workers who were counting down the hours until closing. Noah gathered up their packages and they made their way through the crowds and out into the cold and dark night.

The drive home was quiet and mellow, not the loud singing and music blaring from earlier, tonight was more reflective. Noah was learning to appreciate the quiet moments along with the adrenaline rush of being a cop. They both had their purpose.

Noah found himself humming to an old favorite Christmas song and Kate joined him. As the miles passed, they reached for each other's hand. Still humming, Kate thought she had never been this happy. Could it ever get any better than this?

Noah slowly pulled up to the house and they walked up the front steps, always admiring the twinkling porch lights. He carried all of the packages upstairs, to be wrapped tomorrow. Everything could wait until tomorrow.

Tonight was about them. Noah didn't want this night to end and neither did Kate. They slowly undressed and kissed in the dark. It was slow and romantic. They made love as the moon rose higher in the sky.

There was no hurry, they would get to know every inch of each other's body and then search some more. They didn't worry about the time. They had each other. They had forever.

Chapter 35

When Kate woke up, she was alone in bed. She sat up and tried to focus. Noah was not here and must have already gone down to breakfast. Kate rubbed her eyes and looked around.

When she sat up she saw the note, 'Meet me at the waterfall,' it said. Noah must have gotten up pretty early and she wasn't sure what was going on. She got dressed and went downstairs to grab coffee first.

Kate bundled up and went to the barn. Kate smiled as she saw a horse already with a saddle and was patiently waiting for her. She got on and rode towards the waterfall. It was cold and crips outside, it felt good after being inside the mall all day yesterday.

Noah heard Kate approach and produced a thermos of hot coffee. "I knew you'd want some when you got here," he said.

Kate confirmed that she did want more coffee. She also wondered what brought him out here. Noah said there was something he wanted to discuss with her and didn't want anyone else to hear it before she did.

Noah went on to explain that he had gone to the Summer Hill police station and inquired about the job. He said that they would hire him whenever Noah said he was ready. He admitted to doing it behind her back, but he wasn't sure it was something he wanted to do until now.

"I was up front about being shot on the job and how it affected me. I told them everything, I don't want any secrets anymore," Noah explained. "And I didn't want to hide it from you either, I was only waiting for the right time to tell you."

This was all a surprise to Kate. She was glad he wanted to stay in Summer Hill, glad he was ready to put down roots and live and work here. She was just afraid for his safety. She didn't know if she could handle him being in danger everyday.

"You don't look happy," Noah said. "Please tell me why."

"Well, I guess I'm just afraid of you getting hurt, again."

Noah knew it was always a possibility, no matter what city he was a police officer in. All he could do was promise to be careful.

"What else are you afraid of?" Noah asked.

"That you will like being a cop more than the ranch," Kate said quietly. She knew it was a selfish thing to say, but it was true. He might decide that it was more satisfying to be a cop than shoeing a horse or harvesting the corn.

"Never," Noah replied. "You are my priority. I will always love being here with you, I just also feel my duty of a police officer still. I can make it work, all of it."

Kate didn't want to argue, she was too cold and hungry to anyway. "Let's go back. It's a longer discussion than we can have here in the cold."

Noah conceded and they rode back to the barn. He wanted her to understand that he wasn't going anywhere. He was here to stay and it shouldn't matter what job he had, he loved her.

They put the horses back in their stalls and stood for a moment in front of Marigold. "I remember the night she was born," Noah said.

Kate smiled. "I do, too. You stayed with me that night, through the storm."

Noah came over and kissed her, "I will always be here."

Deep down, Kate knew it was true, she knew it with every fiber of her being that Noah was here to stay. She just had to trust him.

Cold and hungry, Kate suggested they go inside. As they approached the house, they noticed there was an unfamiliar pick up truck in the driveway.

Noah immediately felt chills run down his spine. It couldn't be, not after the talk they had at the hospital. Noah and Kate had been as clear as they could that he was to leave them alone. Mason had even cried when he apologized for goodness sake.

Kate was afraid, too. Was Mason waiting inside for them? Was he only pretending to be sorry at the hospital just to make them complacent and let down their guard? There was only one way to find out, they had to go inside.

Noah pulled out his Glock from where he kept it tucked into his belt at his back. With arms straight and the gun ready, he asked Kate to stay outside. Noah approached the front door, taking each step up to the porch one at a time, slowly making his way to the front entrance.

Noah hesitated when he saw a box on the floor. He lowered his gun, although still cautious and picked up the small red box with a large white ribbon. It was a Christmas gift with a card attached.

Curious, Kate joined him on the porch and stared at the wrapped gift. "Who do you suppose left it?" She asked.

Noah slowly shook his head and put his gun away. Without an imminent threat detected, he felt at ease enough to open the card that was addressed to him. Noah and Kate quickly glanced at each other, still unsure who it was from.

As Noah read the note, he felt the hairs on the back of his neck stand on end.

"To Noah,

Merry Christmas.

Mason Fisher."

What kind of game was he playing? Noah slowly unwrapped the box and what he saw inside made tears come to his eyes. It took Kate a minute longer to realize what was happening. Inside the box were keys. Keys that he knew were to a bright and shiny new black pick up truck, just like the one parked in front of the house.

Mason Fisher had been sincere in his apology. So sincere that he had a brand new truck from his dealership delivered to Noah. Whether it was motivated by guilt or apology, it didn't matter. Mason did something so selfless, it made Noah emotional.

Kate hugged Noah, not knowing what else to do. Noah took the keys out of the box and hit the unlock button. The truck responded by unlocking its doors. Noah was weak in the knees as he descended the steps and walked to his brand new truck.

He felt guilty for assuming the worst, but with a man who tormented him for so long, it was hard to believe that an accident that he created had changed him so completely. It had. Noah didn't have any words to describe how he was feeling other than gratitude.

There were so many things in his life that he was grateful for, if he were to name them all it would take all night. Right now he would enjoy the moment. Noah looked again at the keys before putting them in his pocket. He was willing to give Mason Fisher a second chance.

Inside the house, dinner preparations were in full swing. Tomorrow was Christmas and pies and side dishes were being made and prepared. The house smelled fabulous. Vegetables were being chopped, potatoes peeled and flour being measured, all in advance of tomorrow's big dinner.

Kate joined in to help with the meal and Noah walked out to the living room. His head was still spinning about how wrong he had been about Mason that he needed time to process what had just happened. He stood at the window and stared at the new truck.

Henry came up behind him and asked who's truck that was. Noah went on to explain that it was his and briefly why. Henry was impressed that Noah could tame such a horrible man as Mason. Then Henry had a surprise of his own.

"I've decided to go to college after all," Henry said.

"That's great," Noah replied.

"I wanted to tell you first, before anyone else, because you encouraged me so much," Henry said. "I'm going to continue to work on my music but I'm going to take some business classes at the community college so I can manage my own money."

Noah laughed as Henry smiled. "Sounds like a solid plan," Noah said. "It also sounds like you might need transportation."

Noah took out the keys to his old truck and handed them to Henry. "As long as you don't mind driving a beaten up truck, and your parents approve, it's all yours."

Henry gave Noah a hug and thanked him. He was so excited he would go and talk to them now, about everything. Henry ran out of the room, eager to share his news. Noah was proud of him. He came to that decision all on his own, even though he had helped by putting the idea in his head. Henry would give college a try.

Noah was realizing that he was not responsible for the actions of other people, no matter what he might think. It didn't matter if Noah was a good person or tried hard, people were still going to do what they wanted to do. That was both comforting and off-putting at the same time.

Noah heard a notification on his phone letting him know he had a text. When he saw it was from Steven he looked at it immediately, not sure if this was going to be good news or bad.

'I'm coming down for a few days after New Years,' Steven wrote. 'I can't wait to see you again, buddy.'

Noah texted back, 'There's always a place for you here.'

'Actually, Teri offered.' Steven replied.

Noah actually laughed out loud when he read Steven's last text. Well, he didn't see that one coming, or did he? Noah simply replied that he couldn't wait to hang out with him when he got here.

Kate said she was going upstairs to lay down. Today was so overwhelming, she needed to rest for a while. Noah understood, but he wanted to stay busy. He walked back out the front door and called for Pepper. The dog came running up to Noah and they went for a walk.

Noah walked along the fence line while Pepper ran alongside. This fence brought back a lot of memories for him. It all started here, this strange twist of fate. He came to this town for one reason and stayed for another one.

Noah took this time to make some phone calls. He called his parents and talked about everything that had been happening. His new job starting soon, his new truck and his plans for Christmas. Noah's parents were so happy things were finally working out for him.

They promised to come and visit this coming summer. Noah would love to show them all around the ranch. Having such supportive parents was a blessing.

Next he called the Harris's. He wondered if there was anything he could do for them. Noah offered to bring them some Christmas dinner if they wanted him to. They said that people have been so nice dropping off hams, pies and other items that they could feed an army.

Noah was glad to hear it. He reminded them to call if they ever needed anything. They said they would. It made Noah happy to hear that the Harris's were doing well.

His last call was harder to make but it meant the most.

"Hello?" Mason asked.

"Hello, it's Noah." There was silence on the other end, probably wondering if he had seen the gift. "I just wanted to call and say thank you."

"You're welcome," Mason replied.

"Hey, if you ever need anything or help doing something, give me a call," Noah said. "Also, I've accepted a position with the Summer Hill police department starting early next year, so I'm gonna need you to stay on your best behavior or else."

Mason laughed on the other end. "Yes, sir, officer, I promise."

Noah hesitated before saying, "Do you need any food brought over tomorrow? I'd be happy to bring you Christmas dinner?"

"No, I'll be okay," Mason replied. "But thank you."

"No problem, Merry Christmas, Mason."

"Merry Christmas, Noah."

Noah realized that he had lost track of time and started heading back towards the house. He felt lighter after that last phone call. He and Mason had a new understanding. It was still shaky, but with proper maintenance, he felt like it could really be a tentative friendship. Who would ever have guessed that he and Mason Fisher could even consider trying to being friends?

Certainly not Noah.

Chapter 36

It was Christmas morning and a light snow was falling. It left a white blanket on everything outside. It was like one of those movies Kate liked to watch on television. Noah rolled over and kissed Kate. She blinked a few times and then smiled.

"Merry Christmas, Katie."

"Merry Christmas, Noah."

They already heard the commotion downstairs so they knew everyone was awake and probably waiting for them. They put on robes and went down to get some coffee and muffins. The family were in various states of eating, drinking and just a general ball of energy as they stared at all of the presents under the tree. Teri was even there.

"Now can we start?" Asked Lorna.

"Yes!" Replied Kate.

Gifts were passed around to the appropriate recipient and one by one, everyone waited for the gift to be unwrapped. Clayton and Ashley loved the coffee mugs, puzzle books and novels they were given by their children. Lorna squealed when she saw her new games.

Henry appreciated the gifts that Noah helped pick out and said he needed new guitar strings. Teri thanked them for the luggage they got her and the blender from her parents. It was so special to see all the joy on their faces. Everyone looked so happy.

Noah looked at Kate and said, "I'm sorry, but yours isn't ready yet."

Kate wasn't sure what he meant. He was obviously being deliberately secretive, but so could she. She also had something she wanted to give him, but not here, not yet.

Everyone enjoyed their morning with their new gifts. It was like they were young again and they all got new toys. As all of the gifts were given out and opened, it was fun to see and share what everyone received. It always came down to the thought behind the gift, not the dollar amount.

Christmas music was playing and the food was cooking. It left them with time to just enjoy the moment. Noah didn't need anything else, he already had everything he ever wanted and more. He looked at Kate trying to play the game that Lorna got for Christmas.

Noah called his parents, again, and said Merry Christmas. He missed them, but it was different. It would be good to see them in a few months, so he looked forward to that. He asked if they opened the gift he sent them and they confirmed that they had. He had sent them travel vouchers for a vacation and they couldn't wait to use them.

When dinner was ready, everyone rushed into the kitchen. Dinner smelled delicious and everyone sat down and started passing platters back and forth. Clayton said the blessing and they all started eating. There wasn't time to talk, only enjoy the savory meal until every bite was eaten. Noah felt blessed to be sitting around the Patterson table this year as part of the family.

There were offers of seconds and eager hands reaching for thirds. The empty dishes and platters were a testament to the cooks. Even Pepper was enjoying his bone that was longer than his leg. Noah was just thankful to be included in this warm family gathering and wanted it to last forever.

Everyone pitched in when it was time to clean up. Pots, pans, platters and dishes were washed and dried with care. It didn't matter who's job it was supposed to be, the men washed as the girls dried. It all got done without complaint.

Desserts would be enjoyed later, now was the time for sports on television, video games and playing guitar, depending on who you were. Noah excused himself upstairs and went looking for a paper and pen. It was time for another note.

Kate went back into the kitchen to pour herself another cup of coffee when she saw the note Noah had left her by her mug. Kate was starting to wonder if this was going to be a regular thing and what on earth did he need to discuss in private, again.

The note read, "Meet me at the waterfall."

Kate went out to the barn and saw the horse all ready to ride. She got on and rode out to the waterfall. Kate didn't know if there was more news that Noah needed to reveal and it made her a bit nervous on the ride over to meet him.

Her stomach was already not feeling well from overeating an hour ago and wanted to just get off. The ride to the waterfall seemed to take longer this time, or was it just her?

Noah had needed more time to prepare for Kate's visit to the waterfall today. Everything had to be perfect. A lot of planning went into it. So when Kate arrived, she was greeted with red roses, rose pedals and a blanket laid out on the snow.

Kate got of the horse and walked slowly to Noah all the while wondering what was going on. Noah got down on one knee and held out a small velvet box. Kate stopped walking and both hands went to her mouth. Was this really happening? Now?

Tears were coming to her eyes when she realized what Noah had planned. Noah gestured for her to come forward and she did. Her hands started shaking and she felt like she needed to sit down. It felt like a dream.

"Katie, from the moment I met you I knew you were the one. It took a while to admit it to myself, but from that moment I knew I had to fight for you. I didn't realize it would mean literally fighting, but I did."

Kate laughed and cried at the same time.

"Katie, you have never left my thoughts even when I wasn't here. It only made me know for sure that you were the one for me. I want to grow old with you. I want to have a family with you and I want to live here with you. Forever. Will you marry me?"

It took Kate only a second to find her voice, "Yes!"

Noah stood up, put the ring on Kate's finger and kissed her. He held her tight and lifted her feet off of the ground. This was always their special place, but now it would be even more so. Perhaps even a good spot for a wedding.

"You've made me so happy, Katie," Noah said.

"You've made me more happy," she replied.

There were no more words needed between them. Noah had offered himself to her forever. It answered all the lingering questions she had or would ever have. It told her where he saw himself in five, ten or fifty years. It told her he wanted kids and they would have a family.

"Let's go tell the family," Kate said.

They rode back slowly, in no hurry to include anyone in their happiness right now. At the barn, they released the horses back to their stalls and returned to their family as an engaged couple.

Kate couldn't wait to tell them. She brought everyone back into the living room for the news. She was beaming! Kate cleared her throat and wiped at her eyes.

"We have an announcement," Kate started. "Noah asked me to marry him and I said yes!"

There were shouts of joy, handshakes and hugs. Everyone asked to see the ring. Most of all, there were congratulations and Clayton and Ashley welcomed him to the family. Noah had already asked

Clayton for permission the other day in the barn, so he knew and, of course, he told his wife.

It was only a surprise for a few in the room. Kate had something else to say.

"Noah, there is one more present for you," Kate said.

Sure enough there was a box wrapped in green paper with his name on it. Noah thought she must have put it there when he went outside. He was curious why she would make such a big deal about another gift. Kate handed Noah the box and he slowly opened it.

He didn't need to wonder any longer. Tears came freely down his cheeks as he read the shirt she had wrapped for him. He looked at Kate as if asking if it were true, she nodded her head. Her own tears streaming down her cheeks.

Unable to stand the suspense any longer, Teri asked what it said. Noah turned the shirt for everyone to read, not trusting his own voice at the moment.

The shirt read, "Best Dad Ever."

It took but a moment for Clayton and Ashley to realize that not only were they gaining a son-in-law but they were having a grandchild soon! Everyone was happy for the new couple and future parents.

Noah stood up and hugged Katie. His future wife, his fiancé and mother of their unborn child. Life didn't get better than this, did it? They realized that they each at their own surprises, not knowing about the other.

When emotions finally calmed down, the reality of what was happening hit them. They needed to plan a wedding and prepare for a baby. It was all happening at once and they felt so blessed.

Teri texted Steven right away to share the news and Noah felt his phone buzz as texts came in. He called his parents with all of the good news and they were so excited. They would let them know as soon as they made any plans.

First they needed everything to sink in. Noah took Kate into the other room and asked her when she found out. She said she hadn't been feeling well the last few days and decided she'd better take a test, that was this morning.

Noah had never felt more in love with anyone or more protective over someone as he did right now for Katie. He was even more ready to protect and serve this town if it meant it would make it safer for his future wife and child.

Kate would start taking it easy, but she still had work to do. Spring and summer would be here before they knew it and they had so many plans for the ranch. Also, there would be a wedding, maybe it would be their first one on the ranch.

Kate knew her life was just beginning. Everything up until now didn't even matter.

Noah reflected on how the trauma of the home invasion that changed his life forever was not the moment that defined him. He was able to keep moving forward, however slowly, and push through it. Sometimes every two steps forward resulted in a step backward, but he kept going. He knew in his heart that if he made it to the other side, it would be worth it.

Life was worth living, even the hard parts because they won't always be hard. People deserved second chances.

Life will surprise you when you least expect it.

Sometimes in the form of a girl named Katie.

Acknowledgements

To my husband, Yoshi, for giving me the time and space to write. To my daughter, Alisa, for reading my first draft and loving it.

To my son, Leo, for his constant encouragement.

To Rick Ross, a friend from our Club Med days, for providing the answers for all of my gun related questions. We were, we are, we will always be.

To my sister for always being there for me.

To my friends for always being willing to read my first drafts and saying that they were perfect, even when I knew they weren't. Your encouragement has brought me to where I am now.

To Maggie Stiefvater for creating a writing seminar that provided life changing inspiration.

To my parents, who are no longer with us, for their constant love and support.

About the Author

Amy Iketani lives in Stockbridge, Georgia, with her husband and pet cat. Originally from Erie, Pennsylvania, Amy met her husband while working for Club Med and has lived in Florida, Japan and Hawaii. Amy enjoys crocheting, reading, spending time with her two grown children, Alisa and Leo, and traveling with her husband, Yoshi, of thirty-two years.

Follow Amy on Instagram @amyiketaniwrites

Don't miss out!

Visit the website below and you can sign up to receive emails whenever Amy Iketani publishes a new book. There's no charge and no obligation.

https://books2read.com/r/B-A-ALFAB-TLFID

BOOKS 2 READ

Connecting independent readers to independent writers.

Did you love *Second Chances*? Then you should read *I Never Knew*[1] by Amy Iketani!

[2]

Luna Delaney was planning a vacation to Cancun with her friends. When Luna applies for a passport, she asks for her birth certificate and notices something odd. Her father is not the father listed on her birth certificate. Luna finds an online match for her biological father in Italy. Encouraged by her friend, Chad, Luna embarks on a solo trip from Erie, PA, to Italy to meet her father. She meets Antonio who offers to help Luna on her journey. She meets her biological father, Cosimo Vernetti, but a stroke leaves him unable to provide answers.

Luna returns home until she learns that Cosimo has died and Luna is in his will. When Luna returns, she is reunited with Antonio. She learns that her father owns Vernetti Vineyards, whose future

---

1. https://books2read.com/u/3k9Y9R

2. https://books2read.com/u/3k9Y9R

now depends on her. Luna confronts her mother and demands to know the real truth about him. Will Luna's mother reveal the truth she's been hiding for decades? Luna is now faced with a decision that would forever change her life.

I Never Knew shows us that life is full of choices and risks. Sometimes the decisions that scare us the most are also the most rewarding. Follow Luna on an emotional journey as she discovers that there are people in her life who are worth risking it all.

Read more at instagram.com/amyiketaniwrites.

Also by Amy Iketani

Coming Home
The Last Wish
I Never Knew
Second Chances

Watch for more at instagram.com/amyiketaniwrites.

About the Author

Amy Iketani lives in Stockbridge, Georgia, with her husband and pet cat. Originally from Erie, Pennsylvania, Amy met her husband while working for Club Med and has lived in Florida, Japan and Hawaii. Amy enjoys crocheting, reading, and spending time with her two grown children, Alisa and Leo, and traveling with her husband, Yoshi, of thirty two years.

Follow Amy on Instagram @amyiketaniwrites

Read more at instagram.com/amyiketaniwrites.